May's Stony Road

Beryl P. Brown

THREE BEES PUBLISHING

Beryl P. Brown has asserted her right to be identified
as the Author of this Work in accordance with
the Copyright, Designs and Patents Act 1988.

British Library Cataloguing-in-Publication Data
A catalogue record for this book is available from the British Library.

Paperback ISBN 978-1-9163375-3-4
ebook ISBN 978-1-9163375-4-1
ebook ISBN 978-1-9163375-5-8

Published in Great Britain by Three Bees Publishing, 2022.

Cover design by GetCovers

About the Author

Beryl P. Brown's first novel, *May's Boys*, was written as the dissertation for her Master's degree.

It tells the story of May Sheppard and evacuee, Cliff Ewin, as they struggle against hardship and prejudice in a rural Dorset village in the Second World War.

May's Stony Road continues May and Cliff's story a year later.

Beryl has won numerous prizes for her short stories and, after living for many years in rural Dorset, she, her husband and their Dalmatian, Digby, moved to a cottage on the Stour estuary in East Anglia.

Beryl can be contacted via berylpbrown.uk

Also by Beryl P. Brown

May's Boys
A boy wants a mother, a woman wants a son …

For Mike

who always supports my endeavours

Chapter 1

'Peter's missing,' May called, returning to the back-kitchen and uprighting the boots and pails she'd cast aside racing for the clamouring telephone

Two figures, in heavy coats and balaclavas and carrying more metal pails, stared at her.

'What d'you mean missing?' Cliff said, tugging off his balaclava and leaving his hair standing in spikes.

A blast of arctic air swept in as the back door blew open and Jesson went back to close it.

The mustard and black stripes on the gloves and bala-clava, that Rose had re-knitted for Jesson from old woollens, were overpowering indoors.

Incredible as it was that they were making do and mending nearly two years after the war, May thought wasp stripes a step too far against Jesson's dark skin. He disagreed, telling his little son he was a big bumblebee. There was certainly no danger of losing him in the white world they'd inhabited all weekend.

'Rose rang. She said that because the school's closed, the twins' father insisted they help him clear snow off the village paths. Peter refused. When Len got cross and tried to force him to join in, he walked out.'

She turned to Jesson. 'You know they've had problems since Len's demob?'

Jesson nodded as he ran water into a pail in the sink. 'It can't be easy fitting back into the family when he's been at sea for years—'

'His dad's very bossy,' Cliff, red faced, cut in. 'Pete says

1

you'd think he was still on a ship ordering sailors around.'

'How long has he been gone?' Jesson asked.

'Since eight,' May said. 'It's only a couple of hours, but Rose thinks he might try getting here to see Cliff. The lane's blocked by deep snowdrifts and she can't get here today.' Rose was May's mainstay: friend, farm secretary and baby minder. 'The main road from Dorchester's blocked, too, and they don't know how much longer the road to the coast will be open.'

Cliff squatted beside Bess. He patted her damp coat as the retriever settled herself in front of the antiquated cast-iron stove that heated the entire house. They were keeping it alight day and night to prevent the pipes from freezing.

'Pete isn't stupid,' Jesson said. 'He won't risk trying to get through snowdrifts—'

'Arn Mee, Spence 'wake.' A small child, with a halo of dark hair, cannoned into the room.

Hearing the old name Cliff called her when he'd arrived as an evacuee made May smile. She loved that her foster son now used his own version of "Auntie May". But loved it even more that to Cliff, now her adopted son, she was "Mum".

Cliff grinned at his half-brother. 'Hello, Spence.'

'Spencer, you mustn't come downstairs by yourself. I was just coming to get you.' May swung the child up; his solid little body warm in pyjamas cut down from a pair outgrown by Cliff. She smoothed his hair. Rose despaired of his untameable curls.

'Dada,' the boy said, reaching out towards Jesson, still filling pails in the sink.

'Hiya, Sprout,' he said, lifting down a bucket and ruffling his son's hair with his free hand.

May sighed as the black curls settled back into an unruly

2

cloud. 'The village shops are having a run on provisions, so I've asked Rose to collect our rations – if Victoria doesn't put the kibosh on it. Although when we'll get them is another matter.'

If postmistress Victoria Potts could make difficulties for anyone, she would do so.

'What if Pete gets lost in the snow and can't get home? He might get frostbite and …' Cliff's voice faltered with emotion.

'Peter's lived in the village all his life; he knows his way around,' May said. 'He'll find somewhere to keep warm and go home when he's hungry.' She tried to sound confident, but couldn't stop herself from thinking the only warm places were indoors beside a fire. The temperature outside hadn't risen above freezing for three days. Peter was a level-headed boy, likely as not he'd go to a friend's house in the village.

'His dad's a rotter to him. He treats him like a child, even though he's nearly fourteen,' said Cliff. 'Since his dad came home, Pete's been really quiet. He hardly speaks on the school bus – he used to make jokes all the time.'

'We can't take sides, Cliff. Bob gets on well with his father, remember. It's only been a few months; they all need time to learn how to live with one another,' May said, sitting Spencer at the table.

'He'll be okay, buddy. He's a sensible kid.' Jesson patted Cliff's shoulder. 'Those twins stick together like glue. Pete won't go far without Bob.'

May's buckets were a lot less full than they had been when she'd left the house. Slipping and sliding on the frozen ground made icy water slosh repeatedly down her legs. She tried to conjure up those idyllic days of golden summer: the scent of new-mown hay on the air, skylarks soaring in a wide blue sky and life so blissful she didn't want to be anywhere else. She couldn't imagine it in this white-blanketed landscape where her nose tingled with every breath and her toes were losing sensation, despite two pairs of woollen socks.

'I doubt the POWs will make it today, either. Rose said she'd heard Magna Hill's blocked by a lorry wedged across the road. We're cut off.'

'May. If we had a tractor ...' Jesson said.

Not again. Yes, if she'd kept her promise when he'd accepted the foreman's job and bought a tractor last year, they might have been able to get up the lane. Although, she had little experience of driving in snow and Jesson told her they never had snow where he'd grown up in the States, so they might have been no better off.

She was in the wrong, and she would give priority to getting a tractor this year. It hadn't come between them, and they worked well as a team. She knew there was a lot of speculation in the village about their relationship, but it stayed professional during working hours and they were good friends otherwise. It was a delicate balance; her being Spencer's foster mother and Jesson being his natural father, but it worked because Spencer and Cliff's mother no longer had any say in the boys' lives.

'I'm sorry, Jesson, I know we have to get a tractor and we will – as soon as one is available after the weather breaks. You have my word.'

He grinned, his eyes sparkling in the way she found so attractive. 'I'll keep you to that, Mrs Sheppard.'

They broke the ice on the water buckets in the loose-boxes and refilled them. The two farm Clydesdales, Blossom and Ben, clad in undersized moth-eaten horse blankets, drank thirstily. The horses reminded her of a pair of school-boys in outgrown uniforms, but they were snug and would appreciate a day off.

After they'd fed and watered the hens, they walked down the track between the fields to check the rest of the farm. The crust on the frozen snow crunched as they walked. As their boots sank into the wet snow beneath, it compacted and became instantly slippery. May could no longer feel her toes and her mittens were ice-encrusted. She banged her hands together. Ice chips flew off, leaving saturated wool.

Halfway along the track, Jesson stopped, laying a hand on May's arm. His face was rapt. 'Look at it, May.'

He stared around, and she took her gaze off the virgin snow ahead to absorb the magical sight of the snowy hills rising into the distance. Trees, no longer black skeletons, were etched white against a grey sky heavy with more snow. The silence was complete, and only their steaming breath moved. They could be alone in the world.

She took this beauty so much for granted. When Cliff had first come to the village, used to grey city streets he'd been astounded houses could be colourful. She tried to commit the sight to memory to bring to mind on humdrum days. She sighed. 'It is beautiful. We don't appreciate our world enough.'

It was one of those moments they sometimes shared. A deep sense of being in harmony. A feeling she'd only ever experienced before with Seth and, after his death, never expected to feel again.

She moved and her feet slipped. Jesson put an arm out to steady her and they stood close for a moment, sharing the beauty of the landscape.

She cleared her throat. 'I think I'll freeze to the spot if I don't move.'

They walked on, cautiously feeling for their footing on the rutted track.

It was Jesson's second winter in Britain, and it was clear he felt the cold badly. At the end of work on a winter's day, he dragged the leg that was wounded in the war. Apart from concern about him, May knew that if he over-taxed himself and couldn't work, the farm would be in real trouble.

'We'll leave the heavy work until the POWs make it through to us,' she said. 'We've got enough to do caring for the animals and keeping anything vital from freezing up.'

They walked to the stream at the end of the track. Snow, sculpted into petrified waves, lined the banks. From the tunnel beneath, they could hear running water.

'Wow,' Jesson said, shaking his head at the beauty.

It was breath-taking, but as May admired the spectacle, she remembered Peter. If the boy was out here, he could be in serious trouble.

Chapter 2

'Budge up, Spence, you're sitting on the instructions.' Cliff nudged the child off the booklet on the hearthrug.

'Here, play with this.' He used a nut and bolt to fix a shiny girder to the hub of a brass wheel He pushed it back and forth over the floor and handed it to Spence before picking up the book, trying to work out how the metal plates for the crane cab fitted together.

'Brm brm.' Spence ran the wheel over Bess's feathery blonde tail. The dog opened one eye and gave a low groan before going back to sleep. Cliff ran a hand over her head; his adoration for her never ceased.

He picked up the little spanner and began tightening nuts and bolts to link two steel plates together. They'd found Seth's old Meccano set in a cupboard full of old toys when they'd redecorated Spence's bedroom.

The metal bits were silvery steel; the twins' newer Meccano was red and green, but Cliff liked it that Seth had played with these pieces in this house. He'd never known Mum's husband because he'd died before the war and before Cliff's arrival. Mum often spoke about him, and he was sure he'd have liked him.

He joined two more metal bits together. What had happened to Pete? They'd have to wait for Mrs Gale to go back to the phone box and let them know whether he'd come home. He must have done – even shovelling snow and being yelled at had to be better than being stuck outside in this weather.

***

'Can I take my sled down to Little Hill Field?' Cliff scraped up the last of his soup. Mum had stayed indoors, cooking, while Jesson went back out to the farm. She'd made two rabbit pies for tea – one for them and one for Jesson to take to the cottage. She said he mustn't walk up the lane in the dark because there were giant snowdrifts he could slip into, so he'd have to go early and cook his own meal. Jesson had winked at Cliff, making a joke of it, but sometimes Cliff would spot Jesson walking like the drunken sailors he used to see near Southampton docks because his leg hurt so much.

Mrs Gale hadn't rung by the time they'd finished eating. Cliff didn't want to think about how Mr Gale would react when Pete got home. Lynette, Cliff's old mum, used to smack him if he was naughty, and it hurt. Mr Gale was a strong sailor with a temper, and Pete must be scared of going home. Too scared?

'If you take the sled, I want you back within an hour. It's too cold to stay out longer, and it's going to snow again. Take Bess and send her home if you have a problem,' Mum said, clearing the soup bowls.

While Mum and Jesson talked about the farm, he pulled on his coat and took his balaclava and gloves from the clothes horse that nowadays lived next to the stove.

'C'mon, Bess,' he called. The dog jumped up and ran to him, her tail sweeping off a row of drying clothes.

'Sorry,' Cliff called as he slammed the back door.

Bess ran ahead down the track to the farmyard. Cliff followed, dragging the sled behind him. There was fresh snow and he should get up a decent speed.

'Bess,' he called. The dog began barking somewhere in

8

the yard. Cliff waited by the gate. The fields were a blank wilderness. What would it be like to be a polar explorer, having no landmarks to fix on and getting lost forever? He shuddered and shouted again, 'Bess, come.'

She was still barking. It was unlike her to disobey him. He dropped the sled rope and stomped across the yard to where the dog was raking at the snow in front of the barn.

'Leave Bloss and Ben alone. Let's go.' He turned back, expecting her to follow, but she stayed where she was, now pawing the door and whining.

Was it the snow – was she cold? He ran over to her. She felt warm, but pawed anxiously at the barn door. He slid it open and Bess shot inside, making straight for the hay bales. She began nosing something.

Bloss whickered a greeting, hoping for a titbit. Cliff strained his eyes in the dim light. Had a rabbit, or a fox, sneaked in for shelter? He flicked the light switch as a weak voice said, 'Give over, Bess.'

'Pete?'

'Yeah.'

Cliff gasped at the sight of his friend. He was shaking all over. Even his freckles had faded and his face shone white in the gloom.

'I can't go back, Cliff. He's making my life hell.' His voice quavered. Squatting down, Cliff put his hand on Pete's arm. He touched a sodden sleeve. He could feel Pete shivering.

'Come on, you've got to get in the warm.'

Pete shrank away.

'You've got to. You'll get sick if you stay here. Mum'll know what to do. Come on.'

Bess licked Pete's face. He patted her head. 'I'm not

9

going back. I'd rather stay out there,' he nodded towards the yard, 'than get ordered about by him.'

'You can't go anywhere. We're cut off. How did *you* get through?'

'Along the main road and up Magna Hill – there's a lorry stuck halfway, but I got past it.'

That was miles round. He had to be exhausted and he needed to get warm.

'No one's going to get to us; there's more snow coming. You'll be safe in the house.'

Pete sighed, but he gripped Cliff's arm and pulled himself to his feet. Cliff stayed close as the lad trudged to the door.

Chapter 3

'It's Mrs Sheppard from Elem Farm. Could you get a message to Mrs Gale at Briar Row, please, Janice? Ask her to ring me.'

Ringing the village phone box to leave a message was always a bit hit and miss. The only alternative was to call the post office and get Victoria Potts, the prying postmistress, involved, and that was out of the question.

'Janice Harris says she'll ask Rose to ring back.' May told Jesson, staring through the window at the driving snow hitting the glass like a hail of cotton wool bullets. A blizzard. And they had yet to tend to the horses and hens.

'I'll make a start haulin' water,' Jesson said. 'You need to wait to speak to Rose, and Pete needs Cliff right now.' He began pulling on his outdoor clothes drying on the clothes horse.

Seeing the normally chirpy Peter half-frozen, half-terrified of being sent home had come as a shock. She'd got straight down to practicalities and had the boy in a hot bath, with a beaker of Bovril, before he could collapse in the threatened tears. Cliff and Spencer had joined him in the bathroom and the sound of bathwater sea battles was a sign that Cliff's attempts to lift his friend's spirits were working.

'What are you going to tell Rose?' Jesson tugged the bumblebee balaclava over black hair cropped close to his head.

'Just that he's here, and safe, and will have to stay until we can get through to the village. I'll lay it on thick that access through Magna is out of the question, in case Len wants to flex his muscles dragging his son home.'

Jesson, pulling on the bee gloves, gave her a sideways glance. 'I thought you were neutral?'

'I was until I saw the state Peter was in. He's always been a cheerful lad – forever laughing. There has to be more to it than he and his father juggling to be top dog.'

'Be careful; it never works out well taking sides in a family feud.' Jesson picked up the buckets they'd filled and left on the doormat. May fought against the wind to close the door behind him. She knew he was right, but she couldn't let a boy, who was so scared of his father he'd run away in such dreadful weather, go home to be bullied.

She returned to the kitchen thinking she'd have to suggest Jesson stayed with them tonight. Her old cottage, now the foreman's accommodation, was half a mile up the lane. The heavy snow being driven off the fields would have made it inaccessible by now.

Surely the gossipmongers would accept that putting up a friend in such conditions was entirely innocent. Having Peter in the house was a blessing in disguise – another waif sheltering from the storm and a chaperone, to boot.

The telephone bell jangled.

'Rose?'

Her voice, but frantic. 'Have you seen him?'

'He's here.' May explained how Peter had turned up. She downplayed the shaking with cold, the fear of his father and the hiding in the barn.

'He's very quiet – exhausted after his trek.' She couldn't push it too far. Rose was overjoyed he was safe, and she didn't want to take away from that.

She'd get the full story when Rose came back to work whenever that was. Meanwhile, she allayed her fears that

Peter would be in the way and promised to get the boys doing some schoolwork.

'Mum says Parva's cut off too, today and some telephone wires're down.' Peter had just spoken to his mother, who was checking how he felt after a night away. May hoped he hadn't told her Jesson had stayed overnight. Rose would understand, but she'd rather be the one to mention it.

'I hope our phone holds out,' May said, dreading the thought of being unable to contact anyone outside.

According to the radio news, the entire country was frozen and questions were being asked in Parliament about how long fuel stocks would last. They were lucky in the farmhouse – they could burn logs for heat, but elsewhere people worried that the newly nationalised coal industry might not cope.

'Mrs Sheppard, come and see.' Peter was holding Spencer up to the window. The little boy was pointing and laughing. May joined them. Jesson and Cliff had laid piles of hay in the orchard. The horses needed exercise and, over breakfast, May had decided putting them outside for a few hours would ease their boredom and stretch their legs.

The two animals had been let into the orchard and were investigating the snow. Blossom was high stepping, her tail in the air, and Ben was pawing like a dog, sending snow in all directions.

'Boss funny.' Spencer laughed as the mare bucked in the joy of release before wandering over to her hay and getting down to the business of eating.

'Jesson's cutting wood,' Cliff said.

'I'm going out to check how much feed we've got,' May

said. 'You two boys have schoolwork to do. Read the next chapter of your English book and do the exercises at the end. The same with the arithmetic – and,' she carried on before Cliff could interrupt, 'if you do one subject each, you won't have to swap books. You can do the other one tomorrow.'

She left them looking crestfallen, but resigned. They arranged books and paper at the kitchen table while Spencer played with his wooden bricks.

The snow on the track was halfway up her boots. As she struggled to keep her footing, the wind whipped her skin and tried to snatch away the scarf she'd wound around her face.

She'd checked the larder before breakfast. They were running low on most things, but margarine, cheese and milk had run out. With two extra mouths to feed, they had to get to the village for their rations. Meals on the ration were bad enough, but when you hadn't got the basic ingredients, impossible.

Already the children moaned about potato everything: pastry, soup, shortbread. She had some bottled fruit in store, as well as chutney and jam Rose had made in the summer, so she could bring a bit of variety to the food. And Cliff bagged rabbits for the pot. He and Jesson were talking of taking the gun out later, if it wasn't snowing again. Last time, Jesson had brought back a pheasant. It was a liberty because the Squire rented the shooting rights but, with the season finishing at the end of the week, he wouldn't begrudge them a last bird.

Jesson was sawing in the Dutch barn beyond the stackyard that was now reduced to one lonely straw stack. May continued on, past the two horses, who were finishing the last of their hay, to the poultry yard and the feed store.

Mealy smelling dust blasted into the air as May opened

the shed door in the gusting wind. She closed it on the weather and counted the bags of feed in the feeble light. Enough for another ten days, or two weeks if they reduced the rations to two-thirds. The birds weren't burning off weight through exercise, but they needed it for warmth.

In the barn she checked the horse feed. They'd kept plenty of hay back from the summer, hoping to sell it. Without being able to get it to market, they had enough if the horses ran out of oats.

After mucking out the looseboxes, she brought in the horses, who were despondently standing at the gate.

As she changed their damp rugs for others equally disreputable, she wondered whether they should try to get the potatoes out from the frozen clamps. She was reluctant to harness the horses in these conditions, but work must go on and these two were bored with time off. Jesson had pointed out prices would be good – if they could get them to market.

As she approached the Dutch barn, she heard the tap, tap of a hammer.

Jesson was bent over a construction on the floor. At first glance, it appeared to be the prow of a boat – a V shape, each planked arm about five feet long, linked by a bar across the centre. The ends of the planks extended beyond the bar, like wings, and the whole thing resembled a letter A. Bolted on either side of the tip, metal ear-like loops protruded.

'What on earth?'

Jesson grinned, his eyes sparking, 'Meet the Cobb patent snowplough!'

Intrigued, May walked around it. Jesson pointed out the features. 'We harness the horse to the metal loops by a chain. As it drags the plough, the snow gets pushed aside by the

15

arms and leaves a clear path behind – I saw a guy using something like it in Tuskegee. It worked a treat.'

The principle sounded fine, but would it work?

Jesson, fired with enthusiasm, went on, 'We couldn't use it on the tracks – too many ruts – but on the lane ...' He grinned at her. 'We might make it to the village. What d'you think?'

She shook her head. He was mad. Laughing, she said, 'Try it – as long as the horse is safe. But I reckon you'll need a seat.'

'Next job, ma'am.' He saluted.

Chapter 4

'Are you sure you'll be all right with Spencer?'

'Yes, Mrs Sheppard.' Peter couldn't meet her eye; he was so unlike his usual confident self. When Jesson announced they were trying out the snowplough to get through to the village, May thought he was about to faint.

'You've plenty of food. The stove's made up and, if there's a problem, ring the phone box and ask someone to get your mum. I'll phone you when we get there.'

'Righto.'

'Can I drive Blossom?' Cliff asked.

'You'll have to walk with me – we've got to take shovels in case we reach a drift the plough can't get through.'

'Can Bess—'

'She'll be fine with Peter. You don't want her getting too cold, bad enough for us and Blossom.'

There had been more snow overnight, but the wind had lessened by dawn and Jesson insisted on an early start. 'We don't know how long it'll take, or how long the snow will hold off,' he said, urging them to get the feeding and mucking out finished before it was properly light.

Blossom calmly allowed herself to be harnessed to the snowplough. Jesson picked up each hoof and greased the hollows of her feet. If snow packed into them, she would be walking on balls of ice and liable to fall.

The rudimentary seat Jesson had attached to the construction appeared agonisingly uncomfortable, but his expression when May suggested a cushion was enough to make her hold her tongue; this was his project.

Cliff held the yard gate as Jesson gingerly steered Blossom through. The wings of the plough missed the gateposts by fractions of an inch as the plough swung into the lane.

Would it work? She dearly wanted it to. Jesson had worked hard building his plough and she couldn't help thinking all their lives would have been easier if she'd bought a tractor. It *would* be her top priority when the thaw came.

Jesson asked the mare to walk on and, after a slight hesitation, she stepped forward into snow that covered her hooves and the long hair above them. As she moved, the prow of the plough cut through the snow. May and Cliff watched and a snowy path emerged, leaving furled walls of snow on either side.

'It works!' Cliff shouted, running after the plough, his boots crunching on the thin layer of snow left on the road.

May silently gave thanks. Maybe they could get supplies from the village – as long as there was stock in the shops.

Passing the farmhouse, Cliff called, 'Hello, Spence.'

Peter was holding the child in the front window and Spencer waved back with both hands, an enormous grin on his face. In comparison, Peter's face was pale and fearful.

'He doesn't want us to get there,' Cliff said. 'He's scared you'll make him go home.'

She'd deliberately left the lad babysitting to give him an excuse for not going with them. Voicing her thoughts, she said, 'He'll have to go sometime. If we can get through, his dad can get to us.'

'He's more scared of that,' Cliff said, stomping forward in the snowplough's wake.

They rounded the bend where the hedges on either side of

the lane ended. Jesson shouted, 'Whoa,' and Blossom came to a halt.

May shouted, 'What's the matter?'

Jesson pointed. Ahead was a white prairie. It was impossible to discern where the lane ended, and the ditches and fields beyond began.

A few hundred yards in front, Elem Cottage stood out like an iceberg in a frozen sea. It was the halfway point between the farm and the main road, beyond which lay the village.

'We'll have to use the shovels to find the road edge. We can't risk the plough flippin' over into the ditch.'

May and Cliff squeezed past. Blossom's flanks were steaming and Jesson covered her with the horse blanket he'd been sitting on. May grinned, but stopped herself from asking whether it was more comfortable than a cushion. He'd roped a third shovel to the plough, and all three began scraping snow away to expose the ditch line.

'You okay to go on?'

'Yes, you get on the plough. We're not far from the cottage and the hedges start again after that,' May said.

Jesson headed back to Blossom. He was favouring his leg as they watched him walk away. How bad was his limp? He tried to hide it, but it worried her. She must stop him over-exerting himself.

She stepped back to carry on shovelling, but her foot went straight through the snow and she plunged into the ditch. She screamed. Her boots filled with snow and she'd have sworn she'd fallen twenty feet. In fact, when her feet hit solid ground, she was only waist deep. Jesson came running with his crabwise gait. What a fool she was to have screamed.

'Mum? Are you all right?' Cliff had thrown down his shovel and was lurching over to her through deep snow.

She scrabbled to get out before Jesson reached her, but as she struggled, her feet slid and she was helpless. Jesson had rolled up the balaclava, and it sat as a fetching yellow hat on his head. As he bent down to her, a concerned frown on his face, her heart raced. He grabbed her forearm. Cliff clutched her other hand and together they hauled her out.

'Are you hurt?' Jesson asked, still holding her arm.

'Just a bit damp. I'm glad I put on dungarees. And three pairs of socks,' she said, rambling to detract from the heat in her face. She pulled off a wellington boot and tipped out compacted snow. She tugged off a wet, heavily darned sock before shoving her foot back into the boot and repeating the exercise with the second boot.

'I'm fine now, thanks,' she said, struggling to appear normal. 'Jesson?'

He was staring at her. He blinked, saw his hand still grasping her arm, and released her.

Even through the layers of clothing, her skin felt cold as he took his hand away. She smiled at him. 'Thank you,' she said softly. Cliff was watching them. 'And thank you, Cliff. What an idiot I am.'

'All part of the service, ma'am.' Jesson turned away.

Jesson had planned to collect some things from the cottage but, when they arrived at the gate, he said, 'We don't know what's ahead. We'd better mosey on down the trail.' He winked at Cliff.

Cliff laughed. 'Sure thing, pardner.'

May smiled. Cliff loved Jesson using Western film

language, and she loved their uncomplicated relationship.

They moved on but, at the bend beyond the cottage, Jesson stopped Blossom again and asked May and Cliff to go ahead. 'The hedges are only on one side for the next stretch. Take a look at what we're up against, please.'

May and Cliff edged past the plough and waded through to the point of the bend.

'Cor!' said Cliff. 'It's like Switzerland.'

May felt a rush of disappointment. This must be where Rose had said the lane was blocked. To the left was another white prairie but, on the right, the blackthorns formed a barrier and drifts, as high as the hedge, blocked half the lane.

'If you and Cliff mark the left-hand edge, I'll keep us close to that, and we'll see how it goes,' Jesson said, when they reported back.

Blossom didn't falter when she was asked to walk into knee-deep snow. The plough cut in and she strained to haul the weight. May and Cliff pushed the ends of the wings to help the horse and keep the plough straight, and a cleared path gradually emerged.

May ached everywhere. Her legs quaked as if *she'd* pulled the plough. Blossom's coat was saturated and steaming. Cliff's face was red. He'd pulled off his balaclava when they were shovelling, and his tawny hair shone black with sweat. They all needed to beware of getting too cold. May's feet were still damp from her fall and she needed to keep moving.

Eventually, the hedge on the left reappeared, but all four were exhausted and they'd slowed to a crawl.

'Look,' Cliff shouted, flailing over to a snowy post at the roadside. He banged it until a slick of snow slid off and revealed a black X on a white rectangle. The crossroads sign.

He tugged off his glove and gave the victory sign, his face alight with pride. 'We did it!' he yelled.

'Hooray,' May cheered.

Jesson gave a piercing whistle that startled Blossom, who flicked her tail and moved off, making them laugh. May put her arm around Cliff's shoulders and they trudged on.

The main road appeared in minutes and beyond it, the road into the village, which had been cleared of snow. Great white heaps lay either side of the road. Len's work, May guessed.

They stopped at the crossroads. How to suggest that Jesson took the horse back to the farm? Blossom had done so well, and they couldn't let her stand in the freezing temperature while they went into shops. She was the main source of power on the farm; old Ben did his best, but he was past his prime.

Having brought them this far, was it unfair to ask Jesson to return immediately? She was trying to find the right words when she heard a voice.

'Mrs Sheppard?'

'Hello, Mrs Wheaton,' May answered, as a woman from one of the cottages on the village road came towards them. Huddled in a long thick coat with a shawl clamped over her head, she could have been a medieval peasant.

'Good heavens, what's that contraption?' she asked.

After they'd explained, she insisted on making them tea and headed back to her cottage. She'd told them the main road was now impassable in both directions, although they had heard the POWs were being used to clear it from the Bridport end.

'Be able to get to school soon, mebee?' she said to Cliff, who gave a weak grin.

Jesson had unchained the plough and was walking a blanketed Blossom in circles to keep her warm while they waited for the tea. 'May, when you've had a drink, why don't you do your shopping and I'll get Blossom back to the farm.' He stared up at the overcast sky. It was the grey of a herring gull's back. 'Doesn't look like we'll get snow anytime soon. You oughta make it back okay.'

She should have known he'd offer; so often they thought the same way. She asked him for a list of things he needed besides the rations that Rose had collected for them.

'Let's hope Victoria has taken to her fireside,' May said, as she and Cliff made their way to the combined shop and post office.

They'd helped Jesson swing the snowplough around and re-harness Blossom after they'd wolfed Mrs Wheaton's tea and potato shortbread.

'I promised Peter I'd telephone when we got here,' she said, pushing open the phone box door and squeezing in with Cliff.

She put tuppence in the slot and dialled the farm's number.

'Hello?'

'Now, Cliff.'

Cliff pressed the silver button labelled 'A'. The coins clanged down and May said, 'Hello, Peter. We've got here. Is everything all right?'

'Yes … er … well … no. The lights ain't working and neither's the cooker. But Spence is okay. I gave him a sandwich for his dinner and he's having his nap.'

'What's happened? Just a minute.' She turned away from the receiver and spoke to Cliff. 'Can you see any lights on?'

He opened the door and peered up and down the street.

'Nothing. But there's a candle in that window.' He pointed to a house across the road, where a dim light flickered.

'There might be an electricity cut, Peter.' There'd been talk on the wireless of coal stocks running low and cuts having to be made, but she thought they'd have had more warning. 'Keep the fire made up. There are some candles under the sink – be very careful and don't let Spencer near them. Mr Cobb is on his way back. Don't worry, he'll be there soon. We're just getting the shopping, and once we've seen your mum, we'll be on our way back.'

'All right. Mrs Sheppard … you won't let my dad come and get me, will you?' There was a catch in his voice.

What could she say? His father had every right to take his son home, but the boy was terrified.

'I'll tell him it's not a good idea today,' she said. But what would she do about tomorrow?

Chapter 5

'Can I go and see Bob?' Cliff asked.

They were at the door of the butcher's. Mum had only been able to get one National Loaf at the baker's because they were running out of flour. He made her promise she wouldn't buy horsemeat, even if that was all the butcher had.

When he sold rabbits and pigeons to the butcher, he had to take them around the back. He never looked beyond the doorstep because you could see carcasses hung up, and he couldn't bear to think of Ben and Blossom ending up like that.

'Tell Mrs Gale I'll come round when I've done the shopping,' Mum said, opening the door. She said, in a low voice, 'Say I'll explain about Peter when I get there.'

As she went in, he glanced inside the shop. Candles threw ugly black shapes on the walls and the butcher, in a bloodstained apron, cleaver in hand, materialised like Count Dracula. Cliff had read Bram Stoker's book in secret when Mum hadn't let him see the film at the flicks. He shuddered and ran on down the street.

'Cliff!' Mrs Gale was surprised to see him and he had to explain about the snowplough and why his mother wasn't there before she let him go up to Bob's room.

'Who's that?' he heard Mr Gale call out as he went up the stairs. Thankfully, Bob had heard him and was at his door. He was wearing two jerseys and gloves. Bits of sandy hair stuck out from under a too-small knitted hat. There was no fire in the grate.

'We ain't got much coal, so we're savin' it for down-stairs,' he said, as Cliff huddled on the bed, still in his coat.

The weak light reflecting off the snow was all that lit the twins' bedroom, where Bob was squinting at the jigsaw puzzle he had laid out on a tray on the floor.

'Dad gave it to us at Christmas,' he said, 'but Pete didn't want to do it.'

The picture was of a ship battling enormous waves, other ships in the background and a plane overhead. Bob pointed to the foreground ship. 'That's a merchantman. The Royal Navy and the Airforce are guarding the convoy.'

That was why Pete wouldn't have wanted to do the puzzle; too much of his dad's world in it.

'What's your dad doing now? Your mum said something about mending motor cars?'

He knew what Mr Gale was doing, but maybe he'd get a clue to why Pete was so upset.

'Yeah, he used to be an engineer in the Navy, in charge of the ship's engines, sailors an' all that. He's staying on shore now, working in a garage in Weymouth.' Bob fitted a piece of the merchant ship's blue funnel into place. 'Why didn't Pete come with you?'

Cliff had to be cagey; the twins were each other's best friend. They often knew what the other was thinking, or about to say, but Bob was close to his father and he might let something slip that would rile the sailor and make him more angry with Pete.

'He's babysitting Spence. Someone had to stay and Jesson wanted me to come so's I could drive Blossom if he had to dig us out.'

Bob raised his eyebrows. He knew Cliff was only

allowed to drive the horses on the farm tracks in safe conditions, but Cliff hoped he'd think today was an emergency.

To distract Bob, he picked up a random piece of puzzle and tried to ram it into a space.

'That doesn't go there. It's hull, not part of the superstructure.' Mr Gale stood over them.

Heck. He hadn't wanted to see Pete's dad. 'Sorry,' he said, hoping Pete would be grateful he'd made an idiot of himself for his sake.

Mr Gale was a big man, with hands the size of Blossom's hooves. Cliff thought that Mr Gale's hair was like Blossom's, too: reddish with grey bits in it. He had heavy lines on his face and his skin was a mass of brown freckles, far more than the twins had.

He was wearing a short-sleeved shirt. The sight of his bare arms made Cliff feel a sissy for wearing his coat. Mr Gale's right arm had a blue anchor tattooed on it. Cliff tried not to stare. He'd often seen tattoos on sailors in Southampton, and the sight of them brought back memories of his unhappy life there.

'So, where's that jessie of a son of mine?' Mr Gale said.

'Pete's taking care of my brother,' Cliff said, not daring to meet the man's eye.

'Pah! Women's work.'

How dare he? Cliff often looked after Spence, and he enjoyed it. He felt himself flush as he took a deep breath and said, 'Mum had to come with Jesson and me to help with the snowplough—'

There was a knock at the front door. Cliff felt his heart stop pounding as Mr Gale headed downstairs. He could hear his mum's voice talking to Mrs Gale.

'I've got to go,' he said to Bob. 'We have to get back

before it snows again.'

He stood up. Bob said quietly, 'Tell Pete I miss him. If he comes back and just does what Dad says, he'll be okay.'

'I'll tell him,' Cliff promised, knowing that Pete could never do that.

As he walked down the stairs, he heard his mother's voice. '… a bit of a cold. Probably from walking through the snow to see Cliff. Best leave him to recover – you don't want to catch it, Len, might stop you going to work.'

Mr Gale snorted. 'If the Jerries and the Japs couldn't stop me doing my job, I doubt a bit of a sniffle would.'

'Still, better ter be safe than sorry,' Mrs Gale said. 'If we don't get more snow, I'll try ter come ter work in the morning, May, now you've cleared the lane.'

'Waste of time. We'll get more tonight. You won't get there for weeks.' Mr Gale sounded pleased.

'At least we got here today. Thank you for collecting the rations, Rose. Everything would have gone by now.'

'Just hope those bloody POWs earn their keep and get the main road open before we all starve,' snapped Mr Gale.

Cliff squeezed into the hall and picked up two of the bags his mother had beside her. She took another from Mrs Gale and they said their goodbyes.

Just as they closed the gate, Mrs Gale opened the front door and called, 'Electricity's back on.'

'Marvellous,' said Mum, waving.

As they walked along the slippery path out of the village, bending into a freezing wind, Cliff said, 'I didn't know Pete had a cold.'

His mother didn't answer.

Chapter 6

'Come in.'

The back door opened to the sound of voices. May dried her hands and turned to see Rose and two POWs. Thank heavens.

Rose's voice was muffled as she took off her headscarf and unbuttoned her coat. 'I decided I'd get here come hell, or more likely with this bit of a thaw, high water, and I met these two being dropped off at the crossroads.'

'*Guten tag*,' said Walter, treating May to his wide grin. He was unmistakably Germanic: blonde hair, eyes the colour of forget-me-nots and startlingly white teeth.

Alwin said, 'Hallo.' He rarely met May's eye, but thank goodness he'd stopped saluting. She'd found it uncomfortable, verging on ridiculous, but Jesson returned the salute as a matter of course.

'We were sent to clear the roads,' Alwin said. 'Your village now has passage from Dorchester to Weymouth.'

'That is good news,' May said.

'Mum?' Peter led Spencer into the kitchen.

'Arn Ro,' Spencer gurgled, pulling Peter over to Rose.

How was this going to go? Peter had managed to stay on at the farm with May colluding in accepting his exaggerated excuses of fresh snowfalls but, when the thaw had set in overnight, she'd known his time was up.

'Rose. Peter. Go through to the study. I'll sort out the work with Alwin and Walter.'

She'd sent the two Germans off to find Jesson and harness

the horses. The potato clamps had to be opened, and the contents carted up to the barn before the melted snow ran off the fields and rotted the spuds.

Now Rose was here to take care of Spencer, she'd hoped both boys might help outside. The study door was still closed.

'Cliff, can you get ready to help outdoors, please?' she called up the stairs. Should she knock on the study door?

She put the kettle on – a cup of tea would be a good reason to interrupt mother and son.

Before she'd poured the tea, Peter came into the kitchen.

'Mum says did you want me to help, Mrs Sheppard?'

'Thank you, Peter. You would be a big help.' He didn't look as if he'd been crying. Maybe they'd sorted out their problems.

'The boys have gone outside – I'm about to go too,' May said, carrying a cup of tea into the study. Spencer trotted alongside, clutching his stuffed rabbit. 'What do you …? Ah, it didn't go well with Peter then?'

Rose was sitting at the roll-top desk, head in hands. When she turned around, May was shocked; her eyes were dark ringed; her skin sallow, cheekbones sharp beneath. Even her hair had more grey amidst the springy brown curls.

'Peter and Len. I just don't know what ter do,' Rose said, her voice breaking.

She'd never seen Rose like this. Throughout the war she'd been stalwart. Strong. May's rock. Something fundamental had changed since Len was demobbed. The family was adrift, like a family bereaved, not reunited.

'He's welcome to stay on here – if it'll help,' May said.

'That's what he wants,' Rose said, unshed tears in her

eyes. 'I don't know what Len'll do if I don't take him back with me tonight. Bob misses him too; he's been playing with the village lads. It makes me so sad; the twins were inseparable before ... before ...'

Before Len came back, May thought.

Rose went on, 'I had so many plans, you remember?'

May did. Rose had been brimming over with ideas of what they would do when Len came home: how they'd take the boys on trips and holidays; modernise their house; even try for another baby before she got too old.

Spencer was quietly piling up his bricks on the carpet. He was such a good child; his honey-coloured face usually alight with a smile. She'd been lucky with the two lads she was bringing up.

'I think a lot of families are finding it hard to adjust after so long apart,' she said. 'Evelyn Harris had the devil's own job convincing her husband she should be allowed to work in the shop, never mind he is labouring up-country and she was going mad with boredom. Stretching his irregular wages for her and the two girls was a nightmare.'

'At least Len seems to be fine with me working here, at the moment,' Rose said.

At the moment? What on earth would she do if Rose gave up her job?

'If the boys can go to school tomorrow, might Peter be persuaded to go home and get his uniform tonight?' May said. 'If Len's at work today, there won't be much chance for them to see each other – Peter will be tired after the farm work and in need of an early night.' It might placate Len enough to let up his bullying. For a while.

'It's worth a try. I'll ring the school and see whether it'll be open tomorrow, although I expect they'll be as short of coal as the rest of the country.'

They talked for a few minutes about the problems of coal frozen in rail yards before May left. She was glad Rose was more like her old self, even if only by becoming animated over the lack of governmental preparation for the winter.

As she was closing the kitchen door, Rose called, 'I brought the post. The postman was at the crossroads and said he wasn't going ter chance the lane.'

'Thanks. You deal with anything farm related; I'll look at the rest later.'

May insisted the two Germans join the rest of them in the middle of the day for the soup Rose had made. 'It's too cold to sit in the harness room,' she said, as all eight of them sat around the huge old kitchen table. Jesson was at the head of the table, or was that herself at the other end? So often they shared family-like moments, and she tried to hide from herself how natural they felt.

Today, the atmosphere was strained. The POWs covertly glanced about them at the big farmhouse kitchen, like people visiting a posh restaurant for the first time.

Alwin kept his gaze on his food once Rose placed a bowl in front of him. May noticed neither started eating until she picked up her own spoon. Well-brought up, then.

'We've made good progress. How many loads left in the clamp do you think, Jesson?' The cartloads of potatoes had been unloaded in the barn ready for riddling, to separate the sizes, before weighing into sacks.

Jesson said, 'Guess we're about halfway.'

'Two more loads, then?' May said.

He didn't answer. He wasn't pleased that they were entertaining the POWs, that was obvious. His relationship with them was strictly foreman to worker. It must be hard accepting your onetime enemies as fellow workers, but they were human beings too, and no one could question how hard they worked. Today the conditions were foul, a layer of slippery mud and slush overlaying frozen ground, easy to twist an ankle, or worse. The men had coped with it without complaint, and in her opinion, deserved a hot meal.

'At least you have enough sacks,' Rose said.

May guessed she was trying to lighten the atmosphere; Jesson was being difficult and Peter was sulking, barely eating anything and replying only in monosyllables after he'd been told he'd be going home that afternoon.

Rose went on, 'With the factories shutting down because of the power restrictions, they say there's a shortage of hessian sacks.'

'What next – sack rationing? Anything to make life more difficult.' May was sick of rationing. The entire country was struggling to feed and clothe itself, but her last comment was aimed at Jesson.

Everyone ate in a heavy silence.

'You will sell potatoes in London?' Walter asked.

May felt guilty – the POWs sometimes told them how their families struggled to get food in Germany and she was moaning about sacks. 'No, just the local wholesaler,' she said. 'I don't trust the weather – we don't want them snowed up in some railway siding for weeks. It might be difficult enough just getting them to Wareham.'

'I'll go back to the cottage tonight. I've taken your hospitality long enough,' Jesson said.

May flushed. Touché, but she wished he hadn't let it out that he'd been staying in the farmhouse. Why was she so sensitive? The three boys were in the house with them and she had nothing to hide.

He went on, 'But I've been mighty glad of the bathroom – the tin bath on the rug may have to wait until the weather warms up!'

Everyone laughed. The difficult moment had passed, but she'd clearly upset Jesson.

It should have been dark at four o'clock, but the snow-reflected light had prolonged the dusk. The Germans got ready to set out to meet their transport at the crossroads; Rose and Peter walking with them.

'You go too, Jesson, I'll lock up. I'll feel happier that you're all together now that it's freezing again.'

The snow beneath their feet was crisping as they talked. May went on, 'Rose has made something for your dinner – the cottage will be freezing until the range gets going.' She handed Jesson a jar of stew wrapped in a tea cloth. 'Just pop it in a saucepan.' He touched his hat. So, he hadn't forgotten their difference of opinion.

She turned to the others. 'Thanks for your help today. We did well to get the clamp cleared.'

They passed through the gateway Peter, walking like a condemned man, trailing behind. Walter, holding the gate, patted the boy on the shoulder as he passed. After latching the gate, the German strode on and May watched him station himself alongside Rose.

After she and the boys had eaten their stew, she retrieved the pile of letters Rose had sorted from the dresser.

There were a few circulars and two late, very thin copies of the *Farmers Weekly*. Victims of fuel shortage and weather.

Last of all, a long flimsy brown envelope addressed to May with the words *Private and Confidential* typed across the top.

Frowning, she slit the envelope and drew out a sheet of paper headed Thomas, Barker and Frost, Solicitors. What on earth?

Dear Madam,

We are instructed by our client, Mrs Dorothy Ottaway, to put in train an action to challenge the last will and testament of her brother, Thomas Arrowsmith Esquire.

The grounds for the action will be that undue pressure was exerted on Mr Arrowsmith over several years with the intention of influencing him to bequeath his estate to yourself, an employee and non-blood relative.

May dropped the paper as if it had scalded her. This had to be a mistake. Could it be a practical joke? Someone being vindictive?

The only candidate for vindictiveness was Ephraim Potts, but they'd settled their difference years ago and nowadays rubbed along without animosity.

A loud thud came from upstairs, where the boys were playing before Spencer's bedtime.

Almost without knowing it, May went to the foot of the stairs and called up that it was time for Spencer to get ready for bed. She barely registered his wail of complaint.

She picked up the letter. A.D.Frost had signed it; the name followed by a string of letters. The address was Basingstoke, Hampshire.

Why would Dorothy engage solicitors from so far away? It made little sense. None of this made sense, not least the accusation that she'd engineered Tom's bequest. Nothing could be further from the truth. He'd mentioned once that she would inherit, but he'd been ill at the time and she'd assumed he'd been hallucinating.

When the time came for reading the will, she'd been taken entirely by surprise, having assumed that his estate would be sold, and the proceeds would go to his sister.

Dorothy had shown no ill feeling at the time; she'd attended the funeral, thanked May for caring for Tom in his last months and seemed to accept her brother's decision to leave his property to his stepson's widow.

She put Spencer to bed, her mind on the allegations. She'd been fond of Tom and still missed him greatly. No one who knew her would ever consider she'd try to inveigle an inheritance. It was preposterous.

She made up her mind. With Jesson being difficult and Rose having to cope with the Len business, she'd deal with this herself.

Chapter 7

'You'll never believe who's creeping around the village checking everyone's sticking ter the power restrictions.' Rose had moved her paperwork to the kitchen table and was sitting at the end nearest the stove. A Tilley lamp, hanging from a beam above the table, hissed; its glowing mantle a halo of brilliant white light. Spencer, on the hearthrug, played with a wooden zoo animal jigsaw. The old puzzle had come from a jumble sale and so much paint had worn off, the chimpanzee had become a hairy headless torso.

'That puzzle makes me shudder,' said May, who'd come indoors to change her sodden gloves. 'Sorry, Rose, who? No, don't tell me …?'

'You guessed it. Ephraim Potts. I'm waiting for him ter dig out his ARP helmet.'

May shook her head. Ephraim, postmistress Victoria's brother, was pedantic and self-important and in his element as a wartime ARP. 'That man. He can never keep his nose out of other people's business. What's he going to do if he finds someone using power inside the restricted hours? Report them?'

'I reckon so. It's a hundred pound fine or three months inside.'

'He'd better keep away from Magna Farm. Bill has an arrangement with the electricity company to keep his power on for the hatchery. I wouldn't like to be in Ephraim's boots if Bill catches him poking about. He's struggling to keep the hens fed and watered, and, with Sally's baby's due in a couple of weeks, he's stretched to breaking point.'

If things had worked out differently, she could have been expecting Bill's baby. She ruffled Spencer's hair. She wouldn't change either of her boys for one of her own.

'This freeze has ter end soon, surely?' Rose said. 'Len is raging about the conditions we're putting up with. He calls the coal shortage "government incompetence". I told him that, apart from what the weather's caused, we had ter endure all this in the war – especially now the street lights are blacked out again.'

May draped her wet gloves over the fender and picked up a warm, dry pair. 'How are things with Len and Peter?'

A log in the stove snapped with a shower of sparks.

'The boys and I are walking on eggshells around Len. He's frustrated with the lack of work at the garage. With the layoffs and restrictions, firms aren't using their vans or lorries, so there aren't many repairs – even if they could get the parts. When they get any jobs in, they are working outside ter get enough light. Lying on the frozen ground under a filthy vehicle wouldn't make anyone cheerful.'

Especially if they were a miserable devil in the first place, May thought.

She massaged her shoulder through the layers of clothing. Her muscles were agonisingly painful and her right hand had blisters from turning the handle of the metal wheel that worked the potato grader.

The great barn doors were open for light, and an icy wind swept through. This was a job for two people, but the POWs and Jesson were busy outside. The farm work was falling behind because of the freeze and everything took three times as long.

The spring sowing was a pipe dream, and everywhere

farmers worried about failing crops and poor harvests because of the late start.

She checked her watch. Five to twelve. She'd better wait until noon to switch on the lights and close one set of doors. Who knew if there was someone snooping around?

The grader was rattling away; the riddle shunting back and forth, moving the potatoes along. Stones and clods of soil tumbled through the holes in the mesh, together with the smaller potatoes, which would ultimately be used for animal feed.

May left the chuntering riddle to pick over the passing spuds, automatically taking out any damaged or rotten ones before they went down the chute and into the sack at the bottom. In her head, she ran through the letter she'd mentally composed to Dorothy. It had to be the first thing to do, to deal with the accusations that had churned over in her mind all night; she'd write it out later and get Cliff to drop it in a pillar box tomorrow.

Someone switched on the lights and a dim glow made a frugal attempt to pierce the gloom of the barn. She smiled as Jesson joined her alongside the machine.

'This bag's full,' May said, swinging the chute over to an empty sack.

'I'll get it,' Jesson said. He swung the bulging sack on to the scales, tossed a couple of potatoes aside before twisting the top corners into two ears. Once tied, he carried the bag across to where batches of them stood in blocks.

'You've got more than another lorry load here,' he said. 'The Jerries can load them in the morning – shall I do the drive?'

The frozen slush on the roads made driving potentially lethal. Some buses weren't running because they couldn't get up the hills and, after delivering the first load to the whole-saler, May had been too unnerved driving the heavily laden lorry to want to attempt it again. Jesson had taken subsequent loads, although he could be less easily spared from other work.

She was conscious of him next to her and wished the atmosphere between them wasn't still so cool. She refused to treat the Germans with anything less than equality, despite Jesson becoming taciturn whenever the POWs ate in the kitchen. The icy conditions hadn't prevented him from returning to the cottage each night, and May missed sharing the evenings with him.

'If we loaded up tonight, you could drop the boys at school in the morning. They're always moaning that the bus takes an age in this weather and I'm waiting for the day it gets stuck on the way.'

'Tell Rose I'll meet the twins at the junction,' he said, shovelling potatoes on to the grader, then helping May sort them. 'How's it working out with Len?'

'Rose tries to keep him and Peter apart. It's no way to live and, once things get back to a normal routine, they'll be together in the evenings and weekends. Unless they sort it out, it's a powder keg waiting to blow.' As long as it doesn't demolish Rose's job when it explodes, she thought.

Waiting until two o'clock for their meal – to use the power on the farm between twelve and two – meant the afternoons were short. Rose had become adept at using the last second of electricity to heat soup for the workers and have it steaming on the table as they came indoors.

Just as they finished the meal, the break lasting only as long as they took to eat, the telephone rang and Rose called,

'May, it's Bill Tyler for you.'

She picked up the receiver. 'May, I'm desperate for feed,' he said. 'My supplier's lorry's broken an axle in Shaftesbury and mine is off the road – I skidded into a tree and the wheel's buckled. The spare's punctured – one of those jobs I didn't get round to,' he said with an ironic laugh. 'I'm right out of feed and I know you're grading – any chance you've got some feed spuds you can let me have?'

Giving potatoes to hens was a way of eking out feed, but it was time-consuming as most poultry farmers preferred to boil the potatoes first. Bill's main livelihood was selling young hens, and he had an excellent reputation. She knew he wouldn't take shortcuts.

'Yes, we've got lots of chats. I could drop some over to you tomorrow afternoon.'

Jesson wouldn't be pleased: he'd say the priority had to be their own farm. The two men had a long-standing antipathy and avoided each other's company, but Bill was a neighbour, and his wife, Sally, had been the head land girl at Elem Farm before her marriage.

'The hill is still impassable. I'll come the long way around,' she said.

Bill tried to persuade her he could bring his tractor to collect them, but May knew he didn't want to leave the farm with Sally's due date being so close.

'It's just along the main road and up the back lane to Magna Farm. Bill said everyone is going that way because the hill is too dangerous, so the lane's quite clear,' she told Jesson. What Bill had actually said was that the lane was "passable". She went on, 'I'll take the lorry when you get back; the engine will be warm so there won't be a problem starting it.'

'I can do it. If I'm taking the kids, I won't be late back,' he said.

Was it the state of the roads, or the fact she was doing Bill a favour that made him so argumentative? She stood her ground.

Chapter 8

Cliff watched every move Jesson made as he drove the lorry. When they got their tractor – Mum had promised they *really* would get it this year – he was going to drive it into the village. He'd hoot at Old Potty and wave to his friends as he roared down the street.

The twins were squashed beside him on the seat. He'd better not talk about tractor driving in front of Jesson – he'd be certain to say Mum wouldn't approve, although it was okay with the law, so why not?

They rounded a bend, and the school bus came into sight. It would shortly turn off to weave through the villages, but as they followed it, Cliff and Bob urged Jesson to overtake.

'It wouldn't be safe. That frozen slush along the edge could force our wheels into the ditch. We're safer staying behind the old jalopy.'

'Course,' Cliff said, and began talking about his ideas of safe driving. Pete stared out of the side window in silence.

'Okay, Pete?' said Cliff, after a few miles.

Pete turned and nodded, his eyes sunk in a face that had angles and shadows it had never had before.

Jesson said, 'So, what do you guys do in recess this weather?'

The twins looked bemused. 'Dinnertime,' Cliff said, proud of his American translations.

Bob mumbled, 'Not much.'

Pete shrugged.

Jesson said, 'No soccer, I guess? D'you have softball over here?'

'Softball?' said Bob.

'Yeah, kinda like baseball, but indoors.'

'We play rounders in the hall in PT sometimes, but not without a teacher there,' Cliff said.

Bob added, 'Too many girls in the hall at dinnertime. They're too soft.'

'Soft girls can be okay,' Jesson said, and winked.

Cliff felt himself redden as he and Bob laughed. This was men's talk. He glanced at Pete, but he was staring ahead and didn't seem to have heard the joke.

Jesson pulled up at the school gates. 'Okay, guys, this is it. See you tonight.' He kept the engine running.

'Come on, Pete, open the door,' Bob said, nudging his brother.

Pete sat still, hands clenched in his lap. 'I'm not goin' in.'

'You've gotta go. You'll get a black mark if you skive.' Bob shook his brother's arm.

'Don't care. I ain't never goin' again,' he said.

Cliff noticed Pete's lip trembling and shook his head at Bob.

Jesson switched off the engine. 'It's okay, boys. Cliff, you and Bob go in. I'll take care of Pete.'

He climbed out of the cab and the boys inched past the gearstick and handbrake to clamber out on the driver's side. Jesson said, 'It'll be all right, Bob. You go in. Just tell 'em Pete was feeling sick. We're going to see if he feels better by the time I've dropped the spuds off. If not, I'll take him home.'

'NO.' Pete half rose from the seat

Bob, pushing Cliff aside, tried to climb back in. Cliff

44

tugged him away. 'Jesson'll look after him. Don't worry.'

Jesson patted Bob's shoulder before climbing back into the cab. He raised a hand as he drove off.

Pete sidled around the door during the mid-morning break. There was the usual uproar in the form room. Cliff was firing a paper airplane across the room when he caught sight of his friend's hunched figure heading to his desk.

'You okay?'

Pete shrugged. Cliff scanned the room for Bob. He was flicking rubber bands at a target stuck on a desk lid. Cliff caught his attention and nodded towards the door.

'Come on,' he said, leading the way to the alcove under the stairs where the janitor kept his buckets and brushes. Bob followed.

'What did you tell the office?' Pete asked, moving his face back from the grey head of an up-turned mop.

'Just what Jesson said,' Bob told him, 'you thought you were gonna spew.'

'They asked if I felt better when I came in,' Pete said.

'What was wrong?' asked Cliff. 'Summate to do with your old man?'

'He wrote to the school. Said I wasn't working hard enough. Just cos I got low marks in the maths test.'

Cliff thought back to the test the previous week. He'd done all right. As usual, Bob had beaten him, but Pete always found sums hard, and it wasn't unusual for him to come be-low the two of them. This time though, he'd been bottom of the class. Cliff was pretty certain it was because he'd been in such a stew lately.

Pete mumbled, 'He wants the Head to beat me.' He aimed a kick at a metal bucket. It gave a loud clang.

Bob threw a furtive glance over his shoulder. Cliff peered past him, but the noise hadn't attracted anyone. He hated seeing his friend so low and wished Mr Gale had never left the Navy.

'Dad only wants you to do well,' Bob said. 'You rile him all the time. If you do what he wants, he's okay—'

Pete's face turned puce, and he shoved the mop aside to push his face into Bob's. 'I ain't one of his sailors. I hate him. We and Mum was crackin' before *he* came back.'

Bob moved forward; shoulders squared. 'Well, he ain't going nowhere.'

Pete shrank down inside his blazer. 'I bloody know it.'

Chapter 9

'I should be back by dinnertime,' May said, slamming the lorry door. 'I'll ring Rose before I leave Magna Farm.'

'Take it easy. There's black ice everywhere,' Jesson said.

'Right you are,' she called through the open window as she eased the lorry into the lane. Creeping up the road, she saw Jesson in the rear-view mirror. He was standing at the gate watching her progress.

Was it better to drive in the tracks of other vehicles, or with the wheels in the frozen snow to the side? She gave the wheel a slight turn. The lorry moved as easily as one of Spencer's Dinky cars, despite the weight of the feed spuds in the back.

As the wheels hit the slush, frozen into jagged peaks, the lorry lurched and jolted as if it was alive; the wheel juddered in her hands and a crunching, tearing sound made her panic. She swung back to the ruts, but the lorry veered on over to the far side slush. One of the sacks fell over.

Her hands were sweating inside her gloves. She gripped the wheel and moved it the tiniest amount. The vehicle responded by settling in to the comparative smoothness of the twin tracks. She ran her forearm over her brow. She should have let Jesson do this.

The hedges on either side of the turning to Crompton Magna were walls of frozen snow, and May gingerly guided the lorry into a white tunnel. Although Bill had told her all the traffic used it, the lane was single track and in a worse state than their own.

The heat of her earlier panic had abated. She felt clammy and shivery in the unheated cab.

She stared hard out of the windscreen at the road ahead. Her head ached from focusing on the whiteness surrounding her. There was a bend ahead. Surely Magna Farm was just beyond it?

'What's that?' As she crept to the point of the corner, something dark red came into sight, lying at the edge of the road. She stopped just ahead of the object and craned towards the passenger side to look out. It was a relief to see colour, even though the maroon metal arch stood out like a gash on a beautiful face. A mudguard. The paint had a deep gouge scored across it and the underside was encrusted with snow and mud.

She accelerated gently, rounding the bend, gaze sweeping the road. As the lane straightened out, she braked again. Black mud and splinters of wood lay spread across the furrowed snow. She stood, crouched, in the cab, looking down in to the nearside ditch.

A ragged rut ran towards it. Someone had skidded off the road here. There was no sign of a vehicle, but a telegraph pole on the bank listed alarmingly. It bore a deep scar where the black tarred surface had been ripped away, exposing the yellow pine beneath.

The pole seemed in no immediate danger of snapping or falling further, and the people involved must have been able to drive away. Lucky, May thought, putting the lorry into gear. Something caught her attention before she raised the clutch: black, icicle-encrusted wires dangled through the hedge.

Muffled up to the eyes, Bill came out from a shed as May pulled into the yard. His battered felt hat, faded to dark olive green, was almost in contact with the brown knitted scarf wound around his nose and mouth. He suffered with chest problems and Sally was clearly insisting he protect his health as much as possible.

'Let's get these spuds off and we'll go into the house for a drink,' he said. 'Sally's looking forward to seeing you; she's lonely stuck out here. Even my POWs haven't turned up today – sent to clear a road somewhere, I suspect.' He lowered the tailboard and heaved himself aboard the lorry. After hefting the sacks to the rear, he jumped down and May helped pile them on a hand truck to ferry them to the feed store, just off the hatchery.

Inside, Bill added a couple of logs to the pot-bellied stove and scooped some potatoes into the huge caldron simmering on the top. 'This'll keep 'em going until the supplies get through,' he said. May noticed some yellowing cabbage leaves and other vegetable peelings in a bowl on the window-sill. Kitchen scraps had become an essential supplement to the meagre poultry rations during the war, and showed no signs of changing soon.

When he decided that the reject potatoes were cooking, Bill led the way to the farmhouse.

May had visited here once when Bill was still a bachelor. He'd had a housekeeper who was a wonderful cook. She fondly recalled the slice of melt-in-the-mouth apple cake Bill had given her that day.

The warm kitchen smelt of beeswax. The room had received a fresh coat of distemper since May's last visit and a cream-coloured Aga replaced the old range.

'Sit down, May, I'll find Sally,' Bill said, after they'd

taken off their outdoor clothing.

She surveyed the room. Sally certainly had an eye for décor. The room was revitalised. A vase of teasels, brought to life by orange Chinese lanterns, sat in the centre of the table. She should instigate something like this transformation at Elem Farm. She'd done little with it since she'd inherited the place; only Cliff and Spencer's bedrooms and the guest room had been redecorated. Thirty-six years old and living like her late father-in-law!

'MAY.'

She jumped to her feet at the sound of Bill's shout.

'Bill?' she called at the foot of the stairs.

His anguished face appeared over the bannister. 'Sally's gone into labour – it's early. Can you call the midwife? The number's beside the phone.'

'Of course.' She dashed back into the kitchen. She'd noticed the telephone on the kitchen wall and thought, what a sensible arrangement; no shedding boots and standing in a cold hallway to answer it.

She picked up the handset and listened for the dialling tone. Nothing. She flipped the receiver rest. Silence. The phone felt wrong, empty. Hell. The wires hanging in the hedge.

She ran back to the stairs. 'Bill?'

The sound of quick footsteps and a white-faced Bill leaned over the rail. 'Is she on her way?'

'The phone wires are down – something hit the telegraph pole.'

'Christ.' He convulsed in a cough. May could hear the rasp of his breath.

'May,' he gasped, 'please help.' He dashed back out of sight, calling, 'I've brought calves and sheep into the world, but I know nothing about babies.'

You and me both, thought May, already halfway up the stairs. Her children had come to her after their birth; Spencer, only three weeks after, but she'd had no involvement. Apart from the time a farmhand asked her to pull on a calving rope when a cow was in difficulty she'd only ever seen her mother's cat give birth.

Now, she had a child's father, well used to birthing animals, panicking about his wife's labour and getting himself into more of a state than his wife appeared to be as she lay on their double bed.

'Sally.' May took Sally's hand. She looked hot but, otherwise, fairly composed, even her wavy blonde hair remained immaculately in place. She'd spread the mattress with towels and, feeling something squelch under foot, May realised she was standing on damp carpet.

'Sorry, May. I'd had a few twinges and went for a lie-down. As I got up to make some tea, my waters broke. I should have had hours before the contractions started, but I'd only just got the towels and so on when—' She squeezed May's hand as a spasm caught her. 'Ow!' she gasped. 'We need to time the contractions; the closer they are, the sooner the baby will come.'

May turned the bedside clock to face her. There was a notebook and pencil on the table beside it. She'd forgotten how organised Sally was: notebooks, towels. She probably didn't need any help at all.

May noted down the time, twelve thirty-five. She should be ringing Rose to say she was on her way home.

Bill was fluttering around, asking if he should get hot water or scissors. He had a hand on his chest, and May saw Sally's calm expression falter as she watched him. She looked pointedly from May to Bill and back again.

'Bill. I don't think we need hot water just now, other than for a cup of tea. I'm parched and I bet Sally would love a cup, too,' May said.

'But—'

'Just what the doctor ordered,' Sally said. She mouthed, "Thanks," to May as Bill turned away to go downstairs.

'He mustn't get too worked-up. His chest is bad in this weather and with no help, he's in with the hens too much. The dust affects him badly; sometimes he can barely catch his breath.' Sally lay back on the pillows.

May said, 'I'm here now, so this is one problem he doesn't have to cope with. Just rest. I'm going to wash my hands. Tell me what I need to do when I get back.'

By four o'clock, Sally was having contractions every five or six minutes and she told May to sterilize the scissors and fetch antiseptic, water, soap and flannels, and a soft white towel for the baby. In the corner of the room, a cot was already prepared to receive the infant: nappies, flannelette nightgowns and tiny vests already laid out on a chest of drawers.

May drew the heavy raspberry coloured velvet curtains and shut out the view of the dark farmyard where a dim light glimmered through the hatchery window. Bill had to care for the chickens, but he spent more time calling up the stairs than he did in the yard.

As she turned around, she admired the room. Pink rose-bud wallpaper and white paint gave the bedroom a fresh, modern look, notwithstanding the clutter of confinement scattered about.

She added a couple of logs to the fire that glowed in the

grate.

'May.' Sally was looking less relaxed; her forehead glistening with perspiration. Her knuckles were white as she gripped May's hand, riding the waves of the contractions. 'I don't want Bill in here for the birth – I don't want him to see me like that – I'm sorry this has fallen to you. If only the wires hadn't gone today.'

May felt the same, but mainly because she had no way of telling home where she was.

Chapter 10

'Mum'll have yer guts fer garters.'

'I ain't goin' home when she's not about. He'll use his belt on me.' Pete sounded defiant, but Cliff heard the wobble in his voice.

'Go on home, Bob,' he said. 'I expect we'll meet your mum in the lane and she'll make him go back with her.'

'But what'll I tell Dad?' Bob said, still hesitating to leave the bus stop. Perhaps he wasn't as sure he wouldn't come in for some of his dad's temper as he made out.

'Tell him I ain't being pushed around no more,' Pete shouted over his shoulder, marching across the main road and into Elem Lane. 'Coming, Cliff?'

'He'll be okay,' Cliff told Bob. 'I've gotta stick this in the postbox, but I'll catch him up.'

He pulled a crumpled letter from his school bag and tried to slide his way right across the road on the ice. After dropping the letter in the box, he skidded his way back to Pete, who was stomping on frozen puddles as if he wanted to kill them.

As they passed the cottage, Cliff said, 'What did Jesson say to you this morning?'

Pete gathered a handful of snow from under the hedge, balled it between his gloved hands, and aimed it at a telegraph post. It landed on the wood with a splat.

'Good shot!'

'Humph.' Pete walked on, hands in his coat pockets. 'He said they'd bullied him in America cos of his skin colour and the fact that his family had a farm – not many black people work for themselves over there. Their fruit trees got smashed up and then, when they got to pick their plums, people wouldn't buy them. They had to take them miles away to sell.'

Cliff had heard some of this before, although Jesson rarely talked about his childhood.

'Blacks have ter use different parts of buses and trains. They're treated like dirt. Even when he got into university and then into Tus … Tuskey—

'Tuskegee.'

'Yeah, Tuskegee, to get to be an airman, it didn't count for nothing.'

The farmhouse chimney stack came into sight above the hedge. Cliff always looked out for the soot-blackened chimney pot as he came down the lane. Today, smoke was curling into the grey sky.

'It's why he came here. We treat him right,' Cliff said.

'Yeah. He said I've got the chance to get an education without being despised and I should take it and get a proper career.'

'Makes sense.'

'Yeah, but it's the old man he should tell. Get him off my back. He thinks if I don't wanna go in the Navy, I'm not worth a light.'

'Maybe—'

'Oh gawd, it's Mum. What's she looking for? Not me? If Bob's phoned her, I'll kill—'

Mrs Gale had been standing at the farmhouse gate. She ran up to them. 'Cliff, you haven't seen your mother or the lorry, have you?' She had her coat clutched around her shoulders. She was wearing her apron and didn't look ready to go home, even though it was getting dark. Her face was serious, with no sign of her usual smile. Only then did she realise Pete was beside him.

'Peter. What are you doing here?'

'Mum?' said Cliff, a stab of fear in his chest. 'What's happened to her?' Mrs Gale was always calm; if she was in the lane looking for his mum, something bad was going on.

Mrs Gale told them Mum had gone over to Mr Tyler's farm and hadn't phoned, like she'd promised, or come back.

'We've gotta look for her,' Cliff said, dumping his schoolbag in the farmhouse gateway and turning back the way they'd come. 'Comin' Pete?'

'Cliff, stop. You can't just go off. You need ter talk ter Jesson; he's already planning ter look for her.'

'He's got a bad leg. I'm okay.'

Mrs Gale's voice dropped into schoolteacher tone. 'No arguing. Come indoors and we'll sort this out. And we'll sort out why you're not at home, Peter,' she said, standing with her hand on the gate, making them enter the path first.

Jesson refused to allow Cliff to go with him to look for his mother. 'The lorry probably won't start and Mr Tyler's isn't working, so she's probably had to stay there. Mrs Gale phoned the post office at Magna and they think the line to the farm is down.'

Jesson was trying to make it sound as if it was nothing much, but he and Mrs Gale didn't worry about nothing. And he was going out just before dark in the freezing cold. He had to be more worried than he let on.

Mrs Gale had spoken to Pete alone in the office. As Cliff came downstairs, he heard Pete shouting and, when they came out, Mrs Gale said Pete was going to stay the night with him and Spence, so that they had company while Jesson was out. She didn't look at Pete.

The POWs knocked at the door, ready to head off for their lift. Cliff and Pete almost pushed Mrs Gale out of the house to get her to walk up the lane with the men. Jesson left with them. The empty house immediately felt huge and cold.

Cliff unlatched the flap at the front of the stove and threw some logs on the fire. 'I'm starving. Want your dinner, Spence?'

There was a casserole in the oven, and the boys decided to eat straight away. Cliff turned the oven down low to keep Jesson and his mother's food hot.

Spence climbed on to his chair.

'Pete, do his bib, will you?'

Pete tied the strings around Spence's neck and the little boy picked up his spoon and sat with it clutched upright in his hand.

'You look like Oliver Twist,' Pete said.

It was good to hear his friend making a joke. He never used to be lost for something to make you laugh.

Cliff ladled out the casserole. It was mainly carrot and potato, but he spotted some bits of meat – rabbit from the last ones Jesson had shot, probably.

Pete sliced bread from the loaf in the bread crock and laid a slice beside each spoon he'd set on the table. 'Marge?'

'In the safe in the back-kitchen. We're supposed to be getting a refrigerator – icebox, Jesson calls it. Could just put it outside in this lot.' He nodded his head towards the darkened windows outlined with what looked like piped icing. He carried the plates to the table and then drew the curtains, trying not to look out. He didn't want to think of Mum out there alone, maybe hurt, or trapped in the lorry …

Chapter 11

Bill insisted on seeing Sally for a few minutes between bouts of pain. May shooed him out, suggesting he made some sandwiches. She was hungry and although Sally said the thought of food made her feel sick, Bill needed something useful to do.

She mopped Sally's brow; the pains were severe and lasted longer each time.

'May, can you check to see whether the head is visible yet?'

May had been dreading this. She'd known Sally for six years; they'd had their differences, but this intimate examination would take their relationship to a new level.

'Pleeese, May,' Sally gasped, her face contorted in agony.

May washed and dried her hands, before lifting the hem of Sally's cotton nightgown.

She tried to forget this was her friend and take a clinical approach.

There was something dark and wet in the orifice between Sally's legs. 'I think I can see the head,' she said. Sally gave an animal-like gasp as a huge contraction racked her body. May caught her breath as a bloody head emerged. It looked at once miraculous and macabre, this mutation of woman and child. 'The baby's head is out,' she said. 'Come on, Sally, one push and it will be over.'

Sally's face contorted again, sweat streaming like tears, as she gave a groan deep in her throat and, with a shudder, the baby slithered out on to the towel-covered mattress.

'It's here!' May said, as elated as if she'd given birth herself. She remembered watching the cowman and wiped mucus from the baby's face and checked that it was breathing. 'Well done, Sally.'

'Is it all right?' Sally, nightgown sticking to her breasts, hair plastered to her face, craned forward towards her own lower body as she issued instructions to cut the cord.

May's hand shook as she prepared to sever the bloody rope between two pieces of tightly tied tape. What if she hurt them?

'Come on, May, I want to see my baby,' Sally said.

May steadied her nerves. You've come this far, she told herself, and holding her breath, she snipped.

The baby was free. It gave a great wail, causing May's heart to lurch, before she realised it was what Sally had been waiting for. She swaddled the baby in the white towel and passed it to its mother. 'Your daughter,' she said.

Sally's expression was wondrous – as if she was looking at a holy vision. May felt a tear in her eye, both for the beauty of the moment and for the experience she would never have. She stamped out envy. She had Cliff, and Spencer was as good as hers; the love she felt for them could never be supplanted.

'Can you tidy me up? I can't see Bill looking like this. Ooh.' Sally put a hand on her belly. 'It's the afterbirth, May. I'm sorry, it's the last thing – can you …'

May dealt with the expulsion of the placenta. Sally insisted the midwife would need to check it and May wrapped the mass of blood and membrane in some newspapers from the hearth. She removed the soiled towels from the bed and helped Sally change into a fresh nightgown.

Sally freshened her face with a damp flannel and ran a

comb through her hair while May held the baby. The child's crumpled red face had an angry expression and May guessed she wanted to be fed. As she jogged the infant, May couldn't see any obvious resemblance to either parent unless there was perhaps Bill's reddish tinge in the layer of fine hair.

May had just tucked the sheets around Sally and the baby when there was a light tap on the door.

'Come in, Bill,' Sally called.

Carrying a tray, Bill appeared. May leapt forward to prevent it crashing to the floor as the new father caught sight of his wife and child.

Placing the tray on the dressing table, May put a couple of lopsided sandwiches on a plate for herself, collected the newspaper bundle and towels and struggled out of the door unnoticed.

'We can never thank you enough,' Bill said as May pulled on her coat and boots. 'Are you sure you won't stay? It's getting late.'

She just wanted to get home. Sally and the baby were asleep. She'd eaten the sandwiches and helped herself to a cup of tea an hour ago. Now, she was exhausted and longing for bed. Besides, she had to get back; the family would be panic stricken until they heard from her.

Stepping outside, she trod into a low dam of fresh snow. Hadn't they had enough of this?

Bill came out with her. She was worried about him in the bitter wind, but she wasn't strong enough to swing the handle if the lorry failed to start.

The lorry tyres were buried in snow up to the wheel rims and flakes were eddying blizzard-like in the light of their torches.

She tugged the door, praying it hadn't frozen shut. It opened, and she climbed on to the seat. After the warmth of the house, the leather beneath her felt like a slab of ice. Bill stood beside the open door as she turned the key and pressed the starter button.

The engine turned over before firing hesitatingly and coming sluggishly into life.

'Take it easy, May, the lane won't be too bad yet – the hedges on either side will protect it – but once you get to the main road, it'll be drifting.'

'I know. Don't worry. And I'll make those calls as soon as I can.' She had a list of numbers in her pocket: the midwife, Sally's parents, and Bill's cousin, all of whom needed to be told about the baby's arrival.

As Bill had said, the lane was much as she'd found it on the way to the farm, except for fresh snow lying a few inches deep on the surface. The hedges loomed like people with sheets over their heads pretending to be ghosts.

Without its load, the lorry moved with the lightest nudge of the wheel and she steered dead centre of the road.

'Look out for the broken mudguard,' she told herself, 'then it'll only be half a mile or so to the main road.'

Mesmerised from staring at the yellow glow of the head-lights on the white road, she felt disorientated. How long had she been driving? She must see the mudguard – at least the buried shape of it – soon.

Was this the bend? She eased her foot off the accelerator, and the lorry slowed to walking pace. She stared at the edge of the light pattern; if she ran over the mudguard, she'd likely damage the lorry and be stranded all night. Her hands were icy in her gloves as she clutched the wheel, forcing it to keep on course. Was that a hump in the snow? She risked a glance towards the verge, looking for the leaning telegraph pole.

Everything was shrouded in snow, and it was impossible to identify one post. She looked back at the road.

'WHAT THE—'

Something tall and black reared up in the lights. She jerked the wheel. The lorry slid towards the left bank, light as a ballerina. She spun the wheel towards the other side and, as she slammed a foot on the brake, she remembered Jesson's warning about not braking on ice. Too late. Like a horse with the bit between its teeth, the lorry bolted for the right-hand ditch. May wrestled with the wheel before everything went dark.

Chapter 12

'May … May … wake up.'

Someone was shaking her arm.

'May. Come on, you've got to get out.'

She wished he'd stop shouting; she wanted to sleep. Why was he shaking her? She opened her eyes. Her head hurt. A light blazed in her face. She groaned and moved an arm to shove it away.

'May. Are you hurt?'

Jesson? Where was she? She'd been at Bill's farm. There was a baby … snow … something on the road. She'd crashed. She was trapped – she had to get out.

She threw her arms about; there must be something she could get hold of. The wheel was useless; it was angled steeply down towards the side window, the same as the seat. The light flashed again and lit the side of the cab. All that was visible through the window was a wall of compressed snow.

Jesson grabbed her arm. 'Take it easy. I'll get you out if you stop fighting me.'

He held her wrists and spoke deliberately, 'Are you hurt? Can you move your legs?'

His hands on her skin calmed her. He'd help; he'd always come to her rescue. She focussed on her legs and feet. There was no pain and, although they were icy cold, she could move her joints and wiggle her toes.

'I'm all right, but it's too awkward to climb out.'

'Push with your feet as I lift you,' he said, clamping his arms around her ribcage.

She had a momentary feeling of embarrassment, knowing her breasts rested on his forearms, but, through her many layers, she doubted he would notice.

'Now,' he said.

She shoved her feet against the door and her body inched past the gearstick and the gap between the seats.

Jesson's upper body crouched above her. 'If you put your feet against the side of the seat, you'll be able to push yourself up and outta the door.'

The light she had seen was coming from a torch, now balanced on the dashboard. Its beam lit the furrow of the ditch, running at a shallow angle in front. Hell. If the driver's side was in the ditch, then the other side was up in the air.

She wrenched her body up and back and shoved with her feet. Jesson, thrown off balance, staggered and fell backwards through the open door.

'Jesson,' she shrieked. 'Jesson, are you all right?'

She snatched up the torch and, standing with her feet on the edge of the seat, shone the light down to see him clambering to his feet from the snowy ground. It was the figure that had appeared in the road before the accident. She'd nearly run him down.

'If that's the way you treat your knight in stripy armour,' he said, straightening the bumblebee balaclava, now rolled up into a cap, 'next time, I'll stay by the fire.'

'I'm sorry,' she said, leaning out of the door. The ground was too far away to step out; she'd have to jump. As she straightened up, her head swam, and she clutched at the bodywork.

Jesson called, 'Turn around and come out backwards. I'll help you, but throw me the flashlight first.'

She dropped the torch down to him. He shone it upwards.

Marvellous. Now he could watch her flailing, backside first, out of the lorry. What an elegant distressed damsel figure she cut.

'I won't let you fall,' Jesson called.

To hell with it. What else could happen today? She brought one foot up to the sill, then the other, before releasing her grip and letting herself drop.

She landed heavily in Jesson's arms. He set her down gently. As she stood upright, her head started spinning again, and she grabbed hold of his arm.

'Whoa! What is it?'

'Dizzy.'

He steadied her and led her to the side of the lorry, where she leant against the wooden body, feeling nauseous.

'Does anything hurt?' he asked, running the light up and down her length.

'Just my head.'

He focussed the beam on the side of her head. 'Can you take off your scarf?'

She unknotted it. The air was full of ice chips, and she was shivering.

Jesson parted her hair, gently feeling her head where she'd hit the side window.

'No blood, but there's already a bruise on your temple. I reckon you're concussed. I need to get you home.'

May gave a mirthless laugh. She looked around. Only the offside wheels were in the ditch; the nearside tyres were still in contact with the road, but the cab was half-buried in deep snow. It was hopeless. They were going to have to walk – at least half a mile to the main road, and then over three miles to the farm.

She replaced the scarf and turned up her collar. Jesson

was kicking snow away around the wheels.

'I think we might drive it out – look, the other back tyre is only just on the edge of the ditch. If we had something to give traction, we might make it.'

He was mad. Her head had a steam hammer pounding away inside it. They had to start walking. Jesson was asking whether there was anything in the cab that might provide grip for the tyres – a blanket, or a rug, perhaps?

She couldn't think of anything; there had been a bit of old carpet, but it got soaked from their boots, and she'd taken it out a few weeks ago.

He began digging about, kicking in the snow along the hedgerow. He soon gave up.

There was nothing that would help. When she left home, the only thing in the back had been the spuds and—

'Jesson.'

He dashed over, feet sliding on the ice beneath the snow. 'What is it? Are you feeling worse?'

'Sacks.'

'What—'

'Sacks. Bill gave me a bundle of empty sacks to replace the ones with the spuds in. I threw them in the back.'

'Good girl.'

Cheek. But now wasn't the time.

Jesson placed a foot on the wheel rim and the other on the mudguard, hauling himself up to look over the planked side of the body.

'I see them. Right over the far corner.'

'Don't get in, Jesson. I'll never get you out if—'

'It's okay.' He jumped down and snapped off a whippy branch from the hedge. He climbed back up and, after a few seconds, triumphantly brandished a hessian bundle.

It wouldn't work. They'd be here forever, or they'd die on the road home. Her mind was a fog, and she was so cold.

He'd got it all planned out and had laid the sacks behind the wheels.

He said, 'She'll come out like a cork from a bottle, and I want you right outta the way.' Everyone gave her instructions. She was supposed to be the boss. Babies, lorries, they thought she knew nothing. He was shouting again.

'May. Listen to me.' He gripped her arms. 'You have to move away.'

She stared at him. He wasn't the boss. Nor was Sally. She was in charge.

'May? May? Come on. Come with me.' He took her arm and walked her along the lane, away from the lorry and into the darkness. 'Wait here,' he said, pulling her to him and kissing her cheek.

She watched him head back into the dark, taking the light. Had he kissed her? She felt herself waver as a gust of wind whipped at her coat. She fought to remain upright on the slippery road and stared into the distance as the glimmer of light disappeared.

The lorry door slammed. She knew it wouldn't start – it was temperamental at the best of times, although did she recall it started at Bill's without the handle? She crossed her fingers in her gloves and rammed her hands deeper into her pockets.

The sound of the whirring engine reached her. She knew it. But it fired. Hurray. It cut. Damn it. It whirred again. This time, when it fired, it faltered a little, but then revived and revved up. She released her breath. It was only the beginning. He still had to get it moving. A headlight came on, and it felt like a gift from heaven; even seeing this desolate scene lit up gave her hope.

After the revving came a graunch of gears. Don't say it's damaged. Please don't let it be damaged. She clenched her fists and willed with every ounce of strength. Let it come out.

Nothing happened. She could hear the engine straining. One wheel was spinning; bits of debris were thrown up.

It was hopeless. He'd blow up the engine and then they'd have nothing. Why hadn't she got the tractor? She was useless. Couldn't run the farm, couldn't deliver a baby without instruction, couldn't get a lorry out. What was that? A second yellow light? Yes! The other headlight shining yellow across the snow. She heard branches snap. The two lights moved away from her and swung into horizontal. He'd done it. It was out.

She slithered down the road towards the lorry. From behind the bright lights, Jesson appeared. He caught her as she half-fainted, half-flung herself at him. 'You did—'

He stopped her praise with a kiss. She clung to him. 'Thank you. Thank you,' she murmured into his collar.

'I love you, May,' he said.

She passed out.

Chapter 13

Mum was still so pale. He'd tried not to think about the only other time he'd seen someone unconscious. The outcome hadn't been good, but Dr Haskett had told Jesson on the phone that Mum would be okay if she had quiet and stayed in bed.

The doctor said he would come as soon as the lane was passable.

'Didn't you tell him you'd got through, bringing Mum back?' he'd asked Jesson.

Jesson, who had bags under his eyes and could barely hobble up the stairs, explained that they'd only just made it home; the roads had been frozen and getting worse as the night went on.

When he'd barged open the back door, Mum in his arms, Cliff had thought she was dead and threw himself at her, calling her name.

She'd opened her eyes as Jesson, demanding blankets and hot tea, laid her in the armchair.

'I'm all right, Cliff,' she murmured, her hazel eyes unfocussed.

He reached to hug her and saw a lump on her temple, the size of a hen's egg.

Jesson fetched water and antiseptic and, as he bathed her face, Mum kept on about a bit of paper in her coat pocket. Cliff found it and she insisted Jesson phoned the numbers written on it. Mr Tyler and Sally had had a baby girl; Mum had helped it to be born and had promised to phone and tell people.

Jesson did the phoning as soon as he'd carried Mum up to her bed.

Cliff refused to leave Mum's bedside and spent the night in the chair beside her, wrapped in a blanket.

When he woke, his neck stiff and pins and needles in his arm, he pulled the curtains back to let a little light fall across the foot of the bed. Just to see what he was doing, he told himself, not admitting it was to make sure Mum was still breathing.

Her white face scared him. The bruise had darkened during the night and looked like a ripe plum beside her eyebrow.

There was a light rap on the door.

'Come in,' he called softly.

Jesson came in carrying a cup and saucer and a plate of toast.

'She's still asleep,' Cliff said.

'It's for you,' Jesson replied.

Cliff realised he was starving and took a slice of toast. Jesson sat on a chair by the window and they talked in low voices.

'Mrs Gale won't make it this morning – the lane's too bad,' Jesson told him.

'Pete'll be pleased.' He knew his friend had been hoping his mum wouldn't get there, and he'd have to stay at the farm over the weekend.

'Yeah, but it means the doc won't get here either.'

'The bruise has gone down a bit,' Cliff said, taking a gulp of tea.

They looked at Mum. She'd hate Jesson seeing her like this; her hair was a mess: dull brown, not shiny with gold bits in it like usual, and she was still in yesterday's clothes. No one had felt able to undress her and they'd just helped to take off her two jumpers before pulling the bedclothes up over her blouse and trousers.

'Is Spence up?' Cliff asked.

'Pete's giving him some breakfast. I'd better get on,' Jesson said, getting to his feet.

'I'll come and help,' Cliff said, 'if you think Mum'll be all right?'

'It's up to you. I know you don't want to leave her, but the doc said she needs to rest, so I guess sleep is the best thing.'

He took a long look at his mother, lying oblivious to their worries.

Chapter 14

Someone was inside her head, tapdancing in hobnail boots. She groaned and opened her eyes.

Her bedroom was in semi-darkness, and she turned to check the time. A piece of paper, propped in front of the bed-side clock, bore Cliff's handwriting. "Mum. You MUSTNT get up. There's a bell if you want something. Love Cliff".

The old cowbell she hadn't seen since her father-in-law's convalescence years ago lay next to the clock. It was half-past ten; usually she'd have been up for hours.

She touched the side of her head and winced. A swollen lump felt hot under her fingers. She remembered the crash. She'd driven the lorry into a ditch and Jesson had got her out, after she'd come close to running him down.

Had he rung everyone about the baby? A girl. What had they called her? She kept turning thoughts over in her mind, refusing to dwell on the incident that happened, or that she imagined happened, just before she passed out.

Her mouth was dry. She reached and shook the bell, intrigued to see what would happen.

After a few moments, a hesitant voice sounded at the un-latched door.

'Mrs Sheppard?'

'Come in, Peter.'

The lad came in, eyes lowered. He looks as bad as I feel, May thought. 'Are you all right? You look peaky,' she said.

'Yeah, I'm okay, thanks. Are you feeling better, Mrs Sheppard?' He gave her a quick glance.

'This is a bit sore,' she said, touching the bruise. 'And

72

I've got a whacking headache. I'm thirsty, too. Could you get me some water, please?'

'Of cours—'

'Arn Mee!' A curly haired missile hurtled towards the bed. Peter grabbed the child before he could throw himself on May.

'Spence, your dad said not to make a noise near Auntie May.'

Spencer wriggled away and began climbing on the bed.

May shuffled to sit up. 'It's all right, Peter. Leave him here while you fetch my water. He doesn't understand.'

'Mr Cobb said we wasn't to let you be disturbed.'

'Don't worry, we'll be fine. Is your mum not here to-day?'

'No, the lane's too bad,' he said.

Was there a note of relief?

Peter glanced back as he reached the door, but after a second went on his way.

'Spencer, can you go to the curtains and pull them back for me?'

The little boy gave one of his joyful grins and toddled around the bed to the floor-length curtains. He tugged one back sufficiently to open it halfway.

'Well done. Now the other one,' May said. He pulled again, then changed to a two-handed push and most of the fabric slid to the end of the rail.

The over-white light that spilled into the room told her the world outside was still snow-covered. She should get up, but as she lifted Spencer on to the bed beside her, she realised that even that slight movement exacerbated the pain in her head.

She and Spencer were playing "This little piggy went to

market" when Peter arrived with a tray of tea, water, and toast.

'You are a good lad,' May said.

Peter flushed. She remembered the boy was in the midst of a row with his father and thought how peculiar it was that Len, held up as a paragon of fatherhood whilst out of circulation in the Navy, had become a tyrant to one of his sons on his return. Was it the case of absence making the heart grow fonder, or had the man's character changed during his six years of service?

'I've found some aspirins,' Peter said. 'Mum always takes 'em for her headaches.'

Rose must get through quite a few at the moment, May thought, tipping two from the bottle and swallowing them with a sip of water.

'Come on, Spence. Let's leave Auntie May to have her breakfast. Shall we get the Meccano out?'

The little boy's expression turned from pique to joy. He slid off the bed and took Peter's hand.

A rumpus downstairs woke May. Someone, she thought it was Cliff, was crying out as if in pain. It was just after twelve o'clock. She'd been in bed for fourteen hours.

Enough was enough. She'd changed into a slip when she'd visited the bathroom after eating the toast Peter had brought her, and now she pulled on a sweater, skirt and stockings and, feeling slightly unsteady, made her way downstairs.

She halted in the kitchen doorway. Jesson was bent over the footstool from the sitting room, wrapping a wet towel around Peter's ankle. The lad was ashen and clearly in pain. Cliff was attempting to corral Spencer, who was charging about waving a spikey piece of Meccano and likely to impale anyone who got in his way.

'What on earth is going on?' The words came out stronger than she'd intended, and the tableau froze for a second before four heads turned her way and a cacophony broke out.

'May—'

'Mum—'

'Mrs Sheppard—'

'Arn Mee!'

Spencer flung his creation to the floor and shot towards her. She braced herself as his little body fell against her legs in a bear hug.

It took half an hour before they restored order: Peter's suspected sprained ankle bandaged; Spencer eating a boiled egg and soldiers, the Meccano contraption dismantled and back in the box; Cliff making sandwiches and Jesson sitting beside May at the table updating her on events since the previous evening, once she'd persuaded him she did not need to be confined to bed.

'Everything was under control,' he said with a rueful look, 'until Pete slipped on the ice out back. We helped him indoors, but it became complete chaos.'

'And that's when I appeared,' May said.

'Yeah. The worst possible moment.' Jesson's eyes sparkled as he added, 'Caught us out, didn't she, guys?'

'As always,' Cliff said, laying a plate of sandwiches on the table and grinning at May.

She knew how relieved he was that she was up and about. Her head still pounded, but she wouldn't take more aspirin until she could do so unobserved. No point in worrying them again.

Peter gave a weak smile to acknowledge Jesson's joke, but he was very pale, lying in the armchair, his foot on the stool, a blanket over him.

The lad was having a hard time. Nothing went right for him and May was sure they could lay the blame at his father's door. Why was the man so intractable? Rose was a wonderful mother and had cared for the boys impeccably during the war, despite working in the munitions factory, worrying about Len and coping with rationing and the hardships everyone had endured.

They were close friends, but May found it difficult to broach the subject of Rose's boorish husband. She must try, for Peter's sake, as soon as things returned to normal.

'Did you hear the weather forecast?' she asked as they ate.

'This morning they said no change. There's nothing we can do. It's the ideal opportunity for you to rest. Cliff and I can get the animals done. We've got a good routine going.'

'Are you really better, Mum?' Cliff asked.

'Bit of a headache and I look a fright, especially this,' she touched the purple bump on her head. 'Otherwise, I reckon I'll survive. I'm sorry I scared you.'

'He stayed all night beside your bed. We were all barred from entering,' Jesson said with a grin as he ruffled Cliff's hair, making him blush.

'Just wanted to be there in case you needed anything,' he said.

May smiled. He'd have been anxious; he felt keeping her safe was his responsibility. How had she got lucky enough to have such a caring son?

'Should I tell me mum about me ankle?' Peter asked.

May's heart went out to him. He wanted his mother but was too scared to go home, not that he could walk in his present state, but she doubted his father would show any sympathy if he turned up on their doorstep.

'I'll leave a message for her to call back and you can have a word when she does. Is that all right?'

'Thanks.' He gave a wan smile.

'I'll ring,' Jesson said, 'save you getting cold in the hall.'

'Tell you what, Peter. Jesson and Cliff have got to go back to work, so what about you and I having a game of rummy by the fire? Spencer can play with his cars and you and I can take things easy.'

'Yeah, thanks,' Peter said.

'I found this.' Jesson appeared from the hall carrying a gnarled walking stick. May recognised it as one from under the hat stand, among assorted umbrellas and other paraphernalia that had belonged to her late father-in-law.

'That's ideal. You'll get about with that, Peter, no problem,' May said.

Peter took the stick and laid it next to his chair.

'I've left a message. Your ma'll phone soon, Hopalong.' Jesson teased Peter. 'Come on, Cliff, let's make tracks.'

Cliff groaned and got to his feet. Handing Spencer his favourite toy car, he fetched his coat and boots from the fender where they were drying.

'You'll be all right, won't you, Mum?'

'Of course, and thanks for helping, Cliff. We couldn't manage without you.'

'It's all right,' he said, blushing.

Chapter 15

Cliff had been bored for ten days. It was great having Pete staying with them – Mum had persuaded Mrs Gale that he couldn't get home and should rest his foot – but, even now his foot had healed and he'd chucked the stick, there wasn't a lot to do. At start of winter, he'd never have imagined snow could ever bore him.

The weather was still biting cold, and everything was frozen. Mum and Jesson worried about the farm; no work could be done, so there was no point in the POWs coming. Mrs Gale only made it into work a couple of days a week. It meant Mum could get outside, but Jesson wouldn't let her do much and especially driving.

He'd helped Jesson bash out the dents in the lorry door and touch in the green paint, shocked to realise Mum's accident could have been much worse. He tried not to think of what would have happened if Jesson hadn't gone to look for her.

Sally and Mr Tyler had sent a big basket of posh food from the shop in Magna to thank Mum for helping with the baby. If she hadn't, he thought, she wouldn't have ended up in the ditch.

They were calling the baby Jemima. It sounded silly to him, but they said it was from the Bible. Her second name was May, which he did like. Mum deserved it.

School had given up; there was no coal for heating and, with power cuts, often no lights either. Mum kept him and Pete working on the stuff the school had set. Mrs Gale had brought Pete's books, so they didn't have to share and, one day, Bob came with his mother. He'd tried to leave the twins some time alone, but they didn't get on like they used to. Pete didn't have a pleasant word to say about his dad, and Bob didn't want to run his father down.

Life was dreary and hard and even with eking out the fancy biscuits and tins from the Tylers, the food was usually the same and always had potato in it somewhere.

One thing cheered him up: Mrs Gale collected their post from the village shop and he'd had a letter from Mrs Wallbanks, his old neighbour in Southampton.

She'd written that the houses still left in the street he'd once lived in were going to be knocked down and new flats built instead. Cliff's old home was bombed in the war, but Mrs W. still lived in hers. She said she was looking forward to her new place, but she was being put somewhere temporary until it was built.

I hope it isn't a prefab, she wrote, *them places are really chilly. It won't be until the freeze is over, so I hope we get a good summer. I'll write you my new address when I get it.*

He hadn't seen his old street since he was evacuated, and now it would no longer exist. He shrugged. Life was better here. He'd never want to live in a town again, despite cinemas and fish and chip shops. He was a country boy now.

Chapter 16

May sat at the desk in the study, usually Rose's domain, with mouldering boxes of paperwork surrounding her. When she'd inherited the farm from her father-in-law, decades of forms and correspondence had been boxed and relegated to the old dairy until May found the time to sort through them.

Jesson wouldn't allow her to work outside for more than a couple of hours a day, so she had no excuse to delay the onerous job any longer.

She sneezed as dust wafted up from the boxes as she lifted out papers. The wicker bin had long since been abandoned and sheets of discarded foolscap overflowed sagging boxes, waiting to be burned.

She looked around, easing her aching shoulders. Still a long way to go. She'd have to clear up before the next time Rose made it to work; she was efficient and could lay her hand on anything in her well-ordered files.

The thought of Rose made her remember the atmosphere between them nowadays. In the past, they'd always supported each other, but the subject of Len had made their confidences difficult; May felt the need to censure every comment that didn't refer to work, in case she was seen to be criticising the man.

In her heart of hearts, Rose must know that Len's behaviour and aggressive attitude was bang out of order, but love is love and she'd waited years to have her husband back.

May could see Peter's point of view; she wouldn't tolerate bullying herself, but Rose had divided loyalties between her two boys and her husband. She wondered whether by keeping Peter at the farm, she'd made life easier or worse for Rose.

She stood up, stretched and headed for the kitchen to recruit the boys to carry the boxes of scrap back to the dairy ready for the next bonfire.

She'd got a pan of leek and potato soup bubbling on the cooker when Jesson arrived for his midday meal.

'It's raining!' he said, as he pulled off his sopping coat and balaclava.

Cliff dashed to the window. 'It'll clear the snow, won't it?' he said, eyes alight with anticipation.

He wants to go out on his bike, May thought. But better weather was good news and perhaps the farm work could begin again.

'It won't clear instantly,' Jesson said, 'and, if it freezes at night, we'll have a giant hockey rink to deal with.'

Peter frowned at Cliff, who shook his head, both clearly puzzled about frost turning the ground into a hockey pitch.

The mealtime talk revolved around the differences between American ice hockey and English hockey that girls played at school. Even Peter took an interest, although the haunted expression returned every time they mentioned the subject of the weather clearing. With the boys delegated to wash up, and Spencer curled up on the old settle for a nap, May and Jesson sat in the armchairs by the fire, sipping tea. Jesson's supply of instant coffee had run out, and there was not much chance of replacing it soon. They'd had no post for days with Rose unable to come to work.

'How long before we can plant the spuds, do you think?' May said.

'Reckon this weather can't last much longer,' Jesson

replied, 'so not too long, I hope.'

Ten days later, it was still raining. May and Jesson stood on the track they'd walked along in the snow to inspect the fields. They couldn't get to the sleeper bridge. What had been a small stream meandering between the fields was now a grey lake with only the rows of willows to define the path of the original watercourse. What most concerned May was the hay fields being underwater. Little Hill Field, on a slope, was less affected, but the meadow alongside the stream was submerged and the water rising. Jesson assured her the grass would recover in time for a late cut.

The sodden fields they'd passed wouldn't be ready for cultivation for potatoes for some time, and May was desperate for some good news. The farm's bank balance was holding up, but losing a year's crops would cause serious problems.

'I thought once the snow melted, we'd be back on track. It's even worse,' she said. 'We can't do anything in this slop.' She kicked out at the slosh underfoot and had to grab Jesson's arm to stop herself from slipping. Boots had no traction and yesterday she'd let rip at Cliff who'd fallen over, larking around with Peter. More washing. With all the drying clothes, the kitchen was like a steam room.

Jesson held on to her arm as they retraced their path. 'It's worse other places, May, crops wiped out and folks' homes flooded.'

She felt chastened. 'I know. At least they got some coal out to people before the floods got too bad. I thought the school would have reopened, but they won't risk the buses getting stuck in the floods.' And the boys are getting under my feet, she added silently.

Rose wasn't much help. She'd come back to work, but there was little for her to do, with the paperwork up to date and Spencer being entertained by Cliff and Peter. Len was busy repairing flood damaged engines, so, as far as May could make out, he hadn't made too much fuss about Peter staying at the farm. Rose was still tight-lipped, and May longed for the chats and laughter they used to share.

'I'm cycling to the village.'

The rain had let up, but the clouds were the colour of the pewter tankard they kept for pens and pencils on the mantle-piece.

'It's not safe, May,' Jesson said. 'Let me take you in the truck.'

'I know the lane like the back of my hand. I'll walk if the water's deep. We need shopping and I need a change of scene.'

Four faces looked at her woefully.

'It's all right, I'd just like a bit of time away from the farm,' she said. 'And don't worry, I'll remember the *Beano*, the sweets and the coffee, if they have any.'

Cliff, Spencer and Jesson grinned. Peter looked at his shoes.

'Anything for you, Peter?'

'I ain't got no money,' he said.

'Don't worry about that. Which comic do you have?'

'*Champion* – but Dad won't let me have it no more.'

'Your father won't be buying it,' May said.

She caught sight of Jesson smothering a smile. Pah! Len was just another problem she shouldn't have to deal with.

***

She set off. She rarely used the bike now but, after the accident, she was chary of driving in less-than-ideal conditions.

The lane, in the village direction, was on an incline and with the runnels of water flowing down, a pool at the farm gate was rapidly widening. How long before the farmyard flooded? Jesson had cleared the ditches beyond the entrance, but they were brimming again because the stream at the bottom couldn't cope with the volume of water.

Once she reached flatter ground, water spread across the road several inches deep. She reached the place where she'd fallen into the ditch on their foray with the snowplough. Then the world had looked almost painfully white. Now it was dull, grey and depressing.

She passed the cottage; it was difficult to remember living there before the war with Seth. How would he have handled this catastrophic weather? Better than she had done, no doubt. But then, he'd never had a war to recover from, a shortage of farm workers or a houseful of under-exercised, overexcited children.

She had no choice but to dismount in sight of the crossroads; a dip in the road had standing water a foot deep. She waded through, ensuring it didn't slosh up into her boots.

Once across the main road – signed to say it was flooded in both directions – she cycled on towards the village, navigating outsized puddles and praying the surface beneath was solid. The last thing she wanted was to return home muddied and bruised from a fall.

In the warm shop, the smell from the paraffin stove was all pervasive. Thank goodness Evelyn Harris was behind the provisions counter; old Fred, who'd worked there for the duration, had retired as soon as demob began. Mrs Harris was on hand to fill in while they waited for a suitable candidate but, as none of the applicants suited Victoria's exacting standards, or refused to work for a female version of Attila the Hun, Evelyn stayed on in the post.

'How are you and the girls getting on?' May asked, passing over her shopping list. 'And Mr Harris – not washed away up country?'

'We're doing the best we can in the circumstances. Ron got laid off several times 'cause of the weather, but at least it's made him see I need the job. Can't say I'm sorry to have it either. Bein' stuck indoors for months would've driven me round the bend.'

'I can understand that,' May said. 'Can I take Peter Gale's rations, too, please?'

Mrs Harris busied herself fetching, weighing and slicing provisions, while May collected the comics and other bits and pieces from the depleted shelves.

'Talking of getting washed away,' Mrs Harris said as May laid her collection on the counter, 'there's ructions in the Potty camp.'

'I'll take a quarter of sherbet lemons and two ounces of dolly mixtures for the boys, please. What are the Potties up to now?' She never let the boys hear her refer to the Potts by the children's nickname, but among adults it was a joke, said with relish.

Mrs Harris glanced towards the deserted post office counter. She murmured, 'Miss Potts has had a leak in her bed—'

May tried to contain her laughter, but the prospect of the ghastly Victoria having an embarrassing incident was too much; a guffaw burst out. Mrs Harris looked startled, but then saw the joke. The two of them shook with laughter. Not so much at the prospect of the event, but at the thought that the starchy spinster would ever tell anyone.

'I'll get the sack,' Mrs Harris spluttered, mopping her eyes. 'It was her roof. They reckon snow froze under the tiles and when the thaw came, they cracked and let in the water. With all the rain, the ceiling's half down.

'Victoria was fit to be tied. She keeps stock in the spare bedroom here and asked Isabella if she could move into their house. Her ladyship wasn't having none of it; said that the rules were the post office shouldn't be empty overnight, and she didn't want Victoria to get in trouble. If you ask me, Victoria was angling for Ephraim to camp out in the spare room so she could make herself comfortable under his roof.'

May felt better than she had for weeks. It was incredible what a good laugh could do. She and Rose used to laugh a lot.

Mrs Harris went on. 'Victoria was livid. She "forgot" to order Isabella's posh magazine and her ladyship told her she was being petty when she came to pick it up. They're not speaking now.'

May began packing the shopping into her holdall. 'It's good to see the Potties getting some of their own medicine. Maybe they'll be less spiteful to other people in future.'

'Hell'll freeze over first,' said Mrs Harris, taking a ten-shilling note from May.

Chapter 17

Cliff walked through the school gates ahead of Pete and Bob, leaving them to sort out their family problems. He'd been the one with parent problems throughout the war. Now, when it was over and the twins had got both their parents together, it had all gone wrong.

Could his father have been a bully like Mr Gale? Who knew? His first mum never told him who his dad was. Now she was out of his life and he'd got Mum. That was all he'd ever wanted, although sometimes he felt jealous of Spence, who had his dad with him as well as Mum. But he was never bullied, or hit, and he wasn't scared of anyone, not even old Potty nowadays; he'd kept his nasty trap shut since Jesson came to work at the farm.

After he'd hung up his coat and changed out of his wellies in the cloakroom, the boys hadn't appeared, so he went back outside. Surrounded by a gaggle of boys, the twins stood red faced, shoving each other and swinging punches that, mostly, met fresh air.

'You're right under Smokey Burnage's window,' Cliff hissed, grabbing Pete's arm and hoping that the Head would still be having a crafty fag around the back of the gym, where he thought no one knew he broke his own rules.

Pete tried to shake him off, but an older boy stepped in and pinned down Bob's arms, and Cliff dragged Pete back.

'Pain of Death,' someone growled.

The group split off in all directions as two prefects marched up.

'Heck,' Cliff muttered.

'What's going on, Gale?' Payne, skinny as a yard of pump water, looked down his nose at Pete.

'Nuffin,' Pete said, pulling up the coat that was hanging off his shoulder.

De'Ath, short, round and pimply, flicked Bob's tie, hanging out like a dog's tongue. 'Uniform rules, Gale,' he scoffed.

Bob stuffed the tie down the front of his pullover.

Payne glared at Pete. 'I could put you in detention, Gale.'

'Yeah? Why don't—'

'It's nothing,' Cliff said. 'They just tripped each other up with their bags.' He picked up Pete's satchel and shoved it into his arms.

'I've got my eye on you, Gale,' Payne said.

'Gales,' De'Ath said, sniggering.

'Yeah. Gale warning,' said Payne, pointing a tap-root-like finger from Pete to Bob, 'Final gale warning.'

At dinnertime, Cliff waited at the form room door to go to the refectory with the twins as usual. He'd have to get them talking, they were getting into bother with their stupid feud.

Pete barely slowed down as he passed. 'Come on,' he said.

'I'm waiting for Bob.'

'Suit yourself.'

Pete stalked off and Bob, obviously waiting until his brother had gone, came over to Cliff. He trudged up the corridor, shoulders down, and Cliff's attempts at jokes only produced a grunt. The twins had been the clowns of the class, looked up to for their tricks and jokes, especially Pete, but now no one wanted to get caught in the crossfire of their arguments and they were sidestepped. Cliff liked them both, possibly Pete a bit more, but only because he was the more chummy.

'I dunno what to do, Cliff,' Bob said, stopping at the corner before the refectory. 'There's no talking to him. He hates Dad and I think he'd prefer it if he hadn't come back from the war.'

What could he say? He'd had the same impression. Everyone *had* been happier when Mr Gale was away, probably Mrs Gale, too.

'I think he's mixed up,' Cliff said. 'You and he were the sort of the men of the house, helping yer mum and that, for a long time, and then yer dad comes in and kind of pushes you out.'

'But he's our *dad*. He's supposed to be in charge.'

'I know, but maybe he could've been gentler about it.'

'I s'pose he can be a bit pushy,' Bob said.

You don't say. Cliff kept the remark to himself as they moved on.

They rounded the corner to see Pete at the back of the dinner queue. Before Cliff could call out, Pete glanced over his shoulder. Seeing them, he pushed ahead to get to the front.

Cliff cursed under his breath as a pair of Laurel and Hardy figures emerged from the dining room.

'Heck. Pain of Death.'

Bob sighed. 'That's torn it.'

The chatter in the queue stopped as everyone watched Payne loom over Pete, a smirking De'Ath at his heel.

'Pushing in, Gale?'

Cliff saw the tips of Pete's ears redden. 'Just catching up with me pals.'

'Thought *they* were your pals.' He pointed to Cliff and

Bob.

'I got more.'

'Where?'

Pete looked around. Boys near him dropped their gaze.

'Rotters,' Cliff muttered.

'Looks like detention for definite, Gale,' Payne sneered.

'Wind must've blown your chums away, Gale,' De'Ath sniggered.

'What's going on here?' The words rapped out like so many whacks of a ruler.

'Mr Burnage. Good afternoon, sir.' Payne conjured a toadying smile. 'Gale here—'

'I was just joining my friends, sir,' Pete cut in.

Cliff heard Bob catch his breath.

'Hmm. I've been wanting a word with you, Gale. Marks have dropped. Come to my study before the first period.'

'Yes, sir.' Pete's answer was barely audible as he hung his head.

Pain of Death moved off in the wake of the Head, but Cliff saw Payne mouth, "Lucky," at Pete.

The queue was moving on fast after the delay and a first year called out, 'Gale, come on,' as he held a place for Pete.

'Decent of him,' Bob said.

Cliff nodded, wishing it hadn't been necessary.

Travelling home was hard; Pete sat alone on the bus, leaving Cliff to sit with Bob. What was going to happen when they got off and he and Pete had to walk together to the farm?

The rackety old bus pulled up at the stop at the top of Elem Lane. Cliff was surprised to find Pete waiting for them when he jumped off the step behind Bob and the bus pulled away.

'Give this to Mum.' Pete thrust an envelope towards Bob.

'What is it?' Bob asked, turning the letter over.

Cliff saw *Private* typed across the top. It was addressed to Mr Gale. Pete stalked off down the lane.

'Night,' Bob muttered, turning to cross the main road.

'Night,' Cliff called and jogged on to catch up with Pete, who was half-heartedly dribbling a stone between puddles.

Cliff slowed to a walk beside Pete, who didn't speak but kicked the stone Cliff's way. He whacked it and sent it spinning across the lane, where it came to land in a tuft of grass that was probably on the edge of the overflowing ditch.

'You can get that,' Pete said.

'Nah. Mum'll murder me if I come home with wet feet,' Cliff said, walking on.

'Me ole man'll murder *me* if Mum lets him see that letter.'

'Smokey?'

'Yup. I ain't been working to me "full potential".' He imitated Smokey's voice.

Cliff didn't know what to say. Pete hadn't been working well, but he'd got problems at home. Didn't teachers ever think about that? 'It ain't Bob's fault,' he blurted.

'But he ain't on my side.'

Cliff thought he caught a sob in Pete's voice.

'He's in the middle. He just doesn't know what to do.'

'Nor do I.' Pete gave a great sniff before adding, 'But I ain't goin' back.'

Luckily, they'd reached the farmhouse gate, so Cliff didn't have to reply. He had no idea what to say.

Chapter 18

May stacked the breakfast plates on the draining board before running hot water into an enamel bowl and adding soap flakes. She would have asked the boys to wash up but, ever since they'd got home from school the previous afternoon, they'd virtually ignored each other. Peter was barely speaking at all, and Cliff pretended he didn't care. Spencer, oblivious to the atmosphere, played with them in his usual effusive fashion. Would he become a moody "teenager", as Jesson called the older boys, in years to come?

'I'll wipe up,' Cliff said, picking up a tea cloth.

'What are you doing today?' she asked.

'Nothing, 'til the hens this afternoon.'

'It's not raining. Two days in a row. Maybe it'll stop for a while now.' Her mind was on the farm work; the flooded fields and the crops waiting to be sown.

The back door opened and Jesson came in, shrugging off his coat and stepping out of his boots into the shoes he left by the door.

'Mornin', guys.'

Cliff muttered hello, Peter grunted, and Spencer flew into his father's arms.

'Dadda play.' The little boy wriggled and pointed to the pile of wooden bricks he'd been cajoling Peter to build with him.

'Just a minute, Spence,' Jesson said, putting him down.

'Hello, May. Everything all right?' He moved nearer as she filled the kettle.

She raised her eyebrows and inclined her head towards

Peter, who was picking at the varnish on the arm of the chair.

Jesson frowned a question. May shrugged.

'No rain again,' Jesson said, squatting down beside Spencer. 'Maybe this week we'll be able to get some work done.'

'Fingers crossed,' May said as she reached for the instant coffee jar.

Someone tapped on the back door.

'Come in.' Who was calling on a Saturday?

Rose stepped tentatively over the threshold. 'Sorry to barge in, May.'

Why had she waited? She usually tapped and walked in. Damn. Len was behind her.

Rose wouldn't meet her eye. There must be trouble ahead.

'Hello, Rose. Len. Take a seat. Kettle's on.'

'Arn Roe!' Spencer trotted towards Rose.

Jesson grabbed him, led him to the furthest armchair, and sat the child on his lap.

'We're not here to socialise,' Len said, ignoring the chair May pulled out for him.

Rose stood clutching her bag like a shield.

It was only then May thought to look at Peter. He'd shrunk into the chair, face ashen, hands trembling. Cliff had stationed himself beside his friend. He stood very upright; a centurion guarding a Roman emperor. Len Gale wouldn't brook interference from a thirteen-year-old and she would have to diffuse the situation.

Without warning, something inside her snapped. She was in her own kitchen and refused to tiptoe around a rude bully who had changed her friend out of all recognition and turned his own son into a quivering wreck.

Switching off the kettle, she turned to face Len.

She looked him in the eye. Keeping her voice low and steady, she said, 'So, what can we do for you, Len?'

'I'm taking my son home. Back where he belongs. We've had enough of this nonsense. It's only since he came here, we've had this sort of thing.' He brandished a sheet of paper and shook it in Peter's face.

Peter cringed like a beaten dog. The school heading was visible at the top of the letter, and May guessed the boy wasn't performing well in class. Was it any wonder?

'Peter was left in my care because he wasn't happy at home. He's at liberty to go back with you if he'd like to but if, as I suspect, that the letter is a complaint about his school work, perhaps we ought to look at the cause of his problems.'

Len's face flashed to puce. Rose started to speak, but her husband overrode her. '*We? We* ought to look into it? It's nothing to do with you. You've kept him away from his family long enough. That's why his work is so poor. He's got no discipline in this … this …'

Jesson stood up, sitting Spencer in the chair. He took a few steps towards May. She glanced towards him, but this one she was sorting out alone.

'This *home*, Len? This *family home* where he feels comfortable and protected?' she said, her voice forcibly controlled.

Len's scowl almost obliterated his eyes. 'Women can't discipline children. Not without a man around. Rose was too soft on the twins while I was away. Bob's come round, shows respect, but him,' he jabbed a finger towards Peter, 'he needs proper control. If he knuckles down now, he could go far in the Navy.'

Rose and Cliff pointed out that Peter may not want to

join the Navy, but a commanding voice cut them off.

'Why don't you ask Pete what he wants?'

All eyes turned to Jesson. He was head and shoulders taller than Len, although the engineer was broader and as sinewy as a ship's hawser.

Jesson said, 'Pete, what would you like to happen?'

The boy raised his head and, turning tearful eyes on May, said, 'I want Mrs Sheppard to adopt me like she did Cliff.'

Whenever May recalled that moment, it wasn't Len's bark of contempt, nor the jolt in her own solar plexus, knowing she could never do what Peter asked, that cut to the heart; it was Rose's cry of anguish, as if her child was being ripped from her arms.

Jesson was the quickest to recover. 'Cliff, take Spence and go upstairs.'

'But—'

Cliff's eyes sought May's. He'd moved away from Peter and she saw the look of shock on his face. She understood what it meant; he didn't want to share her again, not after all the agonies they'd gone through to become mother and son. And Peter had his own loving mum – nothing like Cliff and Spencer and their abandoning mother.

So often they were in accord; years of living together through the war had formed a bond nothing could break. She gave him the ghost of a smile and nodded.

He turned and carried his brother upstairs.

'Peter, there's a van outside. Go and get in it,' Len snapped.

'You can't drag the boy out, Len,' Jesson said. 'Can't we talk about it?'

'We have. Rose, collect the boy's things we're—'

'No.' Rose turned on her husband, whose head snapped round in surprise. 'I'm not dragging my son back ter a home where he's terrified of his own father. I don't know what happened ter you in all those years at sea, but it changed you. You aren't the man I married and you aren't the father the twins remember. You got the van to help your parents move some furniture, so do that. I want to talk to my son and the woman who has taken him in out of the goodness of her heart.' She turned her back on Len, who stood open-mouthed.

May's eyes flashed to Jesson, who was also clearly expecting Len's temper to erupt and had positioned himself between Peter, sobbing in the armchair, and his father.

Len was helpless. He looked towards Rose, who was ignoring him, bending over Peter and speaking soothingly to him. May and Jesson were silent, embarrassed to have witnessed the marital scene. Without another word, Len strode to the back door and left.

As he passed the window, May saw his stunned expression and wished it hadn't taken so long for him to learn a few honest truths.

She said, 'Rose, why don't you and Peter go into the study? The fire's alight. I'll bring some tea in a while.'

As Rose and Peter left the room, May leaned back against the sink and sighed. She was glad her old friend had got some of her spark back and glad for Peter that he knew his mum was on his side. But more than anything, she was relieved.

Jesson was beside her. 'How could I have told him adoption was out of the question?' she said. 'I have all the family I want.'

Jesson pulled her into his arms, and before she could

think, he kissed her. As they broke apart, he said, 'I love you, Mrs Sheppard. Will you marry me?'

Chapter 19

Something had changed. It was obvious from the way Mum and Jesson were talking, close together. She couldn't have agreed to adopt Pete. It wasn't fair; he had a mum and a twin brother and even a bad-tempered old man, but Cliff only had Mum and Spence. He loved Pete staying here, but not forever.

'Have you—'

'Oh. Cliff.'

Jesson went to the back door and put on his coat and boots.

Mum's face was pink, and she turned her back to Cliff, putting out cups and saucers. She was embarrassed. She didn't want to tell him about taking in Pete. How could she?

'So, yer gonna do it then?'

Mum spun round, slopping milk from the jug. 'What?' She was bright red now.

'Pete. Adopt 'im?'

She gave a big sigh. 'Good Lord, no. Mrs Gale and Peter are talking in the study. His father's gone and they are trying to sort things out.'

'So, he's going home?'

'We don't know yet. I expect she'll want to talk to me about it. Is Spencer all right?'

'I put the stair gate across.' Jesson had fixed the side of Spence's old playpen to the bannisters as a safety precaution, although Spence was adept at getting down the stairs on his backside.

'You could walk Spencer to the stream and see how

much the flood water's gone down. I'm hoping it's the end of the rain and we'll be able to get on the land before too long.'

She wanted him out of the way. At least she wasn't adopting Pete. It was a stupid idea, anyway.

He wouldn't let Spence take his hand away. The mud made the track as slippery as ice and he'd be in bother if he let him fall over. Across the stackyard, the sound of hammering came from the Dutch barn; Jesson was getting the machinery ready for when they could get to work again. The POWs would help with planting the potatoes. He liked Walter and Alwin; they were just like ordinary men, not like the idea everyone had of Germans in the war.

This year they were going to grow barley on the farm for the first time. It was going to be used to make beer. Jesson said he couldn't wait to try a pint.

When he helped with harvesting on Mr Tyler's farm, they'd bring out jugs of beer and all the boys tried to snaffle a glassful, but they rarely got away with it.

Blossom was nosing around for the last few strands of hay in the orchard. Old Ben was in the corner, head down, looking miserable.

'Spence run.' The little boy tugged at Cliff's hand.

'No, you can't. You'll fall over and get muddy. Look at Bess, she's got mud up to her elbows.'

Hearing her name, the dog trotted up to Cliff and touched her nose on his hand.

'Good girl,' Cliff said, fondling her silky ears.

The dog licked Spence's hand and ran on ahead.

She was the best thing he'd ever had. Better than his bike, better than a room of his own. Not better than Mum or

Spence, but just as important.

They slithered their way along the track, between fields where water-filled furrows reflected the grey sky overhead.

Mum had put a stick in the ground to show the highest point the water had reached, and Cliff pointed it out.

'Look, the stick's high and dry. Let's measure how many steps away the water is.'

Spence stepped his little boots out alongside Cliff's paces and Cliff counted aloud, stopping as their toes reached the edge of the floodwater, where Bess waited for them.

'Eight of my paces and twenty-four of yours. We must remember to tell Auntie May.'

He looked across the expanse of water, trying to imagine the hay meadows in full summer, the grass rippling in the breeze. Now it was just a dreary lake with odd weeds sticking out and a reed or two showing where the stream bank was.

They turned back, Spence warbling, 'Twen four big steps.'

Jesson was still hammering as they passed the orchard. Spence, tired out, wanted to be carried, but one look at his mud-caked boots was enough to make Cliff insist he could walk a little further.

Bess poked her nose through the orchard fence and whined. The horses were used to her and often lowered their heads to sniff at her. It always made the boys laugh when they snorted and Bess shot back in alarm. She never learned.

Today though, Blossom stood forlornly at the gate waiting for her warm stable, but Ben hadn't moved from the place they'd seen him on the way out.

Cliff leaned over the fence to get a better look.

'Stay there with Bess,' he said to Spence. 'Bess, stay.'

The dog sat beside Spence, who patted her head, 'Good gog,' he told her.

'Jesson?' Cliff shouted to make himself heard above the noise.

'Hi, Cliff. What's up?'

'It's Ben. He hasn't moved for half an hour and he's holding up a back foot.'

Jesson laid the hammer down and followed Cliff.

'Hmm. Why's he got himself in that muddy corner?' He squeezed between the rails and made his way to the old horse, who looked very sorry for himself.

Cliff watched as Jesson ran his hand down Ben's hind leg.

'Get me a headcollar, Cliff,' he called.

Telling Spence and Bess to wait, Cliff ran to the barn and came back with two leather headcollars and lead ropes, knowing Bloss would be unhappy if Ben went inside and they left her out in the cold.

When he got back, Spence was crying. 'Want Arn Mee,' he wailed.

Cliff handed the headcollars to Jesson and said he'd take Spence to the house.

At the back door, he called that Spencer was cold, but he was going back to help Jesson. Spence toddled in and Mum came to meet him.

Jesson had the headcollar on Ben, but the horse refused to move.

'Come on, old fella,' Jesson said, trying to encourage the animal to put his foot down.

'It's no good,' he said, after several attempts. 'He's in

101

real pain. Will you stay here, Cliff? I'll speak to your ma.'

Cliff patted Ben's neck and spoke softly to him. Bloss was his favourite, but Ben had always been here and he hated to think of any animal in pain. For him to be like this, his leg must hurt a lot. They shot horses when they were badly injured, didn't they? He tried to wipe out of his head the memory of dark red slabs of horsemeat hanging in the butcher's window.

'We'll make it better, Ben,' he said, 'just wait.'

Chapter 20

May couldn't concentrate on Rose's words; Jesson had asked her to marry him. She kept turning it over in her mind. Not the most romantic proposal, beside the kitchen sink in the middle of a family crisis. Nevertheless, she was thrilled and had been going to accept him when Cliff walked in, oblivious of the moment and concerned only that Peter might be joining the family.

Rose was talking about that now and she must listen and try to keep a smile off her face.

'I don't know what ter do, May. Len's so changed. It's like what he experienced in the war has altered him. I don't recognise my husband anymore.' She wiped away a tear.

'How does he get on at the garage?' Was Len likely to bully other men?

'All right, I think. He doesn't like that he's lumped in with the apprentices when it comes ter jobs being dished out, but he realises he's new and still learning.'

'Hmm.' May could imagine Len didn't take not being top dog very well.

'I'm so grateful to you for taking in Peter. And Len is too, he's just keen for the boys ter do well and he gets carried away.'

'What have you decided about Peter? He's welcome here as long as he likes, but I'd never consider adopt—'

'Of course, I realise that. It was just Peter trying ter shock Len and make him see how unhappy he is.'

To anyone less pig-headed, that was clear. 'How are you going to play it?' she said.

Rose shook her head. The prospect of facing Len again was obviously still daunting. Where was the woman who'd stood up to her husband less than an hour ago?

'I don't want ter jeopardise my marriage, May. But I can't have the boys split up. Peter's in such a state. I don't know what ter do.'

'Does Len know how serious this is for you? Does he realise you won't sacrifice the boys to suit his … his … ideas?'

'I've tried telling him, but I can't get through. Len thinks that unless he's seen as the boss, he's not a real man. He does some kind things. He cleared all the snow from the pavements in the village.'

'That was a very generous thing to do and I'm sure Peter would have helped if he wasn't ordered into it.'

'I know, but orders are all Len understands.'

May thought about how willingly Len had done what Rose had told him to do earlier, when May had been expecting an explosion. Was that it? Was the man at sea, when he wasn't at sea, so to speak? If he was, then how could Rose make herself the one he turned to for direction?

'Does Len ever cook?'

'What? No, never. What a thought!'

'What about washing up, cleaning, shopping?'

'No. They're my jobs as far as he's concerned.'

'But when he was away, you did all those things and the gardening, mending fuses, maintaining your bike, cleaning shoes and so on?'

'You know I did. We all did. I still do those things if Len's at work and they need doing. What're you getting at?'

'When I went to Bill and Sally's and the baby was born, Sally had left out a pile of magazines for me. I'd put them in

104

the lorry but forgot about them after the excitement of the accident.' As she said it, she realised that she hadn't imagined Jesson saying he loved her that terrifying night.

Clearing her throat, she went on, 'Cliff brought them in and I read them while I was recovering. Some of them were silly: make sure you're wearing scent and haven't got your pinny on when your husband gets home. That kind of thing.'

Rose raised her eyebrows.

'Exactly. But, in one of them, there was a piece about couples making rules about who does what.'

'I can't see Len obeying my rules.'

'Not if you put it like that but, in the Navy, he didn't go up to the bridge and start steering the ship, did he? And I'm pretty sure the cook didn't come down and interfere with the engines?'

'Of course not.'

'So, he recognises sticking to your own job. What you've got to do is work out between you a set of, let's say, guidelines, so he and you and the boys know who has responsibility for what and that they have to stick to it.'

Rose frowned. 'I suppose it could work …'

They both looked round as the back door opened and Cliff let Spencer indoors.

May got up to take off his coat and Rose went to the foot of the stairs to call goodbye to Peter.

May pulled on Spencer's slippers as he sat on her lap. He had his thumb in his mouth.

'He'll be out like a light in a few minutes,' Rose said. 'Thanks for everything, May. I'll think about your suggestion.'

'All you've got to do is let Len think it's his idea.' May grinned.

Rose tugged on her hat. 'Is that all?' She gave May a rueful smile and headed to the door.

Collecting letters from the doormat after settling Spencer into bed, May felt her stomach sink like a lift in free fall as she noticed a flimsy brown envelope.

Distractedly opening the other letters, she tried to ignore the one marked *Private and Confidential*. It was as easy as if it was written in neon.

She picked up the letter and her paperknife.

'Can you phone the veterinarian?' Jesson called from the kitchen doorway. 'Ben's injured his off hind; I guess it's his tendons.'

'Hell. Is he in pain?'

'A lot. I can't get him to move and he's in the muddiest bit of the orchard.'

'I'll ring Hughes now.'

Jesson was waiting on the threshold, boots dribbling mud over the passageway flags. 'Hughes has retired,' May reported. 'There's a new man. He's on his way, but how long he'll take with the floods ...'

'Okay. I'll get back to the old fella. Cliff's with him right now.'

It would upset Cliff. He loved the horses and if Ben had to be put down, he'd take it very hard.

None of them had developed the died-in-the-wool farmer's detachment from animals. The hens that had been May's responsibility, before the death of her father-in-law, had to be culled. She coped with that, apart from making excuses for a few favourites, but she'd always detested the job.

She put a pan on the stove; if the new vet was here when

they were ready to eat, they'd have to ask him to join them.

She heard Peter coming downstairs. She'd have to make some response to his outburst; with any luck, Rose would have smoothed the way.

'Is Cliff outside?'

'Yes. Ben's hurt his leg. We're waiting for the vet.'

'Right … umm … Mrs Sheppard, what I said …'

May took pity on him. 'It's fine, Peter. I know you're having problems at the moment, but I think your mum and dad will sort things out. Let's just give them a chance, shall we?'

'Yeah. Right. Thanks.' Trying to hide his flushed face, he grabbed his coat and fled.

The food was ready when May glanced through the window and saw the boys, Jesson, and another man approaching the house. They'd need another dining chair.

She collected one of the Rexine-upholstered chairs from the study. As she entered the kitchen, Seth walked in the room.

Seemingly in slow motion, the heavy oak chair dropped from her hands, collided with a side table, where the boys had a half-completed jigsaw, and crashed down. She stared at the multicoloured jigsaw pieces scattered across the floor, noticed how bald the rug had become, and realised how much she detested those shiny red chair seats, one of which was upturned on the floor.

How could Seth have just walked in?

The man spoke. The idea of looking at him terrified her.

It wasn't Seth's voice. This was better modulated and hadn't that underlying Dorset burr. She raised her head.

It wasn't Seth. But he was the image of her late husband.

Seth as she'd first met him, not as he would have been now, twelve years on.

'Are you all right?' the stranger repeated, reaching to right the chair.

'May? What's happened?' Jesson, still drying his hands, strode across to her.

'I … I must've caught the table with the chair leg. I'm sorry, boys,' she said as Peter and Cliff scrabbled to pick up bits of jigsaw.

She looked at the stranger again, the sensation of stepping back in time making her dizzy. 'What a welcome. I'm so sorry. You must be the new vet?'

'Redvers Norton. Pleased to meet you.' He held out a hand.

Norton. Not Sheppard. But he *must* be related to Seth.

'May Sheppard,' she said, watching for a flicker of recognition.

Nothing. He just smiled at her in a way so familiar that her knees went weak.

Jesson was watching her.

'You'll stay for something to eat with us, won't you, Mr Norton?'

He thanked her, and she asked Cliff to put the chair in the space next to Jesson's at the end of the table.

Asking everyone to sit, she ladled soup into the warm bowls she took from the rack over the stove.

Jesson stood close, holding a tray. 'Are you okay, May? You look very pale.'

'I'm fine. Just embarrassed myself dropping the chair. Talk to our guest; Cliff's interrogating him.'

'He wants to be a veterinarian.'

'That'll save on vet bills, at least.'

Chapter 21

Mr Norton was a brick. He explained that if Cliff wanted to be a vet, he'd have to get good exam results at school, and then study at vet college for six years.

Six years! He tried to work out how old he'd be. If he left school after sixth form, he'd be eighteen, and six years on would make him twenty-four. Twenty-four before he started work.

Mr Norton said he'd show him around the surgery in Bridport if he was interested and he said that most students got jobs in vet surgeries during the holidays to get experience.

The prospect of a career other than farming, was exciting, but there was the problem of paying for it, as well as the worry of what Mum would do if he didn't work on the farm. He looked across the table at her, but she was gazing into space. Had she even heard what Mr Norton said?

Jesson and the vet had discovered they'd both served in the Airforce, different countries and planes, but they were taking about bombing runs and flak and fighters.

'Do you come from Dorset, Mr Norton?'

The men stopped talking and looked at Mum. If he'd interrupted like that, he'd have been ticked off for bad manners.

'My parents live in Dorchester, where I grew up, but I went to my father's old boarding school in Kent and then vet college in Edinburgh, so I can't call myself a local.'

'No local relatives at all?'

Jesson gave Mum a strange look.

'My father came from Kent, hence the school, but my mother's a Dorset girl; grew up in Swanage.'

'*Did* she?' Mum said.

She was about to say something else, but Jesson cut in, 'And you came back here in the end.'

'After demob, I was looking for a post. My old assistant job in Suffolk was long gone, but my father heard Arthur Hughes was retiring and the rest is history.'

'We won't be your most regular customers, not much livestock other than the hens, but I believe the farm's always used Hughes. Isn't that right, May?'

'Hughes and Norton, is it now?' Mum said.

Jesson frowned.

'Yes. Arthur is a sleeping partner, but I'm wet behind the ears on the business side and continually call on his help.'

'I see.'

What was wrong with Mum? He'd never seen her so rude. She was being like Pete, not saying anything, but then butting in.

They'd finished their soup, and Pete had made them tea, when Jesson fixed Mum with a hard stare as he said, 'So, Mr Norton, you'll be back to see Ben in a few days?'

'Yes. You'll have to decide what you want me to do. He's an old horse. Firing his tendons and recovery will take up to a year. If you want to retire him now, once he's out of pain he'll be able to potter about, but he won't be up to work.'

Mum looked shocked, as if she'd just remembered about Ben. Why else did she think Mr Norton was here?

'Ben can't work?' she said.

'No, May. Not for months. He's had a jab, but he's got to stay in his loosebox.' Jesson was cross.

'I … I hadn't realised.'

'No.'

No one looked at anyone else.

Mr Norton stood up. 'I'd better be off.'

Jesson went with him to the door. Cliff followed, sorry the vet was leaving.

'When can I come to see the surgery, Mr Norton?'

'Once the weather's settled, give me a ring. I don't expect your mother would want you to get stranded in the floods …'

Mum didn't say anything.

'Anyway, thank you for the lunch, Mrs Sheppard.'

'You're welcome,' she said, but she looked like she was going to cry. Was it so bad about Ben? Was she worried he'd have to be put to sleep?

As soon as they shut the door, Jesson told Cliff and Pete to go upstairs and fetch Spence because he hadn't eaten.

As Cliff climbed the stairs, he heard Jesson snap, 'What the hell is the matter with you, May? You were damn rude.'

He couldn't hear Mum's reply.

Chapter 22

The sight of the two men standing next to each other had made her feel she was drowning; her past life flashing through her mind but carrying her into the future. Two different men, different in almost every way. Except one. Both had loved her. And, of course, this wasn't Seth. It was a man she didn't know who bore a close resemblance to her late husband. More than a resemblance; a likeness so strong, he could have been Seth's brother.

Jesson was more furious than she'd ever seen him.

'You didn't even ask about Ben. This is serious, May. We're behind with the work and might just have caught up using both horses. Now, down to half the team, we're in real trouble.'

He was right and she should tell him why she'd been so stunned, but he went on, 'I've let this drift too long. You promised you'd get the farm mechanised. I let you carry on with your quaint ideas when I should've insisted ...'

He must have noticed her expression. He and stopped his diatribe.

'I'm sorry if my farm is too *quaint* for your liking,' she said, stung to the quick. 'Yes, I should have pushed harder to find a tractor. In the meantime, we'll just have to manage as best we can. Was there anything else?'

She might as well have slapped his face. His eyes narrowed. 'No, thank you. Saturday is my afternoon off. I'm heading home.'

He'd never taken a Saturday afternoon off.

The boys clattered into the room, Spencer calling,

'Dada.'

Without looking at May, Jesson swept the boy into his arms and kissed him goodbye.

Pulling on his coat, he said, 'Your sick horse needs checking on, but I'm sure Cliff remembers the veterinarian's instructions. I'll see you on Monday.'

Hell, hell, hell.

The boys were larking around, Peter putting his troubles aside.

'Peter, can you feed Spencer? Cliff, come and sit down and tell me what Mr Norton said to do about Ben.'

'Where's Jesson gone?'

'He's taking the afternoon off. He needs a rest.'

'Is he coming back for tea?'

'I don't think so.'

'But he always—'

'What about Ben? We've got him to look after and the hens and Blossom to feed.' On our own, she thought, feeling more tired than she had for weeks.

It was not until the boys were all in bed that she had the chance to open the letter that was haunting her.

She crossed her fingers before slitting open the shoddy envelope. The paper inside was so thin it was almost transparent. Why would the well-to-do Dorothy choose such a cheapskate firm?

The letter wasn't a retraction. It admonished her for contacting Dorothy and reiterated the intention of disputing Tom's will.

A final clause puzzled her: *Our client is minded to consider a reasonable offer to settle without resorting to litigation, should you feel in a position to contact us with such an approach.*

Was this normal, offering her a way out? She didn't know, but she did know that accepting would be admitting to coercion. And she'd sooner lose the farm than that.

Exhausted, she left a bath running while she fetched her dressing gown and pyjamas and the whodunit she was currently reading.

Trying to talk herself out of it, she picked up a photograph from the dressing table and carried it with her.

The hot water was a benison, and she sank back, letting it ease her tired muscles.

Jesson hadn't returned and she, Peter and Cliff had dealt with all the chores. Cliff had proudly delivered Redvers Norton's instructions over Ben's care and the old horse seemed to be comfortable and had eaten a small feed.

While the boys entertained Spencer before tea, she had gone to the old dairy and, in the stark light of the bare bulb, rummaged in the boxes of paper she'd left to burn.

Now, in the lavender scented steam, she took a deep breath, forced her thoughts away from farm business and reached out for her book.

The photograph lay on top of the novel, and she stood it on the edge of the bath.

At first glance, the face of the man who'd been in her house that afternoon smiled out at her and, again, the familiarity made her catch her breath. In the reflected brightness of the white tiles, she studied the picture. They weren't identical; Seth's face in the black-and-white photograph, taken just after they'd met, showed lines beside the eyes, etched by constant exposure to wind and sun. Redvers's skin showed none of the rigours of farming life and she'd noticed his

114

palms were clean and soft compared with Seth's calloused, work-worn hands.

The men's eye colour was similar; a distinctive grey-green, a colour that changed with the light.

Seth smelled of the outdoors, Redvers, horse, which wasn't surprising, giving his morning's work.

Jesson had the aroma of wood and citrus about him. A scent she loved. Some soap he used, she'd always thought. His family must send it over.

His family. If they married, would she ever meet them? His parents had a fruit farm in Texas, and there was a sister. Their life was hard. Jesson would never move back, but she would like to visit.

Seth's family hadn't been straightforward. His father was killed in the Great War and his mother remarried and moved to Elem Farm. He'd always said there were no other relatives, but now?

There had to be a link somewhere and, if Redvers was to be the local vet, she wouldn't be the only one to notice it. Should she raise the matter with him? He'd probably think she was mad, if he didn't already after today's performance. It could cause trouble in his family, as it already had in hers.

She had to resolve the problem with Jesson; he'd asked her to marry him and not only hadn't she answered, she'd caused a rift between them.

She reached for her flannel and soaped her skin. Her white skin. She never thought of the difference between them. She bathed and changed Spencer, seeing no difference between the boys or herself. Likewise, Jesson. She treated him like any other person. But she had to face it. Marrying him would bring difficulties.

She wasn't interested in pursuing Redvers; it wasn't that;

he could be married or engaged for all she knew or minded. But he represented the life she'd had: ordinary, to a man respected in his community, known and liked by most. Life with Jesson would be very different. People would look at them askance wherever they went. Some would take instant dislike; some would sneer or make horrible remarks. In the village he'd been accepted, after a struggle, but even now, it was sometimes a case of tolerance rather than liking. The Potts were a case in point, prejudiced to their bones and barely hiding it.

Did she want that kind of life forever, always fighting, always reading between the lines?

The water was cold, and she switched off her thoughts, deciding to sleep on the mayhem of her own making and see what the following day brought.

'Isn't Jesson coming for breakfast?' asked Cliff.

'You know he doesn't always on a Sunday,' May said. 'After breakfast, please take Spencer up to the cottage and tell Jesson he's welcome to come to us for Sunday roast. And then,' she added, 'come home again.'

'But he always—'

'Please, Cliff. I've got to do the hens and the cooking.'

'I can do the hens, Mrs Sheppard,' Peter said.

He'd helped Cliff over the years, often while waiting to go for a bike ride, but since he'd been staying at the farm, he'd done as much work as the rest of them. And he needed a confidence boost.

'All right, Peter, thank you.' She resisted the temptation to mention closing gates, topping up water and other elementary matters. They could always check later.

She beat the batter pudding mix. This British institution fascinated Jesson: served with meat, veg and gravy for the main course, and the remains with jam for pudding.

She hoped he'd come. Surely, he'd take the olive branch she was extending?

The gamey smell of roasting pigeon filled the air as she removed the sizzling Yorkshire pudding tin from the oven and poured in the batter.

Cliff and Peter were checking the flood level. Yesterday, the stream banks were just visible above the water, and the grass in the hay meadows lay flat and yellow on the sodden soil. If she had a pound note for every time someone told her you couldn't kill grass, she'd be a rich woman. She hoped they were right; hay sales were an essential part of the farm's income.

'Arn Mee!' Spencer crashed into the kitchen. He was carrying a pheasant's tail feather. 'Pessant,' he said, waving it at May.

'Hello, Spencer. What a lovely feather. Let's get your boots off.' She looked up. Jesson was standing just inside the door. Her heart skipped a beat. She hadn't ruined it, had she?

'Come on in, Jesson. The food won't be long. Glass of beer?'

'Please.' He hung up his coat.

He was wearing a button through cardigan that she hadn't seen before. Hand knitted in cream wool, the ribbed design fitted close and showed off his trim figure, the shawl collar flattered his features. A tingle ran up her spine as she admired the handsome man in her kitchen.

'New cardigan?' she asked, handing him a glass of pale ale and trying not to stare.

'Mom sent it for Thanksgiving. Hadn't had a chance to

117

wear it before.' He sipped the beer.

'It suits you.'

'Thank you.'

He wasn't making it easy.

'I'm sorry about yesterday,' May blurted. 'I got such a shock with Peter asking about being adopted and then Len and Rose arguing. Not to mention Ben. It just got a bit too much.'

'And the new vet?'

'Well, yes. Another person to get used to …' Why didn't she tell him he reminded her of Seth?

'New people don't usually bother you.'

'Oh, Lord.' She dashed to the stove, where the carrots were boiling over. 'Can you see whether the boys are in sight, please?'

Jesson gave her a long look before checking through the window.

'Just headin' up the track.'

'Thanks. Could you get Spencer up to the table?'

'Sure thing.'

Hell. The easy-going relationship that she so valued had vanished. She had a lot of ground to make up.

Chapter 23

Cliff sat alone on the school bus. Pete and Bob wanted to talk, so he left them to it and absorbed himself in thoughts of becoming a vet. Mr Norton told him he'd need to pass the Higher School Certificate to get into vet college.

He'd never considered doing anything other than working on the farm, but now it was all he could think about. Seeing Mr Norton examine Ben and then give an injection that helped the old horse, made him see there was a way he could help animals more than only by being kind to them. He just needed all that knowledge Mr Norton had in his head. Piece of cake.

He grinned to himself; if he was going to get the exams he needed, he'd have to knuckle down, as Mr Gale would say.

He would also have to talk to Mum, but she was very peculiar at the moment, hardly talking, and staring out of the window a lot. She and Jesson had had some sort of row and were being extra polite to each other. He preferred it when they bickered over the work and joked about it afterwards.

He felt guilty thinking about a different career. What would Mum and Jesson do without him? And, how much did going to vet college cost? He remembered overhearing Mrs Gale and Mum talking about Dr Haskett's son who'd gone to Oxford University. They were saying how much it must have cost to put him through it for four years. Vet college would be longer. Could Mum afford it? He resolved to save as much as he could from his farm wages and from selling the rabbits and pigeons to the butcher.

The bus pulled up at the school stop. Pete and Bob laughingly jostled him as they got off. They must have made up. He was glad for them. It was good to have Pete confiding in him, but he'd felt bad about siding with one brother when he could see both sides of their argument.

The three of them walked abreast through the school gates.

'Pain of Death, eleven o'clock,' said Bob.

Cliff glanced out of the corner of his eye to see Payne lounging against the wall by the door and De'Ath lumbering around him like a pudgy puppy.

As they reached the door, Payne called out, 'Mornin' Gales, going to entertain us with a punch up today?'

Cliff heard Pete draw a breath. 'Ignore him,' he muttered, marching on, hoping the twins would follow.

They entered the vestibule and he heard De'Ath's squeaky voice. 'They've blown themselves in.' His snort of laughter followed them.

'I wish our name wasn't Gale,' Bob said with a sigh.

'Could be Death,' Pete said.

'Or Glory,' Cliff said.

'Or Pain,' they all chimed.

To get from their form room to the attic-like, art room, "vaulted" the art master called it, meant travelling the length of the school along a series of staircases and corridors. Cliff and the twins had long ago discovered that using a side door, cutting across the playground and up the seldom-used back stairs, was a shortcut that avoided the after-break crush.

As Bob pulled open the door to the stairs, he was almost knocked off his feet by Payne. 'Make way. Prefect coming through.' He brayed, shoving between Cliff and Pete.

'What the—'

Bob regained his balance, only to be swept aside by De'Ath. 'Prefects,' he squeaked, emphasising the "s".

Cliff and Pete jumped back as the scarlet-faced boy charged after his hero.

'Where'd they come from?' Pete asked.

Bob pointed to the door under the stairs. 'They didn't come downstairs, so that's the only place.'

'What's in there?' Cliff asked.

Bob shrugged. Imitating De'Ath's squeaky voice, he said, 'Something only prefects are allowed to touch.'

They laughed, but as Bob and Cliff launched themselves up the stairs, Pete turned back and picked up something from beside the door.

'What's that?' Bob called.

'Fags,' Pete said, holding up a packet of five Woodbines. 'One of 'em must've dropped it when they shoved past us.'

'Gonna give 'em back?' asked Cliff.

'Not on your nelly.' Pete laughed.

'Give 'em to Smokey next time he threatens to send a letter to Dad.' Bob pounded up the uncarpeted stairs as his brother lunged at him.

Cliff grinned. Everything was back to normal.

'Back stairs?' Cliff asked.

'Yeah, but we'll never be first in the dinner queue, now.' Pete nodded towards Bob. His twin was packing away his art materials; he'd spent ages with the master, talking about perspective and his picture of a steam engine on a railway line.

'Come on, I'm starving.' Pete grabbed his satchel and headed for the stairs. Cliff followed and Bob, still stuffing pencils into his bag, brought up the rear.

'What's that smell?' Pete stopped dead, Cliff almost cannoning into him.

Looking past Pete, he saw a haze at the foot of the stairs.

'It's smoke,' he said.

'Where's it coming from?' Bob asked, as all three made their way gingerly down the wooden staircase.

At the bottom, it was obvious the smoke came from the gap beneath the under-stairs door.

Cliff ran to open it, but Pete yelled, 'Don't open it. Dad says you must never open a door on a fire. On board ship they compartmentalise fires to keep them from spreading.'

Cliff stepped back. He'd forgotten all the wartime fire-fighting training they'd had in the village school.

He could hear crackling through the door and noticed brown paint at the top was blistering. The smoke was getting thicker and darker. It smelt like the farm bonfire when they burnt old sacks and rotten fenceposts.

Pete was shouting to Bob. 'Was Beardy still there when you came out of the art room?'

'Packin' up his stuff. I'll tell him to get out.'

'There's a fire point outside the refectory. I'll raise the alarm. Cliff, stay here and don't let anyone come in.' Pete dashed away, letting the door swing back.

Cliff put a hand across this nose and mouth as the draught from the closing door forced a gust of reeking smoke into the stairwell. He went to the door, opening it a fraction to let him breathe. The fire training was coming back to him. *A fire needs oxygen.*

Bob clattered down the stairs carrying a bucket.

'Beardy's left. I shut the door but I can't do nuffin' about the front stairs – there's no door at the top. Where's Pete?'

'He's gone—' Urgent clanging sounded in the distance.

122

'That'll be him.'

Almost immediately, more clanging came from other directions. Hearing Pete's alarm, people were using the fire bells throughout the building.

'Is that water?' Cliff asked, pointing to the bucket.

'Sand.' Bob clamped an arm over his face, and tipped the contents along the base of the door. 'Might stop it for a while,' he said. 'Come on.'

Both boys ran outside, coughing as they reached the open air. Pupils were streaming out from the building. Masters and mistresses, their flapping gowns making them look like flying beetles, herded the agitated mob to the muster point at the back of the playground.

Frenzied clanking added to the cacophony as half a dozen boys, accompanied by the PE teacher and Pete alongside pointing towards the back stairs, lurched into the playground pushing a red handcart. The loaded fire cart carried a great barrel, coiled hoses and metal buckets. At the top, a big brass bell swung madly, its clapper sending out deafening discordant clangs.

The fire team went into action; playing out hoses and unloading buckets. Cliff held the door open for the team as Bob explained about the sand and the art room. Pete nodded at his twin.

'Well done, boys, you've done all the right things,' the PE master said, connecting a hose to the tap on the barrel. 'Now rejoin your form at the muster point. We'll take it from here.'

Everyone was shivering by the time they were allowed back into school. The dinner ladies had kept the food hot and several teachers helped serve. Cliff and the twins reeked of smoke, but the people who came up asking what had happened didn't seem to care.

The fire team was relieved of their moment of glory when the local brigade arrived and quickly dealt with the blaze in what was a store cupboard for old equipment and unclaimed lost property.

They were finishing their rissoles and mash (and the sloppy tinned tomatoes that Cliff left untouched), when a pimply first year brought a message from the Head: could all three come to his study at the end of dinner break?

'Going to congratulate us on our fast action,' Pete said, reaching for the jug of watery custard to pour over his slab of stodge.

'D'you think so?' Cliff asked, remembering the last time Pete had to go to the Head's study.

'Give us a special mention in Assembly tomorrow, I bet,' Pete said through a mouthful of pudding.

'Maybe,' Cliff said, digging into his sponge. Things like that didn't happen to him.

'Come.'

Pete opened the study door and strode in. Cliff and Bob looked at each other before they followed warily. It was never good to be in the Head's study.

Smokey sat in his usual place, back to the window that overlooked the front of the building, his face in shadow. His carved black desk, big enough to have sat round for a tea party, added to Cliff's urge to cringe.

He stood, Bob on one side, Pete on the other, his gaze trained on the carpet. The atmosphere wasn't right; it was like they were waiting to be caned.

Pete hadn't picked up on it and was almost bouncing as

124

he waited for the Head to speak.

'Can you explain what happened in the back stairwell this morning?'

'Yessir.' Pete jumped in. 'We discovered a fire – at least smoke was pouring out from the door under the stairs. We raised—'

'How did the fire start?'

Cliff's stomach felt it had dropped to his feet.

Pete had realised things were looking bad; his voice faltered as he said, 'We don't know. We just found the smoke coming under the door. But we—'

'Erwin, what about you?' He fixed Cliff with a stare. 'You're a sensible boy. How did the fire start?'

'I don't know, sir. We came down from the art room and saw the smoke. We've never been in that place under the stairs.' Cliff felt sick.

'Humph. What about you, Gale Two?'

Bob's voice was almost a whisper. 'Same as my brother and Erwin, sir. We don't know how it started.'

Smokey got to his feet. 'Empty your pockets. All of you.'

'Pardon?'

Why did Pete make things worse?

'What did you say?' Smokey roared at Pete.

'Pardon, *sir.*'

Smokey swept round the desk like a charging bull. Right in Pete's face he thundered, 'Turn out your pockets, NOW.'

They all felt in their pockets. Cliff knew he'd got a half-chewed toffee in a corner of his hanky (Mum always complained if he forgot to eat the remains because it went in the washing). He dragged out the handkerchief and tried to hide the caramel lump as he laid it on the desk.

Bob put a set of compasses and a screwed-up bit of paper on the table. Heck. Was it the picture Cliff had drawn of Beardy during Art? Please don't let Smokey look at it.

Pete pulled out a grubby handkerchief and tried his other pocket. His face drained of colour and he dragged out the packet of Woodbines and laid them on the desk.

'Sir – I found—'

'BE QUIET.'

The Head returned to the far side of his desk and sat in his swivel chair.

'You three went into the storeroom to smoke, didn't you?'

'No, sir.' The three spoke as one.

'Despite it being against the law at your age, and against the school rules, you had your smoke. As if that wasn't bad enough, you failed to extinguish your cigarettes, and they caused the fire.'

This wasn't fair. They couldn't be accused of this. Someone must've told Smokey that Pete had the fags.

Cliff stepped forward until his thighs were digging into the sharp curlicues of the desktop. He fixed his eyes on the Head. 'Sir, I don't know what you've been told, but Pete – Gale One – found those cigarettes by the outside door as we went to Art. They'd been dropped when someone bashed into us in their hurry to leave. We've never been in that storeroom. And we don't smoke.'

Smokey stared back at Cliff. 'Who are you saying dropped the cigarettes?' he asked.

Hell. Cliff looked over his shoulder at Pete, whose face almost matched his white shirt. Pete caught his gaze and shrugged. It was down to Cliff. If he told, he'd be the sneak. If he didn't, they'd all be in serious lumber.

'Erwin. Who dropped the cigarettes?' The Head's voice was sharp.

Cliff took a deep breath. 'Payne or De'Ath, sir.'

He heard Bob's groan. Now they were for it.

Smokey stared at him in silence.

'Do you two agree with this accusation?' Smokey said after several moments, looking from Pete to Bob.

Cliff stepped back in line with the twins.

Bob hung his head and muttered, 'Yes, sir.'

Pete, in a voice that was almost a whisper, said, 'Yes, sir.'

'So, we have a case of accusation and counter-accusation,' the Head began.

Cliff had been sure it could only have been Pain of Death that lied about them, and now Smokey had confirmed it. He felt murderous.

'This is a very serious matter. Arson, albeit not by intent, is an expulsion matter.'

Pete whispered, 'No. No. No.'

Bob gave a loud gasp.

Cliff felt himself reel like someone had punched him in the guts. He couldn't be expelled. What about his vet career? Mum had done so much to get him to this point, he couldn't lose everything now.

'We're innocent, sir,' he pleaded. 'All we did was raise the alarm and try to stop the fire spreading.'

'We'll see what the investigation reveals,' the Head said. 'Take your things – not the Woodbines – and go back to your class.'

Chapter 24

When she came into the kitchen, Cliff was sitting in the armchair, still wearing his school uniform, Bess's head resting on his knee. Spencer ran over. 'Kif. Kif. Spence find eggies.'

'That's good.' Cliff looked away from the excited child.

The little boy stared, confused by his brother's lack of enthusiasm.

Hell, May thought, what was wrong now? Did these problems never stop?

'Put on your slippers,' May told Spencer. He went off to find them.

Rose had left a shepherd's pie in the oven. More potato and onion than meat, she was sure, but the smell of it made her hungry. She thanked her lucky stars for Rose; she was trying to do more than her share of the farm work and, if she'd had to face cooking the evening meal, she would have despaired. Jesson can't have failed to realise she was trying to atone for her behaviour with the vet, but he hadn't mentioned his proposal. That was down to her, and she had no idea what to do about it.

'Come on, Cliff. Something's wrong. Where's Peter?'

'He went home with Bob.'

'Crumbs. Have you two fallen out?'

'No.'

His voice quavered, and she realised he was on the verge of tears.

'What is it then?' She put a hand on his shoulder. There was a smell about him. Smoke?

The back door opened and Jesson called out that he was

going home.

'Spencer, say goodnight to Daddy,' May said.

Spencer, running a toy car over Bess's back, didn't respond.

'Daddy's going, Spencer,' she said.

Spencer didn't move. Both boys playing up. That's all she needed.

Jesson came in as far as the kitchen door. He must have seen Cliff's demeanour because he looked quizzically at May. She shrugged.

'No Pete?' Jesson asked.

'Gone home,' May said.

Jesson raised his eyebrows.

May gave a slight shake of her head. 'Stay to eat, Jesson,' she said. She sounded desperate, but without his support, she was floundering. The last few days had been hell with this rift between them. Besides, Cliff saw Jesson as a father figure. Perhaps he'd open up to him.

'Spence, shall I go back to the cottage?' Jesson said.

'Dada, stay.' The child flung down his toy and ran to hug Jesson around the legs.

His father grinned. 'Okay, Sprout. Thanks, May, I'd like to eat with you.'

That Spencer had learned how to manipulate them took second place to the relief she felt now that Jesson would be sitting at their table again.

May served the shepherd's pie while Jesson sat at the table sipping a glass of beer. She'd offered it, knowing it emphasised her anxiety to get back on good terms, but eager to please him. Cliff had refused ginger beer, and Spencer kept offering him his beaker of milk.

'Wha's up, pardner? You're looking down in the mouth.'

She saw Cliff glance at her as she placed the plates in front of them. He'd changed out of his uniform, but the smell of smoke still hung on him.

'Tell us what it is, Cliff. We've never kept secrets, have we?' she said, sitting down next to Spencer, who dug his spoon into his bowl as if he had a bucket and spade.

Cliff stared at his plate, and then, without raising his eyes, blurted. 'I might get expelled.'

May's hand halted halfway to Spencer's spoon. She lowered it, letting the child continue shovelling. Calmly, she said, 'Well, if that happens, we'll cope with it. But tell us what's happened. I assume Peter's involved, too?'

'And Bob,' Cliff wiped an eye. He looked at May. 'Mum, we didn't do nuffin', I promise.'

His grammar had never failed to slip when he was troubled. She wanted to wrap her arms around him, as she had when he was five years old.

Gradually, the story emerged. May was outraged by the duplicitous behaviour of the two prefects. From the set of Jesson's jaw, she knew he recognised the impotence the boys had felt at being unable to defend themselves.

They finished the meal in silence, Cliff picking at his food. When he'd eaten, he went into the hall and fetched a letter from his satchel.

He handed it to May. 'From Mr Burnage.'

Surely the Head wouldn't expel the boys without proper investigation? She ripped open the letter while Jesson made a pot of tea.

She scanned the letter. Cliff didn't take his eyes off her and looked scared when she folded up the paper and put it back in the envelope.

'We have to attend a meeting on Monday. Peter and Bob and Mr and Mrs Gale will be there and the two prefects with their parents.'

Cliff groaned and seemed to shrink before her eyes.

'Is Burnage having an investigation?' Jesson put a cup of tea in front of May.

'It doesn't say, but he can't make a judgement without, can he?'

Jesson grunted. He'd been judged unfairly all his life for no more reason than the colour of his skin, but he didn't demur.

'Cliff, we'll sort this out,' May said. 'You can't be expelled for something you didn't do, especially when you and the boys saved the school from a serious fire. I'll make that clear at the meeting.' And, if Mr Burnage won't listen, she told herself, the governors will have me to answer to.

The days dragged by with the usual routine of farm work and school. Cliff and the twins were reluctant to go, although they and the two prefects avoided each other.

May had postponed her solicitor's meeting. Enough was going on, and Cliff was her priority right now.

Rose fretted as much as May about the forthcoming meeting. Len, though, was fired up, ready to defend his boys to the hilt. Rose said he was even coaching Peter on what to say about finding the cigarettes.

'Ter be honest,' she said, 'I'd rather Peter used his own words, but I'm not going ter put my spoke in now things are starting ter improve between them.'

May hoped that Peter didn't come across as belligerent as his father. That would help no one. She hadn't relished the idea of travelling with Len, but felt she must make the offer.

Fortunately, his boss at the garage had agreed to lend him a car and May had to find an excuse to refuse a lift.

It was on Sunday evening, after a weekend of trying to raise Cliff's spirits, that Jesson said he would drive her to the school. With Rose absent, he had the care of Spencer, but insisted it would be no trouble. Until Walter and Alwin were back and they had borrowed another horse, the sowing couldn't begin.

It would be awkward being in the lorry cab with Jesson; some of their old camaraderie had returned, and she'd deliberately gone to shop in the village when Redvers had returned to check on Ben earlier in the week, but there was still a distance between them.

Chapter 25

Jesson insisted on allowing extra time to get to Bridport and dropped May off half an hour before the start of the meeting. Although no longer freezing, it was cold outside, and she walked into the school, found the secretary and accepted a cup of tea while she waited in a corridor.

The meeting was set for the period between break and dinnertime, so pupils were in lessons and the school was quiet. May wished Rose and Len would arrive; she didn't want to have to sit alongside the Payne and De'Ath parents making polite conversation if they arrived first.

She checked her watch for the umpteenth time. Drat, why was she the only early one? She heard voices approaching and crossed her fingers.

Thank goodness. It was the Gales. Rose was wearing her best coat with the fur collar; May had grabbed her stalwart pigeon-grey button through that was years out of date. How dowdy she must look. Even Len had oiled down his hair and donned an ill-fitting suit. He carried a trilby May had never seen him wear.

They greeted each other, and the couple sat beside her. Rose whispered, 'Any sign of the opposition?'

May smiled. Rose's sense of humour always cheered her up. 'None. Maybe they're being held elsewhere.'

Rose gave a rueful grin just as footsteps sounded in the corridor and the secretary appeared. 'Would you all like to come with me?' she said.

She led the way to a room where a heavy door stood open. The sound of muted conversation ceased as they entered.

Mr Burnage sat behind a huge ugly desk. Sitting in front on the right were three people: a very upright gaunt-looking man. He looked down a hooked nose to scrutinize them. Next to him, a woman turned cold eyes briefly towards them. She must be his wife. She was muffled in a fur coat balding around the cuffs.

Beyond her was a plump woman in a faded emerald-green hat that clashed with her heavy salmon-pink cardigan. She had a coat, folded lining outwards, on her lap.

The Head gestured to the row of chairs on the left and May, Rose and Len sat down.

Directly in front of the desk, between the two groups, was an empty space. Mr Burnage gave a nod to the secretary and a few moments of embarrassed silence later, the boys filed in. The Head directed them to stand in the centre spot.

'Can't the boys sit down, Headmaster?' May said. 'This could take some time, and I feel uncomfortable with them having to stand.'

A snort came from the man with the hooked nose. His plummy tones carried unmistakable derision as he said, 'Men on a charge always stand to attention. Rightly so.'

'The boys aren't in the Army,' May pointed out. 'And this isn't a court martial.'

The Head, clearly concerned about the hostility building up between the parents, said, 'Very well, Mrs Sheppard. As no one has yet been found guilty of almost burning down the school, we'll let them sit.' He gave a placatory smile to Hook-nose, and the secretary took the boys with her to fetch chairs.

The angle of Hook-nose's lips mirrored that of his beak. May couldn't see his wife's expression, but the lady beyond was plucking nervously at her folded coat.

Rose nudged May and gave her an approving nod. Len stared through the window behind Burnage.

Cliff parked his chair next to May. The tall skinny schoolboy, prefect's badge on his lapel, sat next to Hook-nose, the family resemblance extremely obvious.

Bob, Peter and an untidy florid boy, also with a prefect's badge, occupied the middle. The secretary took a place to the side of the Head's desk, notebook on knee.

The Head cleared his throat. 'Good morning, ladies and gentlemen. You all know why we are here. A serious incident happened at the school last week and these two groups of boys each blame the other for the cause of a fire that could have had very serious consequences—'

'If,' Len broke in, 'my lads hadn't used their common sense, and what I taught them from my time in the Royal Navy,' he paused, glaring at Hook-nose, 'to raise the alarm and contain the fire.'

'That they may have already started,' interjected Hook-nose.

The Head raised his voice. 'Thank you, Mr Gale and Major Payne.'

May heard Rose take a deep intake of breath, trying not to laugh. She bit her own tongue, reflecting never had a name been more apt.

Burnage continued, 'I would be grateful if you could please keep your comments until later.'

He ran through the story of the fire and the accusations and counter-accusations. 'What we have to determine is what actually happened and I should warn you, those found responsible will be liable to expulsion.'

'My son is innocent,' Major Payne interjected. 'Since he

was in the company of … of …' he looked at the woman in the cardigan.

'Johnny,' she said, flushing.

'J …?' Major Payne stopped dead and glared at Mrs De'Ath.

'Sorry. De'Ath.' The woman's face was crimson.

'Since he was in the company of De'Ath, so must he be. My son does not smoke and nor will he until he is of age.'

Payne Junior had a smirk on his face May wanted to scrub off. What a patronising little so and so this boy was; a true chip off the old block.

Len couldn't resist getting his two-penn'orth in. 'My sons could take my fags any time, but they don't. They aren't interested. Erwin lives on a farm; he would never smoke in the yards. These lads *do not smoke*. In any case, they would be far too sensible to leave stubs burning, even if they experimented.'

Marvellous. Why not give them the idea the boys might have tried it out? May sighed.

Burnage ignored the superiority contest between the fathers. He looked at young Payne.

'Can you explain what you were doing exiting the building just before the second period?'

'Yes, sir. De'Ath and I had been doing our rounds, checking no one was getting up to mischief in the corridors or form rooms, during break. We checked the art room and then came down the back stairs. You often get a few bad eggs skulking around there.' He looked pointedly at Cliff and the twins.

'At the bottom, we saw those three,' he nodded to his left. 'We didn't know where they had come from, but assumed they'd just come in – even though we didn't see them enter.'

'That's a lie,' Cliff burst out.

'You'll have your turn, Erwin.' The Head's voice was sharp.

'Indeed,' the Major snapped.

May's temper was at boiling point.

Burnage said, 'Right, let's turn to Gale and Erwin.'

May said, 'Excuse me, Mr Burnage.'

'Yes, Mrs Sheppard?'

'We've heard from one prefect. Could I ask some questions of De'Ath?'

'Umm …' He glanced that the Major. 'I don't see why not.'

'What did you do when you saw the three boys at the bottom of the stairs?'

The baby-faced boy looked frightened. He turned towards Payne Junior, who studiously ignored him.

May raised her eyebrows. The boy remained mute.

'Did you speak to them, Johnny?'

The Major tutted.

'We – we asked them to move so we could get out of the door.'

'Were they blocking the doorway?'

He looked back at his pal, who again ignored him.

'Yes.'

'All of them?'

'Umm. Mainly Gale One.'

'Where were Gale Two and Erwin?'

The boy wiped his shining forehead. His mother tugged doggedly at her coat lining.

'I'm not sure.'

'So, they weren't in your way?'

137

'I don't remember.'

'Is this relevant?' Payne Senior barked.

'Just one more question,' May said, not giving the Major time to object. 'Johnny, weren't the Gales and Erwin outside the door of the building, about to come in?'

'No. Gale Two was coming through …' The boy halted, looking terrified, bottom lip trembling.

No one spoke. After a moment or two, May said, 'Thank you, Headmaster. That's all.'

Feeling dreadful, she daren't look at Mrs De'Ath. She'd pushed the boy hard, and he was so obviously under the influence of his snooty chum, it wasn't really fair. She cut off the thought. He had a choice, and he was going along with the attempt to get Cliff expelled. She'd happily cross-examine Major Payne if it meant proving Cliff's innocence.

The headmaster swept on before anyone else could interrupt. 'Gale Two, let's hear your version of events.'

Bob began explaining how they'd gone to enter the building and been charged aside by Payne. The Major huffed and his son sniggered when his words about making way for a prefect were quoted.

Bob explained he regained his balance and again went to walk into the building, only to be confronted by De'Ath.

Someone tapped at the study door. The headmaster sighed and snapped, 'Yes?'

It was a young woman May had seen in the secretary's office earlier. The woman looked around nervously.

'I'm sorry, Mr Burnage, but there's a gentleman here to see you and he says it's urgent. It – it's about the fire.'

Mr Burnage tutted and looked as if he wished he were anywhere other than trying to run this disorderly meeting. 'Show him in.'

Everyone watched as a middle-aged man in a shabby tweed jacket snatched off a flat cap and stepped hesitatingly into the room.

'Come forward,' Burnage ordered, as if the man was a prisoner.

The man stood beside the desk, half-turned towards the Head. His forehead shone with sweat.

'You have something to say concerning the fire at the school?'

'Not the fire exactly.'

The Head lost his composure. 'Then why are you here, man? I'm conducting a very important meeting. Boys' education depends on the outcome.'

'So, I believe, sir. But I was asked to come here this morning by a gentleman called Mr Cobb. An American.'

The Major looked astonished. Burnage clenched his fists and May's group stared at each other.

What on earth was Jesson doing? May prayed the man didn't mention that Jesson was black. The word "American" had caused the Major to look as if he was about to explode; if he thought a black man was involved in the case against his son, there was no telling what this kind of man would do. Instantly, she felt ashamed. Jesson had every right to be here. He'd fought in the service of his country just as the Major had and he'd chosen to make his home here. He loved Cliff like a son, and morally, he had every right to intervene. But why?

The man was twisting his cap in his hands. He said, 'My name is Alfred Doubleday. I run the tobacconist stall at the station …'

Now she knew. Thank God for Jesson. He'd been through so much persecution he knew how to find evidence.

'… Mr Cobb asked me if I ever sold cigarettes to school-boys. I told him only them over sixteen. He said innocent boys were being blamed for the fire at the school and asked me to come along and identify anyone I sold fags to.'

The Major had no idea who Jesson was. He appeared delighted that someone had been invited to vindicate his son.

'So, my man,' he said, speaking over the Head. 'Do you recognise your underage customers?'

'He told me he was of age, sir, and I do recognise 'im. He's a regular at my stall. Five Woodbines, Monday and Friday, regular as clockwork. It's 'im.' He pointed at Payne Junior.

'Preposterous,' thundered the Major, although one look at his son's paper-white face told another story.

In the ensuing uproar, May heard the Head thank Mr Doubleday for coming in, and the man scuttled out.

May, Cliff and all four Gales left the Head's study jubilant. Burnage hadn't said what he was going to do, but it was pretty obvious when he asked the prefects and their parents to remain behind.

'You won't hear any more about that now,' Len told the boys.

'Are you sure?' Cliff asked.

'No doubt,' Rose said. 'Your mum and Jesson sewed it up pretty tight. Serves the little blighters right.'

May thew a swift hug around Cliff's shoulders, much to his embarrassment.

'I feel sorry for Johnny, though,' May said. 'He's led on by his slippery pal.'

'It was a masterstroke calling him by his Christian name,' Rose said.

But I didn't want to make him cry, May thought.

'He's just as nasty as Payne,' Peter said. 'He didn't *have* to lie.'

'You're right, Peter, he didn't,' his father said and ruffled the boy's hair.

Rose looked at May and winked.

They rounded a corner and there were Jesson and Spencer chatting to the attractive young woman who'd brought in Mr Doubleday.

May's heart leapt as she saw Jesson; he'd saved the day.

When they approached, the young woman retreated to her office, her cheeks pink. May noticed father and son clutched drinks, and a plate of biscuits lay between them. She'd better watch out. Someone else had spotted what a wonderful man Jesson was.

Chapter 26

Cliff wanted to jump for joy. Mum and Jesson were smashing. Because of them, he'd be able to stay at school and have a chance of getting to vet college.

They all walked to the parking area. The twins' father was going on about getting an apology from Smokey and moaning about having to take a morning off work to come to the meeting.

Cliff didn't care about an apology. He just wanted to forget it all. He suspected the twins felt the same because they said nothing and just let their dad ramble on.

Mrs Gale was getting a lift to the farm in the lorry, so Mr Gale could go straight back to work. Everyone cheered up when he drove off. Lifting Spence into the cab, Cliff heard his mum mutter, 'Damn.'

He looked round as the Major strode up to Jesson. Heck.

'Mr Cobb?'

'Yes, sir.'

Would this never be over? Why did they have to use those flippin' stairs that day?

The Major just said, 'Payne,' and held out his hand.

'Sir.' Jesson didn't seem surprised, but how many bossy posh men were there likely to be at school today? He shook hands.

'Good job with that tobacconist, Cobb. Bad show for my lad, but you did the right thing.'

Cliff saw his mother's look of astonishment.

'Thank you, sir.' Jesson's face didn't flicker.

'Worked with some of your kind on the Front. Good

workers. No hard feelings, Cobb.'

They shook hands again and the Major walked off towards his big shiny Rover, where his wife and son were waiting.

Mum was cross about him saying "your kind" to Jesson.

'As if you're different from the rest of us,' she said.

'I am,' Jesson said. 'I'm American.'

They all laughed and, by the time they drove off, Mum had calmed down.

They walked across the playground to the refectory. Pete said, 'Payne didn't have his prefect's badge on. Reckon we won't see any more of him around here.'

'Good riddance,' Bob said.

'Yeah. And what about "Johnny"?' asked Pete.

They all sniggered.

'Won't miss him either,' Bob said.

Pete said, 'Your mum played a blinder, Cliff. She and Jesson got us off buckshee.'

'We were innocent, but I suppose that isn't always how it works out,' Cliff said.

They were silent for a moment while they digested the alternative outcome.

'Come on, let's get some grub,' called Pete, breaking into a run.

They caught him up. With a cheeky grin, he said, 'Tell you what, after dinner let's celebrate with a fag—'

They cut his words short by rugby tackling him to the ground.

The boys were waiting at the bus stop in Bridport High Street when one of the strangest cars Cliff had ever seen drove past, hooted with a sound like a strangled cockerel, and screeched to a stop. The driver put an arm out of the window and beckoned them.

They looked at each other, bemused, before running over to the great car, half made of wood.

'It's like a shed on wheels,' Pete said, looking at the panels of varnished timber and the row of windows that made up the sides and back doors of the vehicle. The fawn front of the car and the rear mudguards were metal and looked just like a normal car.

'It's a shooting brake,' Bob said. 'Mum's magazine had a picture of the King in one at some castle. Dad thought it was great.'

The front passenger door swung open, and Cliff felt a pang of delight to see Mr Norton leaning across from the driving seat.

'Hello, Cliff. I'm going your way. Would you like a lift?'

'Yes, please.' The thought of travelling in this monster was too good to miss.

'What about your pals?'

'Yeah! Thanks,' the twins yelled in unison.

'Hop in then, boys.'

Cliff commandeered the front seat in the blink of an eye and the other two piled in the back seat.

Mr Norton swung the car out just as the bus pulled up behind them, and they set off. The car felt as big as the farm lorry, but far more comfortable. From the jingling at the back, and the faint whiff of disinfectant, Cliff guessed the vet had plenty of room for the bottles of pills and medicines that he always carried.

Bob asked endless questions about the car: Its make? A Lea Francis. Its age? New, but owned by Mr Norton's dad, who had loaned it to him for work. How many miles did it do to the gallon?

Cliff switched off from the conversation. Cars didn't interest him like they did Bob, who'd got the bug from his father. Bob was sure to pass on every piece of information, word for word, when he got home.

They'd dropped the reluctant twins at the crossroads, when Mr Norton said, 'The weather's getting better, Cliff. Do you think you'd be able to make it into the surgery on Saturday to have that look around, if you're still interested?'

'Yes, of course. I can get the bus.'

They confirmed the arrangements as they reached the farm. Cliff got out to open the gate and waved to Jesson, who was in the yard. He grinned when he saw Jesson's jaw drop as the Lea Francis rolled into the farmyard.

As the car stopped beside him and they climbed out, Jesson gave a low whistle. 'Now that's what I call an automobile,' he said, shaking Mr Norton's hand.

He walked round the car nodding. 'Right size and impressive styling. I could be back in the good ole USA. You don't see so many station wagons over here.'

The two men began talking about engine size and consumption, and Cliff made his excuses. He was sure Mum would want to see the car, maybe go for a ride, and he wanted to be the first to tell her about it.

Chapter 27

It had been fun travelling home from the meeting squeezed in with Rose and Spencer, Jesson driving the lorry, and all of them relieved the boys had been vindicated.

At the farm, Rose joined them for a quick meal. They'd stopped at the village shop, where Victoria had enterprisingly acquired a ham that she'd boiled and was selling sliced. The price was extortionate, but they both bought slices on the ration, knowing that the menfolk would welcome a change to their diet.

Evelyn Harris was behind the counter and whispered to May that things were no better in the Potty camp, with the two sides still barely speaking. Victoria had though, ferreted out a roofer and he had made repairs to the roof above her bed.

'She's now pretending that she had no intention of moving in with Ephraim and Isabella.'

May could well imagine that Isabella, doyenne of the WI until May superseded her as chairman some years ago and gave others the courage to stand for the post, would be livid over rumours that her sister-in-law wouldn't deign to share a house, not the other way round.

May and Rose chose comics and sweets for the boys and May picked up a fresh loaf from the baker's to make the most of the ham, her mouth watering at the thought of crusty ham sandwiches.

Over the meal, Rose supervised Spencer eating wafer-thin pieces of ham followed by jammy soldiers, while May and Jesson discussed the farm work. Jesson wanted to summon the POWs immediately, but May persuaded him to wait until the land had dried out a little more.

The atmosphere between them had eased, and she felt an intense gratitude to him for him saving the day for Cliff and, with it, his career dreams. The chance of a profession was no more than the boy deserved after his inauspicious start in life.

Jesson changed into the working clothes he kept at the farm and went out to the yard. May and Rose chatted whilst they cleared and washed up.

'Thank you for your advice, May. I've been trying ter make sure Len has plenty of manly jobs ter keep him busy, even if it means I have to leave the shoes dirty until he has time ter clean them!'

May laughed. 'He was decent with Peter today, defending both of them equally. And he was obviously proud of how sensibly they behaved over the fire. Do you think Peter will move back home now?' She passed Rose a sudsy plate.

Rose dried the plate. 'I hope so, but I'm not pushing it. If it's all right with you, I'd like him ter leave his stuff here, so that if the balloon goes up again, he knows he has a bolthole.'

'That's fine. He can leave it there as long as he likes.' She tipped the washing up water down the drain.

While Rose settled Spencer for a nap, May made a telephone call, and then the two of them sat around the desk in the study, working on farm business.

After a couple of hours, May turned to the farm accounts. They looked healthy – considering how arduous work had been for the past year. With the POWs only receiving a minimal wage, and just Jesson and Rose to pay, the bank balance was better than she'd expected.

'Are you planning some expenditure?' Rose asked.

'I'm—'

'Mum?'

Cliff's voice. Rose and May's eyes met. What had happened? He was more than an hour early. The fears of the morning came flooding back. Had Burnage discovered something else? Instituted a blanket expulsion of all those connected to the fire?

'What are you doing back so early, Cliff?' she said, as he burst into the study.

One look at Cliff's glowing face quelled her worries. It was marvellous to see him so excited.

'Mum, you must come and see. You too, Mrs Gale. We got a lift home in a wizard car. Pete said it looks like a shed on wheels. It does a bit, but only because of the wood. Jesson says it's like an American station wagon.'

May and Rose looked at each other and shrugged.

'I suppose we'd better look after that build-up,' May said.

'Kif, Kif!'

'Right on time, Spencer,' Rose said. 'I'll get his coat. Cliff, can you let him through?'

Cliff fetched the little boy, who was reaching out through the stair gate.

They all put on outdoor clothes and boots.

'Come on, Spence,' Cliff said as they pulled the door closed behind them. 'We're going to see Mr Norton's new car.'

'What?' May stopped dead. 'I thought it was Mr Tyler's car.'

'No. Mr Norton,' said Cliff, being tugged along by Spencer.

'Why did you think it was Bill Tyler's?' Rose said.

'Bill mentioned he was thinking of getting a second vehicle that time his lorry was off the road,' she muttered. 'I just assumed.'

'Are you all right? You look like you've seen a ghost.'

The ghost's in the yard, she thought. 'I've just got a headache,' she said.

Rose looked at her askance, but said nothing.

They rounded the corner into the yard. Jesson told Spencer that all cars in America were this big.

'Crikey!' Rose said, taking in the car.

It was impressive. And enormous.

Cliff came running towards them. 'See, Mum? It's a shooting brake. That's what Mr Norton says, though Jesson calls it a station wagon.'

May looked around. The vet wasn't in sight.

'So, this is what all cars are like in America, is it, Jesson?' Rose asked.

'Yes, ma'am, sure is.' Jesson hammed up his accent, but his eyes didn't leave May.

She pretended to examine the car. She'd seen something similar in a magazine Sally had passed on to her. Ideal for a Royal shooting trip; possibly excessive for everyday. Practical though, she had to admit, for a vet travelling from farm to farm.

On the far side of the car, admiring the features that Cliff enthusiastically pointed out, May noticed movement at the barn door. She refused to let herself look.

Rose gasped. 'Ye gods.'

May stared at the wooden doors of the Lea Francis as if they held some fascinating secret.

'Mr Norton says you could get a young calf in there,' Cliff informed her.

'Hmm,' May said.

'Not that I would want to, of course. Or, not often, at least.' The laugh, so reminiscent of Seth's, brought tears to her eyes.

She couldn't look at Redvers, couldn't look anywhere, but stared blindly at the car.

Everyone was waiting for her to speak, but the lump in her throat made it impossible.

'You must be the new vet?' Rose intervened. Thank God for Rose.

Scarcely aware of Rose introducing herself and telling Redvers how enamoured Len would be of his car, she composed herself.

She walked round the vehicle, held out her hand, and said, 'Good afternoon, Mr Norton. Thank you for giving Cliff the ride of his life. I think he's found a new passion.' She smiled across to where Cliff was lifting Spencer to let him see the inside of the car.

'Good to see you again, Mrs Sheppard. My pleasure. Boys love anything mechanical.'

She was glad his hand was so different from Seth's. As long as she didn't look into his eyes, she'd survive.

'Would you like some tea?' she asked, after the vet explained to her and Jesson how pleased he was with Ben's recovery. Jesson's expression was fixed. He knew her too well.

'Shall I put the kettle on?' Rose asked.

'I'll come too,' she said, desperately seeking escape. 'I've got a tin of special biscuits tucked away somewhere.'

'You *are* honoured, Redvers,' Jesson said without the flicker of a smile.

Damn and blast. She always made things worse.

Chapter 28

May flung herself onto a chair as Rose gathered cups and saucers.

'I thought I was dreaming,' Rose said, filling the kettle. 'He's the image of Seth. He has ter be related. Do you know how?'

At least she didn't imagine the similarity. 'No idea. His father's not from around here, although his mother came from Swanage.'

'Cripes. What a shock for you. Does Jesson know?' Rose poured milk into a jug.

'No, and I don't want him to. It's bad enough I haven't given him an answer—' Hell. What was she saying?

Rose was on it like a magnet to a horseshoe. 'An answer? Don't tell me he's proposed? That's wonderful, if overdue. What's stopping you? You're made for each other.'

May sighed. Perhaps it was time she confided in someone. 'I thought that. Until Redvers arrived and I remembered how it had been with someone without the complications. Today, after what Jesson did at the school, I was certain that I'd accept; he's so genuine and honest and kind ...'

'And black.'

'Yes – no – I don't care about that; you know I don't. I never see his skin colour, he's just a wonderful human being.'

'But?'

'It's just I never seem to stop fighting things: the weather, the staff shortages, the problems with the boys. My life is one long battle, has been for years – for all of us since war broke out, I know – but can I face more, this time for the rest of my life as people look at him – at me – askance, sidestep a dear man, just because his complexion is darker than theirs?'

The sound of Spencer squealing with laughter came from outside.

'Stone the crows, they're here. Where're those biscuits, May?'

May opened a top cupboard and brought out a tin of Jacob's biscuits with a picture of holly and mistletoe on the lid. 'Last of the Christmas treats,' she said.

'I'll stick some on a plate and we'll hide the tin. They'll go in a jiffy if Cliff finds them,' Rose said.

'Or Jesson,' May added, without thinking.

Rose looked at her. 'The gannets of the family.'

May caught her glance, but said nothing.

Redvers left. Cliff accompanied him to the sainted car, having first extracted a promise that she would collect him from the surgery on Saturday afternoon when he'd been on a tour of the place.

Rose had refused a lift to the village, pleading she'd had enough time off today.

Thank goodness; Rose was a trusted confidante, but she would have preferred not to give her a chance to cross-examine the vet about his family.

She buttoned up her old coat, ready to get to work bedding down the hens. It was getting towards dusk and she didn't want to give the fox the opportunity of a free dinner.

As she opened the door to go out, she said, 'Rose, would you and the boys pop down on Saturday morning if you've nothing planned? Len, too, if he wants to come.' She crossed her gloved fingers, hoping Rose's overbearing spouse would be busy elsewhere.

'Thanks, but he'll be working. We'll come along, though. What's it about?'

'Just something I want to show you all. You'll be there, won't you, Jesson?'

He was entering Redvers's visit in the farm diary, a daily routine they'd continued since May had inherited the farm. The dairy had a row of shelves loaded with decades of dusty journals.

He looked up, puzzled. 'Sure.'

She saw him and Rose exchange a mystified glance. Before they could ask more questions, she left.

Cliff was coming up the track. 'I've fed the horses. Did you want me to help with the hens?'

'Have you got homework?'

'Tons.'

'Right, I'll do the birds. You get on and don't waste your time playing with Spencer. Mrs Gale's perfectly capable of entertaining him.' She walked on.

'Righto – Mum?'

'Cliff?'

'Thanks for today. You saved our bacon.'

'It's what mothers do. Jesson was the real hero of the hour, though.'

'I know, I'll thank him too.'

He sprang over to her and wrapped her in a bear hug. 'You're the best mum I've ever had,' he said, grinning.

'Thank you,' she said. There had been little competition; his natural mother had been an utter maternal failure. She ruffled his hair and realised it was no longer a case of bending to do so; he was as tall as her.

Chapter 29

Mum had a secret. She wouldn't tell anyone what it was, but she was going to reveal it this morning.

Because Mrs Gale and the twins were coming, it had to be something to do the farm. His guess was that she'd found a new horse to replace Ben, although when he'd asked her to promise again that Ben would never be put to sleep – put down, as Mr Norton called it – she got cross and said she'd already told him that.

He didn't believe it wouldn't be a new horse but, when he got the barrow from the barn to muck out the hens, he realised the third loosebox was full of junk and a horse wouldn't be able to move in.

Blossom whickered to him, and he pulled a crust from his pocket and broke it in two. The mare accepted his gift with her whiskery lips and lowered her head to sniff at Bess. Ben, always aloof, took his share and went back to searching his empty feed bucket for stray oats.

Cliff grabbed the barrow and set off for the poultry yard, Bess racing him for the gate.

He'd just have to wait and see what Mum's surprise would be. As long as it wasn't something that went on longer than one o'clock, because he had to catch the bus to go on his vet's visit.

He'd got a few butterflies in his stomach. What would it be like having a tour of a business? He hoped he would re-member to ask the right questions; Mum had helped him think of some: What types of animal did the surgery treat? Were there more pets or farm animals on their books? His own question: Which animals did Mr Norton like best?

Jesson had mucked out the horses and put them in the orchard while Cliff had been with the hens. He appeared out of
the Dutch barn and walked with Cliff and Bess to the house
for breakfast.

'Big day, Cliff. What's your ma going to surprise us
with, any ideas?'

'She won't say, but I reckon it's another horse.'

'But why the Gales? They're not interested in horses, are
they?'

'Dunno.' He shrugged. 'Mum's determined to surprise
us.'

'Looks like she will.' Jesson didn't sound very excited
about it.

Everyone was sitting with hot drinks when the phone rang.
Mum jumped to her feet saying, 'I'll get it.'

All they heard was, 'Right you are,' before she was telling them they had to get down to the yard.

'Wos all this about?' Pete said. He and Bob were throw-
ing sticks for Bess as they walked down the track. The dog's
tail thrashed wildly as she looked from one twin to the other,
waiting for the next throw.

Mum called, 'Boys, can you open both gates, please?
Cliff, put Bess in the barn for now.'

Bess let him know she wasn't happy to be shut away
from the surprise with a wistful whine as the door slid closed.

They stood around waiting until Spence said, 'Motor,'
and pointed to the gateway. Seconds later, there came the
sound of a heavy engine, followed by a crunch of gears as a
vehicle slowed and, taking a wide swing, crept between the

gateposts.

'Cor! A low loader,' said Bob, staring at the low-slung trailer tracking behind the pillar-box-red cab unit. Gold sign-writing above the windscreen said "Bristol Haulage".

'A semi?' Jesson said, looking at Mum, eyebrows raised. Cliff made a mental note of the American word for something he'd rarely seen before.

The driver lowered his window and said, 'Mrs Sheppard?'

'Good morning,' Mum called. 'Can you unload here, please?'

The driver and his mate jumped from the cab and began untying the ropes of the tarpaulin that covered whatever was loaded on the trailer.

Jesson, Pete and Bob started helping with the ropes and Spence, jumping up and down with excitement, dragged Cliff over to the vehicle.

'Big lorry.' The little lad pointed at the huge truck, his eyes wide.

'It is, Spence, and it isn't a horse, is it?'

Spencer giggled. 'Silly Kif.'

At last, all the ropes were free, and they stepped back as the two hauliers tugged the tarpaulin back.

'A Fergusson,' Cliff said, recognising the make of the dove grey tractor sitting at the front of the trailer. How soon could he drive it to the village?

'Wow!' Bob was on the trailer, examining the tractor's controls. Pete stuck his head near the back, asking Jesson how the equipment fitted on.

Jesson scratched his head and squatted to get a better look at the bars extending from the back of the machine. The driver explained it was fitted with a revolutionary three-point linkage, so they weren't likely to have seen it before.

'And hydraulics. Gee, that's something else.' Jesson was in raptures.

Mum winked at Cliff; they always shared the joke when something British was new to Jesson; he'd nearly always seen things before in America.

Mum watched with a beaming smile as the tarpaulin slid to the ground and two more pieces of equipment were revealed.

'A plough. And a rotary cultivator,' Jesson said. His eyes sparkled, and he grinned at Mum, whose face was going very pink.

'Would you chaps like a cup of tea?' Mum said. 'You're welcome to come up to the house.'

'No thank you, ma'am, but a refill of our flasks would be just the job,' the driver replied, dragging the tarpaulin out of the way while his mate tugged some heavy metal ramps off the back of the trailer.

Mrs Gale took the men's flasks away and the rest of them helped to push the cultivator down the ramps. It was a thing on rubber tyres, with an arched metal lid, a bit like two oil drums sliced lengthwise and joined end to end. Jesson lifted the lid and beneath were some vicious looking rotating claws. He explained the claws pulled out weeds and broke up the ground, like the cultivator the horses pulled, but they could also use this one like a harrow to make a seedbed.

'Then Bloss will come along with the seed drill,' Cliff chipped in.

'You got it, Cliff, but it'll be a heck of a lot quicker than just using horses.'

'The plough will have to be lifted off,' the driver said and Pete, Bob and Cliff stationed themselves among the men, grabbing a bit to lift.

They staggered down the ramps and everyone sighed as they rested the plough on the ground.

Mrs Gale came back carrying two flasks and something wrapped in greaseproof paper. She laid them on the step of the lorry. 'A couple of slices of cake to keep you going,' she said.

'Much obliged,' the driver said, and the mate touched his cap.

The driver turned to Jesson. 'Mr Sheppard, would you like to back the tractor down the ramps?'

Mum flushed bright red, Mrs Gale coughed to cover a laugh, and the twins looked confused. Jesson just said, 'I'm the foreman, Jesson Cobb, but thanks, I'll get the tractor off.'

He jumped up and climbed into the seat, fiddled with a couple of controls and then, with a puff of smoke from the chimney-like exhaust, the Fergie fired and Jesson reversed smoothy into the yard to a round of applause.

Elem Farm had her first tractor.

Chapter 30

May waved to Spencer as she drove off, and the little boy gave her one of his banana grins. She'd left him in his father's charge and fortunately, with the distraction of the new machinery, Jesson barely registered that, as well as shopping in Bridport, she would be collecting Cliff from Redvers's surgery.

The morning had gone better than she'd dared hope. Since the tractor had arrived, Jesson was like a bee in clover, delighting in dashing about moving the horse-drawn equipment and fitting the new implements into the cart sheds.

Rose hadn't been able to resist teasing May about the "Mr Sheppard" remark. May had taken it in good part, relieved that the atmosphere between her and Jesson had lifted.

Rose and Bob left after the low loader had driven away, but Peter wanted to stay and help and he'd volunteered to take care of the poultry duties that afternoon. Jesson, delighted he'd be able to spend more time with his new playthings, readily accepted.

If only Peter's father could allow the boy some slack, he'd discover a willingness he'd never thought his son possessed. The boy was showing a new side to his nature, and he worked well alongside Jesson. She smiled to herself as she pictured the scene as she left: Jesson, Peter and Spencer heaping sacks and tarpaulins over the tractor in the Dutch barn, to ensure it wouldn't freeze overnight. A newborn baby couldn't have had more care.

The lorry motored along the Bridport road; there was very little traffic on a Saturday afternoon. Ditches at the sides of the road were still full to the brim, but the standing water on the fields had largely dissipated. A tractor was working the land at the top of a hill and she watched to see what progress it made.

It didn't seem to have any trouble, and she hoped they'd have a similar experience on Monday morning when the POWs arrived and they all got down to making up for lost time.

The orange tractor passed from view. Cliff had been crazy for a tractor when he'd first seen one on Bill Tyler's farm; he'd plagued her about getting one for years. Now, instead of being cock-a-hoop as she'd expected, he was far more absorbed in his visit to the vet's surgery.

It was to be expected; he was growing up. His career was his decision, and she'd do everything she could to support him. It wasn't as if farming was in his blood, and he'd worked hard enough since she'd inherited Elem to earn the right to reject the life if he chose.

If the threat from Dorothy's solicitors came to anything, there might not be a farm, anyway. The idea was incomprehensible – not that the farm wouldn't be hers. She'd had no expectations of that kind, but that someone could believe she could bully an elderly man for her own benefit.

If the case came to court and *if* they found her guilty, what would happen to the profits she'd made since Tom's death? She didn't know, but she had no intention of keeping money aside in case someone wanted to claim it. The tractor was essential and she'd spent money on it. She would do so again if necessary, and to hell with those trying to steal what was legally hers. She was seeing her solicitor next week, and she'd tell him to fight tooth and nail.

***

She spotted Sally Tyler on the opposite pavement in Bridport High Street. She was pushing a pram.

They greeted each other with pleasure. May had only seen her friend once since the calamitous day of the baby's birth. The doting couple had brought their daughter to the farm to thank May for her help, a few weeks after the event. It had been a freezing wintry day and May had had only a glimpse of a tiny swaddled face.

'She's grown,' she said, peering under the pram hood at a sleeping Jemima, who had her father's gingery hair and Sally's blue eyes.

'She grows so fast her clothes are hardly worn before she needs bigger ones,' Sally laughed. 'I hear you've got a tractor at last.'

The gossip machine was astounding. They'd only had the thing a few hours and already the news had spread to Magna.

'Have you got time for a cup of tea?' Sally asked.

In a spotless tea room, where Sally tucked the pram just inside the door, Jemima slept on.

Sally took off her coat, and May marvelled at her immaculate appearance; you'd never know she'd had a baby only two months before. Her sky-blue twinset looked new. It was perfect against her blonde hair and fair skin.

May's old cardigan had darns at the elbows and her blouse had been through the wash so many times the paisley pattern was indiscernible. She felt old and dowdy beside Sally, who was only a couple of years younger than herself.

They ordered a pot of tea and two rock cakes and, while they waited, Sally asked how May had come across the tractor.

'When Ben went lame, I knew I had to do something – find another horse or take the plunge. I'd been putting it off for years because I knew how difficult tractors are to find, but then I remembered that in Tom's old paperwork there were some ancient auction catalogues. I dug them out and rang some auctioneers in Bristol on the off chance they were still in business. By coincidence, they'd just had instructions to sell the Fergie by a farmer in Devon. He'd had a nasty accident digging out sheep from the snow and was unlikely to farm again.'

'How awful,' Sally said.

'That's how I felt, especially as he'd bought the tractor with a bank loan and had hardly used it when the accident happened. He couldn't meet the repayments and needed to sell it as soon as possible to keep his head above water.'

'Lucky you. You got a bargain. What about the War Ag though, did you have a permit to buy the tractor and stuff?'

May was unhappy Sally might think she'd take advantage of someone's misfortune. She explained she'd made a fair offer based on the auctioneer's recommendation and that the purchase had the War Ag approvals.

The waitress brought their order, and Sally poured the tea. 'I bet Jesson's delighted, isn't he?'

'Like a child with a new toy.' May bit into a rock cake that lived up to its name.

She went on, 'The auctioneer had his eye on his commission and persuaded me to take other bits as well. It saved me a search for implements, and I'm not sorry I bought the plough and rotary cultivator as well.'

Sally looked impressed. May suspected that they didn't have a rotary cultivator at Magna Farm. It felt good to be ahead of the game for once.

'Sounds like you're making big changes at Elem. Have you done anything with the house?'

May thought about Sally's modernised kitchen, decorated in pastel shades, and contrasted it with the chocolate brown woodwork and featureless off-white distemper of her own kitchen.

'I'm planning to redecorate and replace the cooker,' she said, having just that second had the idea. 'And have the phone moved to the kitchen,' she added, deciding to do just that as soon as the weather settled.

'Just have a phone extension put in,' Sally said. 'That way, they'll always be a phone handy – especially if Rose is working in the study. And if you want to escape the noise of the family to take a call, you can.'

Two phones? May smiled to herself. She wouldn't recognise her home soon; mechanised and modernised. Poor old Tom would turn in his grave.

Feeling rather guilty about the carrier bag she was carrying, the words *Miss Martin's Modes* emblazoned across it, May returned to the lorry. She'd allowed herself to be tempted by the sale posters in the window of a womenswear shop, only to be attracted by the new spring range and not the replacement winter coat she'd had in mind. Sally's example, of course. Her handbag also contained the name of a painter and decorator Sally recommended.

May drove to the vet's surgery. Cliff had expected to be ready at four o'clock and she pulled up at five minutes to the hour.

Should she go into the surgery? It could seem churlish if she sat in the lorry, so she took her handbag and mounted the steps to a weathered oak door. She tugged the bell pull hanging beside a shiny brass plate engraved, *R. Norton MRCVS, Veterinary Surgeon*. Inside, the bell clanged and footsteps approached.

'Mrs Sheppard. Do come in.'

Redvers Norton was wearing a sleeveless maroon pullover over a checked shirt and a lovat tie. Seth would never have worn red and green together and when she shook the vet's smooth hands, she found she could look at him objectively for the first time.

His face was finer than Seth's; although that might be just the absence of weather-beaten lines. She'd loved the creases around Seth's eyes; the skin within paler than the rest of his complexion, and usually visible only when he slept.

There were more differences between the men than she'd first imagined.

It was a pleasant change to feel more relaxed in Redvers's company. She hoped she'd come across as a normal person, not the batty woman she must have presented.

They walked along a passageway lined with chairs, past a half-glazed door with *Surgery* etched into the glass. At the end, he ushered her into a sitting room and offered her a seat on a sagging sofa. She glimpsed a kitchen opposite.

'I'm afraid Cliff may be a while. A bitch needing a caesarean came in just before you arrived and he was mad keen to watch. I hope you don't mind?'

'No, of course not,' she said, feeling awkward and in the way.

'Can I get you a cup of tea?'

'If you're having one. Thank you,' she said.

Redvers went across to the kitchen and she looked around. The furnishings were past their best, but it was a comfortable room; one end occupied by a great bookcase where she could see an inordinate number of veterinary books and bound copies of *The Veterinary Record*.

He came back, carrying a tray. Amid the crockery was a plate of higgledy-piggledy piled custard creams and he unloaded everything on to the ringed top of an ancient coffee table.

'Mrs Sheppard, would you …' he gestured to the teapot.

'Of course. And please call me May.'

He smiled in the familiar way she'd never thought to see again. Her composure began to slip. Keeping her gaze on the tea things, she carelessly placed two cups on mis-matched saucers, her shaking hands rattling the china.

'Do call me Redvers,' he said. After a slight hesitation, he cleared his throat. 'May, my mother always tells me I charge at things like a bull at a gate but, at the risk of being thought impertinent, I must ask why you are so uncomfortable in my company?'

Heat flooded her face. She picked up the milk jug and dribbled milk into the cups. Now was the time. She gripped the handle of the heavy brown teapot and poured without looking up, knowing he was watching her.

She moved a cup towards him, sat back and reached into her handbag. Without speaking, she pulled out her purse, flipped open the notes section and handed it to him.

He took it, a puzzled expression on his face, and looked down at the well-worn black-and-white photograph slotted into a cut-out window.

He looked up at her, dumfounded. He got to his feet and carried the picture to the window, tilting it to the daylight.

'Who is this?' he said, turning to face her.

'Seth Sheppard, my late husband. He died in 1938.'

165

Redvers dropped into the armchair and returned the purse. 'At least I understand your reaction to me,' he said, picking up his teacup and taking a big gulp. 'He's my double.'

'It was an enormous shock and I apologise for being rude,' May said. 'I don't know how, but you and Seth have to be related somehow.'

'My family is so proper; I can't believe we've got a skeleton in the cupboard. When was Seth born?'

May told him what she knew of Seth's family history and they worked out that Redvers was eight years younger than Seth. He had been born in May 1915, a month after Seth's father had been killed at Ypres.

'Seth felt strongly about the sacrifice those poor men in the trenches made,' she said. 'While his mother was alive, they never missed the Service of Remembrance in Bridport; his father's name is on the Column of Remembrance.'

'I've always felt privileged that I still have both my parents, but maybe …'

May felt a stab of guilt; the man's perception of his family had been changed by what she'd told him.

'Redvers, we don't know he was a close relative of yours,' she said. 'Perhaps he was a cousin, or something?' she ended lamely, knowing that the resemblance was too strong to be so tenuous.

They talked round the subject while the tea got cold, May half wishing she'd never told him. They decided May would look out a photograph of Seth's father, Hector, and Redvers would make tentative enquires about the whereabouts of his parents at the time of his conception. May was glad she didn't have to be part of that conversation.

Cliff, wearing a long white coat, strode into the room. His face alight, he looked grown up. She had a fleeting impression of the man he would become: self-assured, confident, nothing like the reticent boy who'd arrived on her doorstep all that time ago.

Someone came in behind him and May expected to see old Mr Hughes. But, instead of the retired vet, an attractive dark-haired young woman stepped towards May, hand extended.

'I'm sorry to have held you up,' she said. 'Cliff was keen to see the operation. I can tell you, he made a first class assistant.' She shook May's hand.

Cliff flushed scarlet, but May could see he was thrilled with the praise.

'Thank you.' May wasn't sure how to react. Who was this woman?

'Sorry, sorry,' Redvers apologised. 'I need to introduce you. May Sheppard, Cliff's mum, this is Fliss Yates MRCVS. My fiancée.'

Chapter 31

He'd helped with an operation! When Mr Norton began showing him around, he'd found it bewildering; so much that didn't involve direct contact with animals. A cupboard full of packets, bottles and jars of tablets, medicines and ointments. How did anyone remember what they all were for and what they were called?

Mr Norton asked if he was studying Latin and he said he was – he didn't mention he hated the subject and didn't try very hard. He'd have to try now, if he didn't want to sound like a clot when he couldn't pronounce the names of the drugs he'd have to prescribe.

There were files of clients and invoices and bills, piles of *The Veterinary Record* magazine that arrived every week and you had to read to keep up to date. So much to learn.

He'd seen the animal cages where they kept patients while they were having their treatment. A huge black cat was asleep in one. He had a bandage on his paw where he'd lost a nail in a fight, and the wound had turned septic. He'd wondered how big the other cat had been – this one was a monster. Mr Norton had laughed and said sometimes it paid to be small and agile.

Mr Norton told him sometimes you had to get up at night to give medicine or check that the animals were all right, as well as getting called out to calvings and other emergencies. Was he trying to put him off? He'd also made a big point of saying he'd never get rich as a vet.

Cliff didn't want to get rich; he wanted to help animals and couldn't think of a better way of doing it.

His visit had confirmed his ambition, and the icing on the cake had been being allowed to assist in the caesarean in the operating theatre, the most exciting room in the place, even though it was just the consulting room with green cloths spread on the examination table.

Miss Yates was a wizard vet; she'd been the only woman in her year at veterinary college but she'd slogged it out and passed all her exams.

'First, we anaesthetised the dog. She was a golden Labrador,' Cliff told Mum on the way home. He hadn't stopped talking since they left the surgery. 'Then Miss Yates had to cut open her side and get the pups out. There were three golden and one black. I had to clean their mouths and noses and rub them if they weren't breathing. I laid them on a towel and then we had to stitch up the mother and bring her round.'

He remembered the bubble of joy he'd felt when the mother had started to lick her pups. Miss Yates had a big smile on her face, too. He hoped he never got to the point when he took births for granted, although he'd see loads of them when he was a vet. A vet. Clifford Erwin MRCVS. Wizard.

They'd arrived at the farm already. He jumped out and opened the gates. The place was in darkness. Blossom whickered from the barn as he walked past. He called to her and jogged on up the track to help Mum with her shopping bags.

'Have you remembered you're going out with the Gales tomorrow?' she said as they walked up to the farmhouse. He had forgotten, but it would be fun going to Weymouth for the day; Mr Gale wanted to show them the garage where he worked – trying to get Pete interested in engineering, Cliff suspected – but they were going to get fish and chips and go on the beach.

Lights shone through the kitchen curtains and as they opened the door, the smell of cooking met them.

'Arn Mee.' Spencer launched himself at Mum's knees, and Bess licked Cliff's hand. He ruffled the silky hair on her head and imagined how relieved the Labrador's owners would have been that she and her pups had survived. Once, he'd thought of breeding from Bess. Mum had persuaded him that there were so many dogs it was better to have her spayed than to breed a litter that no one wanted. He hoped the Labrador pups would go to kind homes.

'How did it go?' Jesson asked. He was sitting at the table reading the Fergie handbook.

'Smashing. I was allowed to help at a caesarean. She had four pups, and they were all healthy.'

'That's great. What's next, calving a herd of cattle?' Jesson grinned at him.

'Yeah, all with twins.' Cliff laughed.

'He did well,' Mum said. 'Mr Norton was very pleased.'

'Kif, look. Twactor.' Spence handed Cliff a Meccano construction that sort of resembled a tractor.

'Is that the Fergie?' he asked, realising he hadn't even thought about the tractor since he'd left the farm that morning.

'Yes. Furry,' the little boy said, with a grin that grew even bigger when everyone laughed.

Mum had left a stew ready for Jesson to reheat, so they ate soon after getting home. Sitting around the table was different from normal, as they all had things to tell the others. Jesson talked about his plans for the Fergie and explained how the hydraulics worked. Bob would have loved it, but Cliff wasn't that interested – although he liked it that the tractor lifted the implements itself.

Mum had had tea with Sally Tyler and talked about her clothes and how she'd got a car of her own now. Jesson said something about Mr Tyler having no money left soon.

Cliff only wanted to talk about the surgery, but he didn't get the chance until they finished their cold rice pudding and Mum had made tea and coffee.

He was about to describe the drugs cupboard, when Mum interrupted.

'Cliff, while I was waiting for you, Mr Norton asked me something, which he felt should be my decision, but I think we should all discuss it. He would like to offer you a Saturday job at the surgery—'

'A job? Smashing!'

'Just hang on. If you work at the surgery, you won't be able to do your work here. It'll be too much for Jesson and me to take on when we get back to proper farm work and the hens are in full production. We need to discuss it.'

Heck. He hadn't thought about his job at the farm, but he couldn't lose this chance.

'Did you have something in mind, May?' Jesson asked.

'First, as I understand it, today was an exception. You wouldn't be involved in operations very often; you'd be cleaning out animal cages, sweeping up, checking the stock of drugs, and that sort of thing. Mr Norton says he would let you sit in on surgical procedures, but they only get emergencies at weekends. It could be boring most of the time.'

He thought about it. Without the operating theatre excitement, had he enjoyed his day? Yes, he had. He'd enjoyed reading the little cards on the cages saying what was wrong

171

with the animals and when they'd eaten and had their medicines, and he'd like to help make them feel better, even if it was just putting fresh newspaper in their cages.

Mum said, 'I don't want you to decide now. You're still excited about the day. Wait until after the weekend, but we should think about what to do about your job in case you go to the vet's.'

Jesson put down his cup. 'The obvious thing is to get someone else, and the obvious choice is Pete. He's a good worker, and he seems to enjoy it. He knows what to do and we know he's reliable.'

Cliff wondered what Mr Gale would say if Pete told him he was going to work looking after chickens. He'd been trying to persuade the twins to get weekend jobs at a garage; Cliff knew Pete would never do that, although Bob was mad keen, and that must be what tomorrow's trip was about.

'I agree,' Mum said, 'but we can't offer him just the Saturday. The job's always been both days, and it's less chopping and changing if it's the same person. You need to think about giving up two days' wages for one, if you take the surgery job. You'll get paid but you'll have your bus fare to take from that.'

Jesson must have seen Cliff's expression because he chipped in, 'There's bound to be other farm work on Sundays that you'll be able to do. If he does a man's job, we should pay him like one, shouldn't we, May?'

'Yes, of course, but there won't be that much in the winter, remember that.'

Cliff couldn't sleep. The decision he had to make turned cartwheels in his head. He loved the surgery and working there would be a good start to his career. But he'd have less money to do things, and less to save for vet college.

He wasn't allowed to say anything about the job to Pete, but he knew he'd jump at it. His father was stingy with pocket money and the twins had hardly anything to spend on themselves.

He fidgeted and turned over. The picture of the blind pups nuzzling their mum for milk made him smile as he nodded off.

Chapter 32

The heather twinset felt wonderful; she'd forgotten the softness of new lambswool. When had she last had new clothes apart from underwear and stockings? Not that she wore stockings very often nowadays – they weren't conducive to bedding down hens or muck spreading.

With her charcoal-grey costume skirt and her late mother's pearls, she felt almost fashionable. She brushed her hair before checking her appearance in the wardrobe mirror. Not bad. The sales woman had been right; the delicate purple mix suited her; it brought a brightness to her face. Her eyes were clearer and even her hair looked to have more gold strands.

The smell of roasting meat tempted her as she laid the table for two. She hoped Jesson wouldn't be late for the meal. It was only a couple of pork chops, but she'd roasted potatoes as well and the carrots were boiling. Gravy would add to the pretence of a traditional Sunday dinner.

A few butterflies flitted in her stomach; she'd asked Jesson to eat with her, even though the boys had gone on their trip with the Gales. He'd accepted, but he'd be surprised to see her dressed up.

She was pouring two glasses of parsnip wine when the back door opened, and Jesson arrived.

'Am I late?' he asked.

'Just right,' she said.

He was wearing the tan sweater that flattered his colouring. Her heart skipped a beat.

'Wow!' he said. 'Who's this beautiful doll?'

May blushed. 'I thought I'd get myself something new.'

'Sally's influence?'

Did he think her shallow? 'Not really, it's—'

'Just teasing, May. You look gorgeous, and you deserve a treat.' He took her in his arms and she felt her cares melt away as she responded to his kiss.

'Come on,' she said, gently pulling away. 'We must eat or it'll be ruined.'

Over the meal, they discussed the work for the following week and May said she'd need to use one of the POWs to help clear out the henhouses and prepare them for the poults that would be arriving from Bill Tyler's hatchery soon.

'I was thinking,' Jesson said, 'why don't we hire a full-time poultry keeper – the job you did before you inherited this place?'

'We tried when the last land girl left, but no one wanted the job. I could put a postcard in the post office, I suppose, it would take the pressure off.'

After more discussion over the mocha pudding she'd made especially for Jesson, she suggested they move to the window seat. The wine had gone to her head and her reflection showed her flushed cheeks.

'Let's not talk about work anymore,' she said. They looked out at the two horses mooching about in the orchard, searching for the first spring grass. It was a bright day, and she hoped the boys were enjoying their time at the seaside.

She took a sip of coffee before trying to appear nonchalant and mention Cliff's vet visit.

'Did he tell you it wasn't Redvers who did the caesarean?'

Jesson sat a little straighter in the seat. 'No. I just

assumed it would be Norton.'

'He had another vet staying for the weekend, and they operated to give Redvers a break.'

'Okay.' Jesson was looking at her with a wariness in his eyes.

'Yes. So, he chatted to me while the operation was going on.' He frowned and she wanted to smile. 'When it was over, he introduced me to her.'

'Her?'

'Yes, Fliss. His fiancée.' She watched as he digested the news. 'Just before I left, they invited me to their wedding. It's not until the summer, but it will be the first wedding I've been to since Bill and Sally's. Unless my own comes first.'

She watched him. He nodded before what she'd said hit him and he did a double-take any actor would be proud of.

'What did you just say?'

'If the offer's still open, then I accept.' She smiled, only the tiniest bit of doubt remaining. What if he'd changed his mind?

'Jeez. You are the most confounding woman I ever met,' he said.

Before she could speak, he enveloped her in his arms. 'Of course, the offer's still open, you maddening woman.'

She emerged from his kiss and laid her head on his shoulder. It was so long since she'd had someone to lean on, metaphorically and physically. The joy of having someone to share her life; the burdens, the worries and the pleasures; someone she loved and who loved her back was like a dream.

Abruptly, Jesson sat up. 'You're not marrying me because Norton's not available, are you?'

A flash of anger swept through her, but she extinguished it with an instant decision.

'Of course not, but there is something you need to see.' Grasping his hand, she led him to the stairs.

He followed her up, but hesitated at the door of her bedroom.

'Come in.'

She sat on the bed and patted the coverlet beside her. He came in tentatively, looking around the room that he'd barely set foot in before. He sat on the edge of the bed next to her.

She reached over to the bedside table and put a silver photograph frame in his hand.

He raised it, looked at the picture. 'Norton?' he said, disgust in his voice.

'Look again.'

He frowned and looked closer. 'It's not Norton, but he's his double. Who is he?'

'Seth.'

'*Seth?*'

'That was taken when I first met him. He was about the age Redvers is now.'

'How are they related?' Jesson stood the photograph back on the table.

'No idea. I only mentioned it to Redvers on Saturday and he's as confused as I am. I felt I had to explain why I was so peculiar in his company.'

'That time you first saw him—'

'It poleaxed me; it was like seeing a ghost.'

'Why didn't you say?'

'I couldn't. I was so mixed up; that's why I couldn't answer you. Seeing Seth again – well, not Seth – but it seemed like it. And I questioned what it would be like being married to someone so different.'

He turned to face her, a glint in his eye. 'And what do

you think it will be like being married to me?'

His arms were around her, and she was flooded with longing for him. 'Wonderful,' she murmured, running her hands under his sweater.

Watching Jesson get dressed was a pleasure. His muscles rippled under skin the colour of burnt sugar. As he bent to pull on his trousers, she noticed the operation scars on his knee. If the shell that hit his plane had caused a fatal wound, her life would have been very different. But it hadn't, and she had fallen in love with this wonderful, kind man. And now she had a new life to look forward to as Mrs Jesson Cobb.

Chapter 33

Weymouth was fun, apart from the visit to Mr Gale's garage. Mrs Gale waited outside with Spence while Cliff and the twins had a guided tour. Bob was eager to see the pit where the men worked on the underneath of cars. Cliff asked what happened if more than one car needed to be worked on at once and Mr Gale grumpily said that they had to get under and lie on the ground while it was on ramps. It didn't sound much fun.

The garage was dirty and smelled of oil, the way Mr Gale often smelled. The endless chain they used to lift out engines sounded interesting when Mr Gale talked about it on the way, but it proved to be just a loop of chain on a pulley. Cliff pretended to be impressed, but was really wondering how long it would be before they could leave. Pete said nothing all the time they were in the garage. His father got snappier as it became obvious Pete didn't want to be there and didn't agree that garage work was the ideal job unless you joined the Navy.

They finally left. You used to tell the twins apart from behind because Pete was always bouncing around. You still could, but now it was because Pete was the one dragging his feet and staring at the ground.

Mrs Gale tried being jolly and also told them how lots of American troops had left from Weymouth for the D-Day landings. There was still an atmosphere, though. Mr Gale looked thunderous, and Pete stayed far away from him while they walked to the beach. The best bit of the walk was when they came to a road and a train was running up the middle of it, right among the pedestrians.

Spence loved the locomotive, waving and kicking his legs to get out of the pushchair. Cliff moved him right away from the rails until the train had trundled past.

'Let's get a drink,' Mrs Gale said, as they reached a seafront café with a red canopy above chairs and tables that overlooked the beach.

'Can we have Coca Colas?' Bob asked.

Mrs Gale said they could and, when the waitress asked if they wanted "floats", she said they did.

What were they going to get? No one could guess, and Mrs Gale just smiled.

The waitress brought glasses of Coca Cola with ice cream floating on it. Smashing!

Spence, who'd never had Coca Cola before, got the bubbles up his nose. Everyone laughed at the faces he pulled and, by the time they got to the beach, they were all in better moods. Even Pete joined in a game, jumping back from the waves before your feet got wet.

Another family was playing French cricket, and they joined in. Mr Gale had a go, but stopped when the others wouldn't play it his way.

Mrs Gale bought Spence a bucket and spade. He built a sandcastle, and everyone added shell doors and windows. It was fun, but would have been better with Mum and Jesson.

After a while, Mrs Gale called them all together and passed round newspaper parcels of fish and chips, and they ate sitting on the sand. The smell of vinegar on chips always reminded Cliff of Southampton; his old mum often brought home a fish supper to save her the bother of cooking.

No one wanted to leave, and Mrs Gale talked the twins' dad into fetching the car he'd borrowed, to save everyone the long walk back to the garage.

'We're home,' he called, wheeling Spence indoors.

Mum came to meet them. She wore a new jumper and was very smiley. Jesson was wearing his smart jumper and was smiling more than usual, too. Something was up.

'Have you been out somewhere?' he asked.

'No, just here,' Mum said. Her cheeks looked a bit pink. 'Did you have a good time? What did you see?'

They left Spence sleeping in the pushchair. Mum made tea, and Cliff told them about the day.

'So, Pete wasn't persuaded to become a grease-monkey, then?' Jesson said.

'A what?' Cliff asked.

'Mechanic.'

'No hope of that,' Cliff said, loving the idea of calling Mr Gale a grease-monkey.

'About Peter,' Mum said, 'have you thought about your Saturday job?'

He'd known as soon as he woken that morning. As Jesson would say, it was no contest. 'I want to take the vet job,' he said, 'if it's all right with you.'

'I'll speak to Rose tomorrow. Hopefully Peter's father will agree.' Mum looked worried.

'It's only a weekend job. He's not joining the Foreign Legion,' Jesson said.

'True,' Mum said. 'Umm, Cliff. There's something we want to tell you.'

He knew it.

Mum reached out and took Jesson's hand across the table. 'Jesson has asked me to marry him and I've agreed,' she said in a rush, her cheeks bright pink. 'It won't make any difference to you, other than Jesson will live here, but you'll still be my son and Jesson could become your adopted father if you'd like? You could change your name to Cobb, too.'

He'd thought it had upset her that he hadn't chosen to be called Sheppard when she adopted him.

'Are you pleased, Cliff?' Mum looked anxious.

'Course I am,' he said. 'The reason I didn't want to change my name before was because I didn't want to change it twice.'

Mum and Jesson looked puzzled.

'Erwin to Sheppard. Sheppard to Cobb,' Cliff said.

Mum and Jesson stared at each other, then burst out laughing.

'You're incredible, Cliff,' Jesson spluttered. 'When did you decide this?'

Cliff shrugged. 'When you came back from America.'

Mum got up and gave him a big hug, laughing. 'To think I worried about telling you. You're the best son I could ever have – as well as Spencer, of course.'

Jesson had gone to bed down the hens, Mum had carried Spence up to bed and Cliff sat in the kitchen thinking that, for the first time, he was going to have two parents.

More exciting was that he was going to work at the vet's. A proper job where he'd learn. But he still had to pass his exams. School life was going to be different; he'd have to work really hard and get his homework in on time. It was the Easter holidays soon, and it was a good thing he wouldn't be working so much on the farm; he'd have more time to study.

He thought about the homework he hadn't finished. Should he do it now? Maybe not. He'd turn over his new leaf tomorrow.

Chapter 34

Monday morning was busy: Cliff had gone off to school; Spencer was still asleep; Rose and the POWs were coming to work and Jesson was getting the tractor ready to cultivate the top field. May had tended to the hens first thing, and the plan was to use Alwin to help her clean out the henhouses ready for the new stock, while Walter took Blossom and cultivated the smaller of the top fields. Jesson wanted to have at least one field drilled by the end of the week.

The POWs and Rose passed by the kitchen window. Rose got on very well with the Germans; Len wouldn't approve of the easy way she chatted to them, Walter in particular.

Having issued instructions to the men, telling Alwin she'd join him soon in the poultry yard, May said to Rose, 'I hear you had a grand day at the seaside. Spencer's still flaked out.'

'The boys enjoyed it and it was good ter get out for the day,' Rose replied, drying the plates May had just washed. 'What about you? Did you have a peaceful Sunday dinner for two?'

May kept her gaze fixed on the washing up, hiding her blushes. Cliff was certain to mention her engagement to the twins and there was no reason not to tell Rose, but her friend knew her too well and she had no intention of letting slip what had happened after lunch yesterday. She'd forgotten about making love; how close to your partner you felt afterwards, but it wouldn't become a habit before the wedding – not that it could in a house with two children in it.

She upturned the enamel bowl, and the water gurgled through the plughole. She shifted round to face Rose. 'I've accepted Jesson's proposal, so I suppose we're engaged.'

Rose's face lit up. 'That's wonderful. I'm so glad. Congratulations. Have you set a date?'

'Nothing like that. He's talking about going to Dorchester to buy a ring. We're so busy with farm work, I'm not sure when we'll be able to fit it in. We've only told Cliff – who had expected it for the last two years!'

'Him and everyone else, I reckon.' Rose laughed.

'Oh Lord, we'll be the talk of the village. Again.'

'I'd love ter see Victoria's face when she hears the news. Ephraim will be incensed. He and Isabella will gossip for weeks about furriners and incomers.'

'Don't make me think about it. Anyway, I've something to ask you,' May said. She explained about Cliff's job and the weekend vacancy. 'We thought about Peter. What do you think?'

Rose hesitated. 'I'm sure he'd jump at the chance …' her voice tailed off.

'Len?' May said.

'He doesn't approve of Peter coming here so much; thinks he's becoming a bumpkin, not expanding his horizons.'

May held back a snort of derision. What did he want the boy to do at weekends, commute to London?

'It's only weekends, not full time. He's got plenty of time to think about his career, but I will say, he seems to like farm work and he's good at it. I have no qualms about leaving him to deal with the hens.'

'He does enjoy it. Thanks for the offer, May. I'll talk ter Peter and Len tonight.'

May didn't envy her the job and was glad she wouldn't have a husband who quibbled over every decision.

'Do you know when Janice Harris leaves school?' Evelyn, the girl's mother, had impressed May. She'd settled well into working at the post office, despite the obvious disadvantage of having Victoria as a boss.

'This year I'd imagine,' Rose said. 'She's not exactly studious and likely ter stay on, is she? She's older than the boys. If she's fourteen, she could leave now. If she's not, the leaving age goes up ter fifteen from next month so she'd have ter stay another year. Why?'

'We think we're going to get a full-time poultry girl – it won't affect the weekend job – and I wondered if Janice would be interested.'

'Blimey. She's quite haphazard, isn't she? When she answers the call box phone, I'm never sure she passes on messages properly,' Rose said, but then went on, 'But I suppose she's always passed ours on all right.'

'I think she deserves a chance, although she might not be interested. I'll speak to her mother later in the week.'

A cry came from upstairs. Spencer was awake.

'I'll leave you to it,' May said.

Alwin was a good worker, albeit taciturn, and they'd got all the henhouses finished by four o'clock.

May sent him off to join Walter and Jesson and headed into the house. She had just enough time to make it to the village and have a word with Evelyn Harris before the post office closed.

It was lovely to feel air that wasn't full of stinging rain or chips of ice on her face as she cycled. Passing the cottage, she saw the daffodils she and Cliff had planted when he'd first arrived, coming into bud. Perhaps there'd be a few in bloom for Easter.

Her appointment with the solicitor was later in the week. It was over a fortnight since the last letter. If Dorothy got impatient, she might embark on further action. She had to avoid that at all costs. Mud sticks, and word here spread like thistledown.

She hadn't told Jesson about the threat over their heads, even though it could affect him more than her.

He hadn't proposed to get his hands on the farm, but would it be different if she wasn't the lady farmer he'd fallen in love with? If they lost the farm, they could live in the cottage, but Jesson would have to find work elsewhere. Herself, too, she supposed. With the prospect of bringing up two boys, one heading for university, they would need two incomes. They might have to move away. Would that be better? If they found her guilty of coercion, would she want to live somewhere she was ashamed to lift her head in public? How would Jesson be received elsewhere? Not everyone took to mixed couples. And what about Spencer? A dusky child in a white school might get picked on. Hell. Why had this thing come now? Come at all?

Propping her bike against the shop wall, May hoped Victoria wasn't standing guard at the post office counter; she didn't want dealings with more bullies right now.

Inside, there was no sign of the dragon, and Evelyn Harris was wiping down the bacon slicer.

'How are you, Mrs Harris?'

'Fair to middlin'.' She smiled at May, wiping her hands down her once-white pinny, stained with grease from slicing bacon and ham and cutting up butter. 'Things getting better on the farm?' she asked.

'Yes, thanks. That's why I've come to see you.'

Evelyn looked puzzled.

'I'd better buy something in case Victoria comes out. Have you any ham left?'

'A little – I'll slice some, shall I?'

'I'll take a half, please.'

Evelyn used a long-bladed knife to carve slices from the ham bone.

'I wanted to ask you about Janice. Is she leaving school soon?' asked May.

'Yes. This is her last week. She hasn't passed any exams – but neither have many people, and they do all right.' Evelyn put the ham on a sheet of greaseproof paper and placed it on the scales. The needle settled at nine ounces, but Evelyn just wrapped up the meat. 'Would you like the bone?'

'Please. Mrs Gale makes a lovely pea and ham soup.' May cleared her throat. 'The thing is, we are looking to take on a poultry girl, Monday to Friday, and I wondered whether Janice would be interested?'

Mrs Harris wrapped the bone and handed both packages to May. 'It would be a good job for Janice and I'll tell her about it, but she's got her heart set on working in them hemp factories in Bridport. She says she'll get good money and make new friends. I'm not so sure, it'll be hard work and some of them factory girls …'

May understood Evelyn's worries. 'I was going to put a card in the window, advertising the job, but I'll give you a couple of days to sound Janice out.'

May handed over the ration books and got out her purse.

'I am grateful to you for thinking of Jan,' Mrs Harris said. 'There's a lot round here that wouldn't have done.' She nodded towards the post office counter. 'How long do you have to live here before you're not thought of as an incomer?'

'Couldn't say. I've been here eleven years and they still think I'm a foreigner.'

Evelyn laughed just as Victoria emerged. The woman gave her a black look. May walked past the postmistress. 'Good afternoon, Miss Potts,' she called over her shoulder, letting the door swing closed behind her before she caught Victoria's reply.

Chapter 35

They finished sowing the top field barley on the Wednesday afternoon before Good Friday.

Peter and Cliff were to work together over the Easter weekend to ensure Peter understood the routine, before starting the job proper the following week, when Cliff began his job at the surgery. How Rose had convinced Len that it was a good idea, May hadn't discovered. Peter's enthusiasm probably had something to do with it, along with Rose's own view that it was a good idea to get the lad out of the house, earning his own pocket money.

The barley fields hadn't yet been rolled and Cliff was using every means to convince them he was competent to do the job using the tractor. Legally, he could drive it, but that didn't convince Jesson he had the ability. And he had no experience.

'You just don't want to give it up, do you?' Cliff snapped at Jesson over their snatched evening meal.

Things were getting heated, and May didn't want a family row to start.

'That's not fair, Cliff,' she said. 'I'm sure Jesson will let you drive it, but perhaps you should get in some practice first.' She looked at Jesson. 'What if Cliff drives the tractor up to the barley fields? You can follow and make sure he's okay. The roller is already up there, so he can help you hitch it on.'

Jesson grunted a grudging acceptance, and she wondered whether Cliff was right. Maybe she should test the situation by asking for a go on the Fergie herself?

No. She decided it was better to let the menfolk establish their own hierarchy. After all, they would soon effectively be father and son.

Cliff and Jesson had just gone outside to roll as much as they could before dark, Jesson concerned the pigeons would have feasted on the seed by morning, when Cliff popped his head around the door and called, 'Mum, someone to see you.'

May went to the door. Evelyn Harris was waiting. 'Come in, Mrs Harris, would you like a cup of tea?'

'No thank you, Mrs Sheppard, I've got to get back. I apologise for disturbing your evening, but I didn't want to ask to leave work early – you know how nosy Miss Potts is.'

'Indeed, I do,' May said, pulling out a chair for her guest. 'We've known each other a long time, please call me May.'

'Thank you. And it's Evelyn.'

'Right you are. So, what can I do for you, Evelyn? I assume you've come about Janice?'

'Yes and no,' Evelyn said, a look of apprehension on her face.

'Now you've got me baffled,' May said.

'Jan, as I thought, has set her heart on the factory and won't be talked out of it.' She hesitated before rushing on. 'So, I wondered if you'd consider me for the job instead?'

Trying to marshal her thoughts, May said, 'Now I know why you didn't want to ask Victoria for time off.' This was a surprise. She'd imagined a young person taking the job, although she'd done it herself well into her thirties.

She said, 'It's a very different job from the shop – out in all weathers, mud up to your ankles sometimes, lifting heavy, smelly bedding, washing eggs in cold water ...'

'I realise that, but when we've helped with haymaking,

I've enjoyed it more than I can say. I love the outdoors – not brought up in the country, of course – but now I live here I never want to live anywhere else. The shop suffocates me. Can't chat, can't do nothing without Victoria's beady eye on you. Even laughing with the customers is wrong. I don't want to go to a town every day to work. I could bike down here. I know you all and I think I'd fit in. And I'd do a good job.'

She'd obviously thought it out, and she had worked hard when she'd joined the villagers for the haymaking during the war; staying on with her two girls after many others had left for the day. If May offered her the job and it didn't work out, Victoria would never take her back. But that wasn't May's problem, although finding a replacement would be, should the worst happen.

Hoping she was doing the right thing for the farm, and for Evelyn herself, May confirmed the wages and they shook hands. Evelyn would start work after giving Victoria a week's notice from Easter Saturday.

May didn't envy Evelyn's task of handing the old curmudgeon her resignation and decided she'd stay away from the post office for the time being.

Cliff reappeared after Evelyn left.

'How did you get on?'

'It was okay. I drove up to the top fields. Jesson made me go slow, but I did all right. He didn't trust me to do any rolling, though.' He went to the biscuit barrel and raised his eyebrows.

'Just a couple,' May said. 'By the way, Rose left a letter for you on the dresser.'

Stuffing a digestive into his mouth, he collected the letter

191

propped in the plate rack. 'It's from Mrs Wallbanks – an Easter card, I bet.'

May was glad his old neighbour remembered him; the woman sent cards at Christmas and Easter and never forgot his birthday.

Her mind returned to Evelyn. Should she have consulted Jesson about employing her? He would soon be her husband, after all. She intended to make him a partner in the business once they married. Tom had put a clause in his will that the farm shouldn't automatically pass to any future husband. He'd must have thought a woman with property would be an easy target for a gold digger. If she married, he requested the farm remain in her name, or she stayed a major shareholder. The solicitor said the clause was unenforceable, but she'd wanted to comply with Tom's wishes and intended to keep a majority shareholding.

Could Tom's clause be something the solicitor could use to prevent Dorothy getting her hands on the property? More likely they would say it showed she was even more greedy, wanting to keep the place for herself.

'Hmm?' Cliff asked her something. She'd been thinking through the possibility of making a new will, leaving her half of the farm to Cliff and suggesting to Jesson that he do the same with Spencer, and had missed what he said.

'So, is that okay?' he asked.

'Yes, yes, fine,' she said, thinking she needed to make a list of points to discuss with the solicitor the following day.

Cliff went towards the hall.

She called, 'Will you check on Spencer, please?'

'Yep. I just want a bit of paper.'

She heard the study door open. He'd be writing to Mrs Wallbanks to tell her about his job. A few seconds later, he pounded upstairs.

Mr Leadbetter's office smelt of musty books. Dust motes floated up as his secretary placed a tea tray on the partner desk.

Although the surroundings were old-fashioned, the solicitor was only in his early forties. He poured tea and offered May a biscuit. Tom had dealt with Leadbetter's for years but, not long before Tom's death, the father retired and the son had taken over. Mr Leadbetter Junior had been invalided out of the Army. Tom had commented that losing a leg hadn't prevented the man from being efficient and astute. He'd earned Tom's respect and May trusted him completely.

'Essentially, Mrs Sheppard, we have two matters here: the question of how to go about administering the gift you wish to make to Mr Cobb on your marriage and, more worryingly, the matter of the threat of litigation from Mrs Ottaway.'

May nodded.

'I would suggest that it would not be prudent to embark upon drawing up the gift documentation until the matter of challenging your inheritance is resolved.'

May felt her hopes of a simple solution drain away. 'The accusation is ridiculous; I would never swindle anyone, especially not Tom. He was my father-in-law. I had no ambition to own any business, much less a farm – I knew nothing about farming, apart from the chickens, and that was only what Tom and Seth taught me. No one who knows me would ever believe I was capable of such a thing.'

'I am sure you are right, and I'm equally certain Mr Arrowsmith came here of his own free will to make you his heir. However, we have to make a case that would stand up in court, should it come to that. The first thing we need to do is discover what evidence Mrs Ottaway thinks she has against you. Have you ever given her, or anyone else, the impression you wanted to live in the farmhouse, or run the farm, or even that you felt you had a right to do so as a daughter-in-law?'

'Absolutely not. It never occurred to me that Tom would leave his property to anyone other than Doro—' A flood of despair flowed through her; if she'd thought that, how many others had? One she knew about: Ephraim Potts. But their battles were scotched years ago, and it hadn't been mentioned again. Could Dorothy have been harbouring a sense of entitlement and resentment finally burst out?

Reading her thoughts, Mr Leadbetter said, 'It seems strange that Mrs Ottaway has never made any suggestion that she was unhappy over the disposal of her brother's estate, yet, out of the blue, threatens to challenge his will. I wonder what has triggered this change of heart? You say she has a comfortable lifestyle, so she shouldn't be short of money, but something must have prompted this action. You haven't heard of any misfortune?'

'We only correspond at Christmas, I'm afraid, but nothing has been said and I've heard nothing on the grapevine, although our social paths don't cross anymore.'

May and Mr Leadbetter talked around the subject for a while, without coming to any conclusions. He wondered why the letter came from an unknown and distant law firm and said he'd put feelers out for information. In the meantime, he would reply with a letter demanding further information.

Driving home, doubts plagued her. Was she doing the right thing, keeping Jesson in the dark about Dorothy's claim? If it came to nothing, she'd have worried him unnecessarily. And, she forced herself to admit, she didn't want him to think there could be any truth in it. Him, or anyone else. She could hear Victoria's sneering voice, "No smoke without fire." The thought that anyone could think so badly of her was abhorrent. She slammed her palm on the steering wheel. 'Hell and damnation.'

Unable to sleep, May tried to remember anything Tom or Seth might have mentioned about Dorothy. Any details about her had been sketchy and, after so many years, were difficult to recall. Had there been some kind of scandal, or a skeleton in the cupboard?

She racked her brains. Seth once said his mother found Dorothy difficult to get on with because she was aloof. Was there something about him only seeing his aunt's little boy once or twice when they'd called in at Dorothy's unexpectedly?

She couldn't remember Tom ever mentioning his nephew. Had there been a tragedy, and the child wasn't spoken of? Certainly, Dorothy never mentioned family.

After hours of twisting and turning, she decided she couldn't let this rule her every hour; Mr Leadbetter was dealing with it, and she had to get on with her life.

Jesson refused to take the day off on Good Friday, insisting on getting on with preparing the sugar beet fields for sowing. He said if he'd had a good run at the work, he would like to take her to choose her engagement ring the following afternoon.

They hadn't had time to discuss plans for the wedding but, as soon as she was wearing a ring, everyone would ask when it was to be. Farming controlled more than the crops; those growing them and caring for livestock had to schedule their own lives according to the workload, seasons and the welfare of their animals. She would like the wedding to be sooner rather than later. At their age, there was no reason to wait; accommodation, furniture and even family were already in situ.

And she longed for someone else to share the load. The war had come and gone, but since it began, she'd never stopped worrying, caring for others and carrying everyone's burdens on her shoulders. She longed for someone to take over some of the decision making, and allow her to take a breather.

Jesson gave up work for the day. She sat him down with a cup of coffee, sent Cliff and Spencer to bring in the hens and horses, and placed a calendar on the table between herself and the bridegroom-to-be.

'Dates,' she said.

Jesson groaned. Tension lines on his face showed how exhausted he was.

'We just need to work out when we can spare a day,' she said, laying a hand on his arm.

'A few days. I'm not marrying you without giving you a honeymoon.'

'Can we spare the time?'

'When was the last time you had any time away from here?' he said.

She thought back. Seth had died in '38. They'd married in '36. Apart from their honeymoon – a week in Hastings – she'd been at the cottage or on the farm.

'Over ten years,' she said.

'Which means you're not missing the chance when

we've got a good excuse.'

'But what about the farm, the boys, the animals?'

'With all these new people you're taking on, I guess we can work something out,' he said, laughing. 'What dates are you thinking of?' He pulled the calendar towards him.

Chapter 36

Cliff steered the pushchair up the lane. He had a letter to post to Mrs Wallbanks, thanking her for the sixpence she'd sent him to buy chocolate instead of an Easter egg.

The only Easter eggs he'd ever had were the painted hens' eggs Mum gave them for breakfast on Easter Sunday. She said before the war, they used to have chocolate eggs. He hoped they'd come back soon, although old dragon Potty was likely to be the last to get them.

'Fast, fast,' Spence yelled. Cliff shoved the pushchair ahead as he ran, zigzagging around the potholes.

Spence shrieked with joy, kicking his legs and waving his arms to get Cliff to go even quicker.

Cliff stopped at the crossroads, breathless. After they crossed the main road, he slowed to walking pace as they went through the village.

Spence kept yelling to go faster, and people on the pavement grinned at them.

'Calm down, Spence,' Cliff said. 'You can't go in the shop all excited; the old dragon will go berserk.'

Spence giggled. 'Serk, serk,' he chanted.

When they reached the shop, Cliff unclipped Spence's harness and lifted him out. He wriggled and demanded sweets.

'Are you going to be good, or shall I put your reins on?'

'No wains, Spence good.'

'Okay. Just stay quiet and I'll get you some sweets when I've bought my stamp.'

Inside the shop, Cliff's heart sank when he saw a queue

at the post office counter. Some customers recognised Cliff and Spence and said hello.

Mrs Harris was serving at the food counter. She caught his eye and raised a finger to her lips. She didn't want him to mention her new job. He nodded. He always said as little as possible to Miss Potts. She disliked him because he hadn't been born in the village. All the Potts tribe disliked Spence because he was black. Cliff and Ephraim Potts had been enemies since he'd been evacuated and Ephraim was an ARP warden. Now he went to school in Bridport, he didn't see the old misery guts, but he couldn't avoid his sister in the post office.

Spence was getting fidgety and swung himself backwards and forwards on Cliff's hand, the shopping bag he'd asked to carry sweeping wider and wider.

'Stand still. We won't be long and then you'll get your sweets.'

One person left the counter, and the others stepped forward. Spence swung the bag and it bashed the departing customer on the leg.

'Sorry,' said Cliff, his face growing hot as the other customers looked round.

The woman gave a half-smile and hurried away.

'Stand still, Spence,' Cliff hissed, 'you're being very naughty.'

Spence stuck out his bottom lip but stayed quiet until they reached the counter.

Victoria glared at Cliff through the grille. 'Yes?'

'A stamp, please.'

'What for?'

'A letter.'

She huffed. 'Where's it going to?'

He knew she'd want to see it. That's why he'd left it in the shopping bag. She always read addresses, even if they were upside down.

'Hampshire,' he said.

She tore out a stamp and slammed it under the grille. 'Tuppence ha'penny.'

Cliff pulled some coins from his pocket.

'I'm surprised you can afford time to come up here. I was told you are all rushed off your feet.'

What was she on about now? 'I'm going back to bring the hens in,' he said. Was she saying he was skiving off work?

'Humph,' she muttered, looking past him and calling, 'Next.'

Cliff led Spence to the little shelf where people stuck on stamps. He took the bag and opened it to get the letter.

'D'you want to lick the stamp, Spence?' he asked, but the child had trotted off, heading for a stack of tins of corned beef arranged on a table.

'Moo cow,' he said, joyfully pointing to the picture of a bull on the labels. He reached out.

'No,' Cliff yelled, dashing forward. Too late. Spence tugged out the bottom tin. The display crashed down, one tin catching Spencer on the cheek. The child let out a great wail and clutched his face.

People appeared from all directions as Cliff tried to check his brother for injury. Spencer was squirming and crying that his face hurt. There was no blood, but already a lump was forming on his cheekbone.

Customers fussed about, collecting scattered tins and asking whether Spence was hurt. Mrs Harris came out from behind her counter and dabbed a damp cloth on the bump.

As people began restacking the display, Victoria swooped out from her lair to stand over Cliff, who was kneeling down by Spence.

'Where's your mother? She should be here looking after this noisy brat, but I expect she's out poaching more of someone else's workers.'

Cliff had had enough. He got to his feet. Holding Spence in his arms, he looked Victoria straight in the face. 'My brother is not a brat,' he said. 'He's hurt. And Jesson has taken Mum to Dorchester to buy an engagement ring.'

There was a collective gasp and the pleasure of seeing Victoria's jaw drop was wiped out by the realisation of what he'd done. His mum hated gossip, and he'd just spread her private business all over the village.

He looked round and saw Mrs Gale and Pete staring at him open-mouthed from the doorway.

'I'll have to tell her,' Cliff said to Pete as they walked down the lane to the farm.

'Do what Mum says, leave it till tomorrow. Don't spoil her day today.' Pete stuck a toffee in his mouth.

Spence had quietened down once Mrs Gale intervened, checking his injury and sending him outside with Pete. She then calmly got her shopping while Cliff bought his bits and pieces and collected his letter to post in the box outside.

They left the shop together, Mrs Gale saying good afternoon to Miss Potts, who looked like she'd bitten an apple and found half a maggot.

Outside the shop, he'd tried to explain what had happened. Mrs Gale had been very nice, but they all knew he'd fouled up.

'Your mum'll be all right about it,' Mrs Gale said. 'They

had ter know someday and now they can get their gossiping over and move on ter someone else.' She gave him a hug. He quickly squeezed away. 'Spencer's all right, that piece of chocolate's made all the difference.' They looked at Spence, who had chocolate dribbling from his mouth and a great purple bruise below his eye.

Chapter 37

She had no thoughts about the kind of engagement ring she wanted, but it had to be different from the diamond cluster Seth had given her. She never wore that ring now, but kept it in its velvet box in her dressing table drawer.

They walked along Dorchester High Street, May a little apprehensive. How much did Jesson want to spend? What if she chose something that over-stretched his budget?

They looked in the windows of a couple of jeweller's shops, but nothing caught her eye. Jesson suggested some rings that she could see were high priced – large stones, one a ruby that she thought far too garish, one a fussy sapphire cluster that would have looked more at home on the hand of a cocktail party hostess than a farmer's wife.

How ungrateful she was; he was offering her her choice and she couldn't even settle on one to try.

'Shall we get a cup of tea? Perhaps you'll think of the type of thing you'd like,' Jesson said, pointing to a side alley where a sign advertised a tea shop.

As they waited for the waitress to bring their order of drinks and apple cake, Jesson picked up her hand and said, 'You've taken it off.'

She looked down at the pale band where her wedding ring had rested for over ten years. It had been heart wrenching to take it off that morning, but she couldn't walk into a jeweller's shop to choose an engagement ring, wearing another man's wedding ring.

Jesson cupped her hand in both of his. 'We'll find something, don't worry,' he said.

May flushed – the waitress chose that moment to bring their order. The woman smiled and said, 'Lovely to see people so happy.'

May dipped her head, feeling like a teenager.

Jesson said, 'Ma'am, I don't suppose you could recommend somewhere to buy an engagement ring in town. Something unusual?'

'Congratulations.' The waitress beamed.

May felt embarrassed that Jesson was broadcasting their business, but the woman asked whether they'd tried the antique shop, Dawson's, further along the alleyway? 'He's a decent chap, won't do you down, and he gets some nice things in.'

'Thank you, ma'am. That sounds a great idea,' Jesson said.

The waitress moved on, and Jesson dug into his apple cake.

Jesson paid the bill, leaving an over-generous tip, and they made their way to the antique shop. It was shady in the alleyway, and the canopy over the shopfront did nothing to improve the view of the display.

May's hopes faded. There didn't seem to be any jewellery but, at the last minute, Jesson pointed out a collection of rings on the far side. He stepped around May so she could get a better view, and there it was. Even in the gloomy corner, it shone out; a gold ring with a startlingly blue circular solitaire stone. It was the colour of the wide Dorset skies in summer.

'I like that one.' She pointed.

'It's very small,' Jesson said.

'I don't want ostentation, I want something I like and

that means something,' she said.

'Whatever you want,' Jesson said, taking her arm. 'Let's go see Mr Dawson.'

They pushed open a creaking door. Inside, a plump man, smoking a pipe, greeted them and cheerfully lifted the ring from the window.

'A blue topaz,' he said, handing it to May. She slipped it on her finger and the man held a mirror for her to see the effect.

'What do you think?' she waved her hand at Jesson.

'If you like it, it's fine. Does it fit?'

Mr Dawson asked to look and slid the ring around on her finger. His verdict was that it didn't need adjustment.

'Go ahead?' Jesson said.

'Please,' May said. She couldn't stop smiling.

Jesson took out his wallet and handed over some notes.

'I'm assuming madam wishes to wear the ring now?' Mr Dawson said.

'Yes, please,' she said, feeling like a callow girl.

The man handed Jesson a receipt and passed May a paper bag with a dark-blue, leather-covered ring box inside. He smiled. 'Good luck. I hope you'll be very happy.'

Beyond the shop, the alleyway was empty. Jesson swung her into his arms. 'Now we are officially engaged,' he said, kissing her.

'Thank you, Jesson. I love you,' May whispered, before pulling away and gazing at her hand and the ring that gleamed like a summer's day.

They'd settled on Saturday 31st May for the wedding. Hay cutting wouldn't have started by then and the rest of the work would be routine. The POWs should be able to cope; May suggested they ask Bill to take a daily look in and resolve any problems.

Rose could manage the house and boys, and May hoped she'd agree to live in for the four days they'd decided they could afford to be away.

As they drove home, they discussed where to hold the ceremony.

Jesson wasn't religious. The church his family attended was an American denomination, and there didn't seem to be a local equivalent. She didn't want a tremendous fuss, and it would be bad taste to have a white wedding in the village church where she'd married Seth. She suggested a registry office, the nearest being in Bridport.

'But what about the reception?' Jesson asked. 'We don't want that in Bridport. And, before you say it, you're not going to do it at the farm. Someone else can take care of the catering.'

Was this what it was going to be like, having Jesson as a husband; someone else taking charge?

'Of course, dear,' she said.

He leaned across and tapped her hand. 'Mind your manners, Mrs Cobb-to-be.'

They decided they'd invite only a few close friends and family to the ceremony and have a get-together in the village for others.

'What about the pub?' Jesson asked. 'They've got a fancy room out back, or their garden borders the stream. That could be a good place, if the weather's all right.'

May thought how marvellous it would be to just walk in and have everything ready. No preparation, no worry, no responsibility. It sounded idyllic.

They discussed the finer points as they drove; every

detail making her realise this was going to happen. She was going to be married. In two months' time.

They decided that they'd ask Sally and Doreen, May's loyal friend from her WI days, to be their witnesses; both had known May for years and Jesson didn't have any especially close friends to call on.

May would ask Rose to be her maid of honour, and Jesson said he'd like Cliff to be his best man, to give him an official role.

Everything was falling into place and they drove into the farmyard full of plans and hope.

'Spencer. What happened?'

They'd found the three boys playing a game of snap at the table. Spencer was absorbed until Cliff spoke to May. Once the child saw her, he hurled himself off his chair and raced into her arms.

'Moo cow hit Spence,' he howled, tears streaming.

'Poor Spencer.' May inspected the lump on his cheek. It was purplish, but the skin wasn't broken. She suspected he just wanted sympathy. She dried his eyes and hugged him.

'Dada,' Spence said, raising his arms to Jesson.

'Whatcha been up to, Sprout?' Jesson asked, taking the boy.

'He got hit by some tins of corned beef that fell over in the shop,' Cliff said, explaining how the tins had toppled when Spencer had touched them, looking at the bull on the labels.

He avoided May's eye; Peter was studiously shuffling the playing cards. There was more to this than they were letting on.

'Did you get a ring? Let's have a look,' Cliff said, over

enthusiastically. May held out her hand, and Cliff peered at the ring.

'Blue,' he said.

'Do you like it?' May asked.

'Yeah. It's nice,' Cliff said.

A boy was never going to enthuse over an engagement ring, and May turned her thoughts to what they would eat that night.

'Are you staying to eat with us?' she asked Jesson.

'Please. I think I'll get an hour on the tractor before I do, though,' he said, unhooking his overalls from the back of the kitchen door.

And that was the day I got officially engaged, May thought, running water to peel potatoes.

Chapter 38

Tuesday morning, after the bank holiday weekend, Rose bustled in, eyes twinkling.

'Let's see it. I've waited all weekend. Peter says it's blue. A sapphire?'

'Topaz,' May said, holding out her hand.

'It's gorgeous,' Rose said, tipping May's hand back and forth in the light. 'Such an unusual colour. I'm very envious.'

'It was just the right one,' May said. 'I'll have to take it off for work. I'm not risking losing it in the fields.'

'How's Spencer?' Rose asked.

'He's all right, showing off his shiner to everyone. Did Peter tell you about it?'

'Umm. I was there actually.' Rose sounded sheepish. 'I thought Cliff might have said.'

May sighed. 'Go on, tell me what happened. I knew the boys were keeping quiet about something.' She sat down at the kitchen table.

Rose pulled out a chair. 'I feel bad about this. Cliff should be the one ter tell you.'

'He's out on the farm with Spencer. I could drag him back but, if I know him, he'll expect you to tell me so he avoids the flack.'

'I didn't see it all but, when Peter and I walked in …' Rose related the tale.

'He said *what*?' May cut in when she heard what Cliff had announced to the shop at large.

'It wasn't Cliff's fault,' Rose said. 'You know what Victoria's like. She could make the Pope swear.'

'So now they all know my business. Damn. Damn that old witch and her gossip.' May was livid. She hated being talked about behind her back. No, it wasn't Cliff's fault; she'd fallen foul of Victoria enough times in the past to know just how manipulative the woman could be.

'And she accused me of poaching her staff? The cheek of it. If she treated her people decently, they wouldn't go searching for new jobs.'

Rose tried to placate her. Gradually, the heat went out of her temper. The Potts clan would never change; they'd always be a thorn in the side of reasonable people.

'When's Evelyn starting work?' Rose asked as they pored over some forms for the War Ag.

'Next Monday. I hope she'll be okay. It's a big change, mucking out hens from slicing bacon.'

'But no devil boss looking over her shoulder. She'll be fine,' Rose said.

'Eat while it's hot.' May carried plates of scrambled eggs to Jesson, Cliff and Spencer for their midday meal.

Rose tied a bib around Spencer's neck, much to his displeasure. He yanked at it, complaining, 'Spence not baby.'

While she wrestled with the child, Rose said, 'Cliff, there's a letter for you on the dresser.'

He grabbed it and sat back down, ripping it open.

'She's coming on Saturday. I told her to get the train to Bridport and I'll bring her home when I've finished work.'

All eyes turned to Cliff.

'Who's coming?' May said.

'Mrs Wallbanks.'

'Coming here? What for?'

'She's staying until her new flat's ready. You said it was

okay.' Cliff was defiant.

May looked at Rose and knew they shared the same thought.

'Cliff, this is the first I've heard of it. We can't invite all and sundry to stay—'

He jumped up. 'She ain't all and sundry. She's my friend. You said I can have friends to stay whenever I want. You said it was okay.' He charged off upstairs.

May stood up.

'Leave him, May. Let him cool off,' Jesson said, in between mouthfuls. 'Did he ask you? He doesn't usually lie.'

'I'm not saying he's lying,' she snapped. How dare Jesson criticise her treatment of Cliff, especially in front of Rose. 'I can't remember him saying anything about her coming to stay. He said ages ago that her house was being pulled down and she was getting a new flat. He got a letter from her before Easter.'

She thought back to the day he'd received the letter. He'd been on the tractor for the first time, and she was thinking about wills and plans for the farm when he'd come in. He'd said something after he read the letter, but she hadn't heard it. She'd brushed it off. Had that been when he asked if he could have Mrs Wallbanks to stay?

'Hell. I said something was all right, but I hadn't heard what he said. Now what're we going to do?'

Jesson laughed. 'Do what you always do, make the best of it; enjoy your house guest.'

She groaned.

'Let her help plan the wedding, that'll keep her busy.' Jesson swigged down his tea and headed for the back door. 'See you later.'

May looked at Rose. 'I'd better apologise to Cliff. Come

on, Spencer, let's find your brother.'

Cliff had apologised for what happened in the shop. He'd explained that Spencer had been playing him up and Victoria had been her usual nasty self, goading him to react.

'I didn't want to spoil your day with your ring and everything, and then I just left telling you until Mrs Gale came,' he'd said.

She'd reassured him she didn't blame him for reacting as he had, and they agreed to put it behind them.

Now, it was her turn to apologise. 'You'd caught me on the hop. I was thinking about things to do with the farm, and I wasn't concentrating on you,' she said. 'We need to decide what we are going to find for Mrs Wallbanks to do. I don't know her, but I get the feeling she's not used to the countryside. Do you know how long she'll be staying?' Only days, she begged silently.

'She said it would be a couple of weeks until the flat was ready. They're chucking her out with nowhere to go – it wasn't fair; we've got lots of room …'

Two weeks? 'I understand that, and you're a kind boy to offer to help her. Shall we put her in Tom's old room? It looks out over the front garden and across the fields to the hills. She might like a view of open country, for a change.'

'It'll be better than our old street.'

May remembered the rubble she'd ploughed through in her search for Cliff's mother. Their street was devastated; blasted homes opened up like sardine cans, leaving their once private contents on show to all.

The idea of living there for another three years until they could move her was something May could never have contemplated. Mrs Wallbanks was certainly due a change of scene.

'We'll make her stay as comfortable as possible. We'll take her for walks and make it like a holiday. What do you think?'

Cliff gave her a hug. 'Thanks, Mum. I'm sorry I didn't make sure you knew what I was on about. We'll show her the farm, too, won't we, Spence?'

'Farm. Twactor,' Spencer chortled.

She'll love a tour of agricultural machinery, May thought, already feeling sorry for the woman.

'What's she like?' Rose asked after Cliff and Spencer had gone outside.

'I only met her once, on her doorstep. The house was almost the only one left standing.

'She's in her late forties, I'd guess. She was offhand at first, but she warmed up when I mentioned Cliff. I think she's genuinely fond of him, and she had no time for his mother. If it wasn't for her, Cliff would have had a much harder time living there.'

'He owes her something, then. It might not be too bad, but I reckon she'll get bored. What are you going ter do about you know who?'

'Don't remind me. I knew you thought of that too, when Cliff said she was coming here. I'll have to warn Ephraim. And somehow we'll have to stop Mrs W. going to the village.'

'That's not terribly likely, is it? There'll be nothing else for her ter do – I bet she shops every day in Southampton,' Rose said.

'Rose, if she sees Isabella and recognises her, our lives won't be worth living. Ephraim stopped maligning Jesson and the boys because I gave my word I'd never tell anyone

213

about Isabella's past.

'But we don't know what her history is.'

'I know, but Ephraim didn't know that. One mention of Isobel Bullock was enough to shut him up.'

'There's one good thing to come out of this visit,' Rose said.

'What's that?'

'We can find out what Isobel Bullock did that was so terrible she changed her name, upped and married Ephraim and left her home for good.'

May looked at her friend. 'You're incorrigible.'

'You know you can't wait ter find out, either.'

May didn't answer.

Chapter 39

May drove into the village on her way to pick up supplies from the agricultural merchant in Dorchester.

She took the furthest turning off the main road to enter Compton Parva from the far end. She didn't need any more gossip.

A dirt track led to the allotments. May hadn't been there before but, from all his bragging about the prize winning produce he grew, she knew Ephraim Potts rented a plot. According to him, the size of his vegetables was entirely because of the amount of care and attention he lavished on them. She'd taken an educated guess he'd be there on a bright spring morning mixing up secret recipe fertilisers, or hand weeding his shallots.

She scanned the precisely laid out tracts of ground with their orderly rows of sprouting vegetables, neatly sown beds and the occasional coop of hens and rows of soft fruit.

It was a peaceful scene, but a figure at the far end, wearing a leather jerkin and overalls, topped by a flat cap, turned in her direction and she recognised Ephraim's miserable expression.

He didn't notice her as she made her way along the newly mown paths dividing the allotments. He was busily watering some plants with a can.

'Good morning, Ephraim,' she said as she grew close.

Startled, he turned around, holding the can behind him.

'May Sheppard. What're 'ee doing here? 'ee aren't an allotment member.'

'No, but I need a private word with you.'

215

He looked around. 'Best come over to my patch,' he said, leading the way back up the path.

'So that's not your allotment?' she said, looking back at the ground where puddles of liquid were sinking in around some plants just breaking the surface. Carrots, if she wasn't mistaken.

'Helping a pal out,' he growled.

He never helped anyone without an ulterior motive. What was he up to now?

He stopped by the most pristine of all the plots. String guides were pegged out to ensure straight planting, and the edges of the path were trimmed in regimental neatness.

He surveyed his domain. Clearly, he expected her to show some sign of admiration. She'd better not say what she thought: it was the vegetable garden of a fanatic. She restrained herself sufficiently to just say everything looked very shipshape, thinking she sounded like Len Gale.

Ephraim approved of the comment; he asked why she wanted to see him, in quite a reasonable tone.

'I'm sorry about this, but it's something that's out of my hands,' she hesitated as a scowl spread across his face. 'You remember I mentioned the name Isobel Bullock to you some years ago?'

He recoiled as if someone had slapped him. ''ee gave me 'ee's word that name would never be spoken again.'

'And I won't mention it elsewhere. But the person who knew Isobel is coming to stay at the farm for a couple of weeks from Saturday. I'll do my best to keep them out of the village, but it won't be easy. There's nothing much to do around here for someone who's used to city life.'

'I told 'ee afore, it'll kill my Isabella if talk about her got round the village.'

You know what harm gossip does, so why are you and she the biggest rumour-mongers in the area? She bit her tongue.

Instead, she said, 'I've come to warn you so that you can take some precautions. I wondered whether you could take Isabella away for a while? It'd give the two of you a break and avoid any possibility of a chance meeting.'

'Go away? Is 'ee mad. It's only April. We don't have a holiday afore August. A week in Weston-super-Mare, regular as clockwork.'

'Well, you could venture somewhere else, Devon or Cornwall, for instance? Easy to get to by train.'

Ephraim looked as if she'd suggested the fleshpots of Cairo.

'What'd I tell Isabella? She'd never agree to the expense.'

She hadn't expected to plan his entire cover story. She sighed. 'I'm trying to help you and Isabella avoid a potentially embarrassing situation. Perhaps you could invent some kind of windfall and decide to take your wife for a treat? I don't know otherwise. Don't you have any relations you could visit?'

'Humph. Us don't want to see any o' they boogers.'

She'd forgotten just how difficult the man could be.

'I've done what I came for; warned you. I've got to get back to work. I hope you'll be able to work something out.' She squeezed past him and headed for the gate.

'I hear 'ee's getting wed?'

She stopped and turned to face him. Now they would come; remarks about Jesson and his colour.

'Yes, at the end of May,' she said.

''bout time that babby had a proper family.'

The babby you called some vile names, she muttered under her breath.

'I'm sure Spencer will like having his father living with us and Cliff will enjoy having a father, too,' she said, knowing Cliff's name would ruffle his feathers.

'Pshaw.' He turned away.

Serves you right, you old curmudgeon. His sourness was ingrained, like a dark cloud looming on a sunny day and however much you wished the sun would stay shining, it inevitably rained on you.

Leaving the agricultural merchant's, May swung the lorry in the opposite direction to home. She had only a vague idea of how to get to the address she wanted. When she found it, she drove on and parked beyond.

Walking back along the pavement that fronted a row of affluent double-fronted houses, she stopped at a maroon front door with a sun ray patterned fanlight above it, and knocked.

The door opened, and Dorothy faced her. May's promise to herself to stop worrying about the threatening letters had been hard to keep. Standing on Dorothy's doorstep, she needed all her courage not to turn and run, but she remembered the nightmares she'd had about Jesson being refused job after job; Cliff, heartbroken not only from losing his home but seeing his beloved horses sold, or worse; and Spencer, facing ostracisation in a new place where he wasn't accepted through no fault of his own. She thought of Tom, who had trusted her with his life's work. She took a deep breath and hardened her gaze.

Dorothy's smile faded quicker than mist in a gale. She glanced up and down the road. 'May? What do you want?'

she said in a low voice.

'Hello, Dorothy. I would like to talk to you about the letters your solicitor is sending me.'

'I don't want to talk about that. The solicitors are handling it.' She started to close the door.

May raised her voice. 'Dorothy, you accuse me of swindling someone out of their estate for no reason and with no evidence, and you expect me not to ask why?'

'Shush.' Dorothy looked up and down the road again. 'You'd better come in for a minute.'

The house was tidy but, even to May's eye, which was accustomed to furnishings decades out of date, it was old-fashioned.

Dorothy didn't offer to take her coat and May perched on a hard sofa, with knobbly cushions that poked into her back.

Dorothy sat mute on the edge of a wing chair. May looked around. In the centre of the sideboard, a photograph of a young man in Army uniform was displayed in a silver frame.

'He's a smart chap,' May said to break the ice, uncertain how to begin.

'Frank,' Dorothy said. She hesitated before adding, 'My son.'

'Oh? I didn't know ...' May said, thinking she hadn't known, not for definite.

'He left to join up, even though I begged him not to. He came home a few months ago.'

'Late being demobbed, was he?'

Dorothy flushed. She lowered her eyes and mumbled, 'Mmm.'

Why is she lying? May wondered. She looked hard at the

picture. Could she discern the badge on the man's forage cap from this distance?

'As I said,' Dorothy's voice was more forceful now; she must have noticed May's scrutiny of the photograph, 'the solicitors are dealing with the claim and I'm not at liberty to discuss it.'

May's hesitancy evaporated. How dare she try to wriggle out of a discussion?

'Why, Dorothy? Why now? You've never spoken before about Tom's will. Why didn't you just come to me?'

'I didn't know what had gone on, but when Frank—'

'What's Frank got to do with it? I've never met him, I didn't know he existed.'

'He saw what had happened, saw what I'd been blind to.'

'What? What did he see? There was nothing to see. In fact, how could he see anything if he was away in the Army for years? And where is Frank? I'd like him to tell me what he thinks he saw?'

Dorothy looked down at her clenched hands. 'He's away on business.'

'Why did Seth and Tom never talk about him? I never heard of him visiting Tom, either. Why wasn't he at family events? Was he living with his father?'

Dorothy snapped her head up and glared at May. 'His father died on the first day he saw action in the Great War.'

Damn. 'I'm sorry you lost your husband, but I don't understand why you didn't let Frank mix with the rest of the family. He might have felt better towards us if he'd known us.'

'I think you'd better go.' Dorothy stood up.

May rose from the unyielding sofa. 'And I think you'd better ask Frank what he's about. I never expected Tom to leave me anything. If Seth had been alive, I would have expected him to inherit his father's—'

'Stepfather,' Dorothy spat.

May replied coldly, 'Tom looked on Seth as a son but, if you insist, his *stepfather's* estate, but it never occurred to me for one moment I would become his beneficiary—'

Dorothy gave a snort and gestured towards the front door.

May moved to the door. 'It was Tom's wish the estate came to me, and I've worked damned hard to build up the farm. I think he would be pleased with what I've achieved. I won't give it up without a fight, and you can tell Frank I said so.' She turned the doorknob. 'Goodbye, Dorothy, I'm sorry you've sunk to this. Tom would have been appalled.'

At the gate, she looked back at Dorothy standing in the doorway; she couldn't meet May's eye.

Chapter 40

Cliff's day at the surgery had gone well. He'd cleaned out the cages first thing, and fed and watered the couple of cats and a rabbit recovering from treatment. Mr Norton liked the animals to feel relaxed and approved of Cliff chatting to them as he worked. He said it helped to stop them pining for home and improved their recovery. Cliff was glad to think that he was helping the animals, just by being himself.

His next job had been to restock the drugs, dressings and equipment in the consulting room from the store cupboard at the rear of the building. He could only do this if there were no consultations in progress, but so far, it was a quiet day with no emergencies.

The restocking took a long time, as he didn't know the names of the drugs or whereabouts the different sizes of dressing and bandages were. It was quite interesting, but it wasn't exciting and he hoped the phone would ring, saying an animal was coming in.

He'd nearly finished when Mr Norton came in. 'Would you like anything from the bakery? I'm going to get something for myself.'

'No, thanks,' Cliff said. 'Mum made me sandwiches.'

Mr Norton brought back a jam tart for each of them, and Cliff made the tea when they sat in the chilly kitchen to eat.

'Enjoying the job so far, Cliff?'

'Yes,' he said, swallowing a mouthful of fish paste sandwich. 'I'm trying to learn the drug names and their different strengths.'

'If you know just some of them, it will give you a head start when you get to vet college.'

They continued eating, Cliff not sure what to say.

'How're things at home – busy on the farm with the fine weather, I expect?'

'Yeah. Jesson's never off the tractor, but he likes it anyway. He and Mum have got engaged; did you know?'

Mr Norton took a swig of tea. 'No, I hadn't heard. That's good news. When's the wedding?'

'End of May. I'm going to be Jesson's best man,' Cliff said. Being asked had been a shock; he didn't know what it meant to be a best man – he'd never been to a wedding. 'It's in the registry office, not the church, cos Mum's been married before, so they say I won't have to do much.'

Mr Norton said, 'You'll do a grand job. Just make sure you don't lose the ring!'

Cliff was going to ask what he meant, but the telephone rang and Mr Norton went to answer it.

Cliff heard him telling the caller to come straight in. Something a bit more exciting to do than file the patient records that had been his job for the afternoon. But he hoped the job wouldn't be a long one; he had to be ready for Mrs Wallbanks, who was going to wait outside for him at five o'clock.

'Dog bitten by another,' Mr Norton said. 'Would you like to observe?'

'Yes please,' Cliff said, clearing their plates and stacking them beside the sink.

Cliff opened the door to a large lady bundled in furs and fluttering scarves.

'An emergency. Mr Norton is expecting us,' she boomed, striding in.

She was carrying a dog, but its colour was so similar to the fur draped around her neck that Cliff couldn't make out the breed.

'Come in,' he said, squeezing himself out of her path. 'Mr Norton is in the consulting room, first door on your right.'

She ignored him.

He followed her into the consulting room, feeling like he'd been trampled by Blossom.

Mr Norton immediately took control. 'Let's have the patient on the table, shall we, Mrs Colindale?' He held out a hand towards the table and the woman sat the dog down. A Pekinese.

'The brute bit Charles right there,' she pointed to the animal's shoulder where a large tear was bleeding.

'What kind of dog attacked him?' Mr Norton asked.

'An enormously large one,' she replied. 'The kind they have as guard dogs. German.' She almost spat the last word.

Did she think an English dog attack would have been better? Cliff didn't look at Mr Norton.

'Hmm,' said the vet, examining the wound. 'It doesn't look too bad. We'll stitch it and give him a jab. He'll be right as rain in a few days.'

'If you're sure. I'm thinking of suing the brute's owner.'

'It's notoriously difficult to prove these things,' Mr Norton said. 'It could be time-consuming and expensive for you. The main thing is that Charles is not seriously injured. Now, if you'd like to take a seat in the waiting area, we'll soon have him back to you.'

Cliff showed her to a seat in the passageway where a pile of dogeared magazines lay on a side table. She sat down without a word, and Cliff returned to the surgery.

Mr Norton asked him to clip off the hair around the bite. The little dog sat still and didn't whimper, even when Mr Norton gave him a local anaesthetic. He told Cliff how he intended to stitch the wound.

Cliff passed catgut and needle and watched as the torn edges of the tear were drawn together.

When they'd finished work on the little dog, Cliff called Mrs Colindale back into the consulting room and Mr Norton explained what he had done, and how to ensure the wound stayed clean. He recommended Charles stayed quiet until he came back to have his stitches removed.

Cliff thought the little dog would have no problem keeping quiet; he never moved. The vet put the animal on the floor, but his owner instantly swept him up and nestled him among the furs draped over her mountainous chest.

'A little gentle exercise won't do him any harm,' Mr Norton said, a note of disapproval in his voice.

'Perhaps. When he has recovered,' Mrs Colindale said, stalking out of the room. 'Send me your bill,' she called over her shoulder.

Cliff watched through the window as she climbed into the driving seat of a large car and pulled away into the path of an oncoming van, making it swerve.

He looked at Mr Norton, unsure whether to say anything about the awful woman. The vet must have read his mind.

'Not all our clients are that bad, Cliff,' he said. 'Don't let her put you off. Charles has the life of Riley. Shame all he really wants is the life of Rover!' He laughed at his own joke. 'Right, can you clear up and then we'll write up the notes for Charles Colindale Esquire over a cup of tea?'

Mrs Wallbanks was waiting for him as he left the surgery. At least, he presumed it was Mrs Wallbanks: a thin woman, in a shabby grey coat and a fawn flowerpot-shaped hat, who looked much older than he remembered, with a suitcase at her feet. She couldn't have been more different from the awful Mrs Colindale.

'Hello, Cliff,' she said with a big smile. He immediately recognised her voice. A hoarseness he remembered comforting him when his mother had left him alone and he'd got scared by the noise of the rollicking sailors in the street.

'Hello, Mrs Wallbanks. You found the way, then?' he said, feeling shy.

'Yer directions were perfect,' she said. 'So, it's the bus now, is it? To Crompton?'

'Crompton Parva, yes. There's two Cromptons. We don't want to go to Magna, it's a long walk over the hill to the farm.'

'I ain't partial to hills. You lead the way.'

'Righto.' Cliff picked up her case, and they set off for the bus stop in the High Street. As he walked close to her, he caught a whiff of a smell he'd forgotten; some sweet scent mixed with fags. Mum wouldn't like it. She detested smoking, and she forbade it on the farm.

On the bus, Cliff told her about his job and the woman who'd come in that afternoon.

'Sounds a right old baggage,' Mrs Wallbanks said. 'Too much money. You get a lotta them snobby people in the country.'

Cliff didn't think this was true, but held his tongue. He wondered how well Mrs Wallbanks would fit in at home; Mum didn't like what she called "generalisations" and said you should judge people by their actions, not by their class or how much money they had. Mrs W. had different ideas.

He pointed out things he thought might interest her: the netting factories; the road down to West Bay; the picturesque harbour. 'Lots of people go there for holidays,' he said.

'Lucky to have the money.' She sniffed. 'I ain't had a holidee in fifteen years.'

'Oh.' It was all he could think to say.

The bus neared their stop. Thank goodness the lorry was waiting at the crossroads. Good old Mum. He couldn't have coped much longer on his own with Mrs W.

Chapter 41

Before she went to collect Cliff and his guest from the bus, May checked Tom's old room. It was transformed from the elderly farmer's bedroom. The heavy dark furniture, brown paintwork and blackout curtains had gone. She and Rose had repainted the woodwork in pale cream and papered the walls with a light sprigged paper.

They'd taken out the old carpet and substituted rugs, leaving the polished oak floorboards visible. Rose had discovered a pair of chintz curtains at a jumble sale and had let down the hems to fit the windows. They were a bit faded but, considering the disintegrating paint on Mrs Wallbanks' front door, not to mention the threadbare pinafore the woman had been wearing when May had met her, it was unlikely she'd object to reused curtains, if she even noticed.

To welcome their houseguest, she'd picked some daffodils and put them in a pretty porcelain jug on top of the tallboy.

She paused at the door; the room was lovely, even Sally would be impressed.

As the bus drew up, she jumped down from the lorry. Cliff and a skinny woman emerged. She appeared a good ten years older than the late forties May had judged her age to be.

'Hello, Mrs Wallbanks,' she said, holding out her hand. 'Did you have an easy journey?'

Mrs Wallbanks' grip was flaccid and brief. She said, 'Yes, Cliff's directions took me straight to the vet's place, and we got the right bus – I didn't want to be trudgin' over hills.'

Puzzled, May glanced at Cliff. He gave a slight shake of the head.

'Put the case in the back,' May said to him, opening the passenger door for Mrs Wallbanks.

The woman, whose lips were fixed in a downward arc of disapproval, stared silently from the two steps up to the cab back to May.

'Can you manage?' May jumped in every day without giving it a second thought. 'Cliff will go in the middle,' she added, in case that was the problem.

Mrs Wallbanks tutted, slid her handbag into the crook of her elbow and, reaching out with both hands as if she was scaling a ladder, hauled herself up and on to the seat. May closed the door, damned if she was going to apologise for the transport. She could have left her to walk.

As they drove, Cliff pointed out the cottage. 'That's where we used to live, before Mr. Arrowsmith died and left Mum the farm.'

'It's an ill wind,' Mrs Wallbanks said. 'Who lives there now?'

May was fuming. Someone else casting aspersions on her inheritance.

Cliff explained Jesson lived in the cottage but would move to the farm after the wedding.

Mrs Wallbanks leaned forward to look at May. 'So, you'll sell it, will you? Worth a bob or two, I expect?'

'We haven't decided what to do with it,' May said, driving to the farm gate and thinking that for all anyone knew, they could be living there again soon.

She'd intended dropping Cliff and Mrs W. at the farmhouse gate but, following the comments, decided the walk from the Dutch barn to the house wouldn't hurt the woman any more than climbing into the lorry had.

Cliff opened the gates and May turned into the yard, driving up the track and reversing into the barn.

'Can you open your door, or shall I do it?' she said as Mrs Wallbanks sat still, clutching her bag on her lap. 'You'll find it easier to get out backwards,' she added, opening her own door and demonstrating the backwards exit.

She reached the far side door as Cliff jogged up to them. Mrs Wallbanks' posterior was hovering over the drop, and Cliff went to assist. May grabbed his arm and shook her head; the woman would not take kindly to a hand laid on her person.

She made it to the ground, smoothing her flimsy grey coat and resettling the scuffed bag on her arm. Watching her, May felt guilty; the poor woman was clearly hard up and she was so slight it looked as if a light breeze would send her tumbling. She resolved to be more forgiving and get to know their visitor before judging her.

Cliff carried the suitcase and as they walked up the track to the farmhouse, Blossom trotted over to the fence, whinnying to Cliff in the hope of a treat.

May watched Mrs W's reaction and was astonished when she moved to rub the mare's nose. 'I love horses,' she said, 'always took a crust to the coalman's old gelding when I was a nipper.'

'Have you always lived in Southampton?' May asked as they walked on.

'I'm a Sotonian born an' bred.' She stepped gingerly over a rut.

As they neared the house, the door opened and Spencer ran out, calling his usual 'Arn Mee,' greeting, only to stop dead when he caught sight of Mrs W.

'So, this is Lynette's other by-blow, is it?' Mrs Wallbanks stared hard at the little boy. 'Don't look like yer ma, does he?' she asked Cliff.

Spencer wound himself around May's legs, hiding from the scrutiny of the newcomer.

'Perhaps he looks more like his father?' Jesson appeared from the house.

Mrs Wallbanks, showing no embarrassment, turned her gaze on him. 'Possibly,' she said.

If she says all black people look alike, I'll swing for her, May told herself, forgetting her resolution about not judging.

Jesson held out his hand. 'Good to see you again, ma'am.'

May held her breath, but Mrs Wallbanks shook Jesson's hand and smiled at him. 'Yourself too, Mr Cobb.'

'I must thank you, Mrs Wallbanks,' Jesson said, ushering them to the back door. 'If it wasn't for you, I'd never have met May and Cliff or even Spencer.'

'That's what happens in wartime. Coincidences,' she said, a magnanimous smile altering her whole demeanour.

If Jesson had picked her up in the lorry, there wouldn't have been any complaints, May thought, watching their guest simper over Jesson offering to take her coat. She's certainly a man's woman. It'll give me a rest from her, anyway. She sighed as she filled the kettle.

'What would you like for breakfast, Mrs Wallbanks?'

It was nine o'clock; Cliff was helping Peter with the hens, May had a chicken in the oven in honour of their guest and Spencer was making a mess of his mashed egg and soldiers when the visitor descended to the kitchen.

May had shown her upstairs the previous evening. The sun still brightened the bedroom and caught the daffodils on the tallboy.

'I hope you'll be comfortable here,' she said, still admiring the room's metamorphosis.

'Hmm. Very nice, I'm sure, but I couldn't sleep with them flowers in the room. Bad for yer.'

'What a shame. I'll take them out,' May said. 'As a matter of interest, why are they bad for you?'

'Take out all the air and put in cardboard dioxygen. They never leave 'em in hospitals at night.'

May turned to look out of the window, trying to keep a straight face. 'Surely you could open a window?' she said.

'Pshaw! Night air's terrible, 'specially in the country, gives yer a chill on the chest.'

'Right,' May said, seizing the jug of flowers. 'I'll take these away and leave you to unpack.'

She left the door ajar but hadn't reached the top of the stairs before she heard it close behind her.

Jesson laughed uproariously when she reported the conversation.

'It's all right for you, you'll be out on the farm all day. I'll have to entertain her while Cliff's at school,' she told him.

'She's a pussycat,' Jesson said, hugging May to him.

'She is if you're a good-looking man. Or maybe any man,' she said, laying her head against his chest.

'Wow. You sure don't like her, do you?'

'I am trying. Don't say anything to Cliff, although I suspect he's got his doubts. I've rarely seen him so relieved to see me as when he got off the bus.'

Mrs W. sat at the table, taking the chair furthest away

from Spencer and his breakfast debris.

May listed the breakfast choices. 'Eggs, toast and marmalade or jam, or cornflakes – Jesson's favourite.'

Mrs Wallbanks was wearing the same navy woollen skirt as yesterday, but with a bottle green sweater that had a pale green darn in the sleeve. Everyone was wearing mended clothes, and had been since the beginning of the war, but most made sure they didn't have food stains on them. May itched to offer to sponge a splodge off the skirt, which she'd noticed had a liberal sprinkling of Bess's hair on the seat.

Mrs Wallbanks wrinkled her nose at Spencer's congealed egg. 'Toast and jam, ta. And a cuppa tea if there's one in the pot.'

'I'll make fresh. The pot's gone cold. Everyone else had theirs hours ago,' May said.

She cut the bread and put two slices under the grill, set the butter dish, filled with margarine, on the table and a jam pot, shaped like a beehive, beside it.

'We'll need your ration book when we get the shopping. It'll be Rose, Mrs Gale, who gets it – she passes the shop every morning on her way to work.'

'I'd prefer to get me own rations, don't want to risk losing the book. Heck of a palaver if yer do.'

For goodness' sake. Wasn't there anything you could say to this woman that didn't provoke an argument?

'It's over a mile each way to the village and we can't use farm petrol for private runs. If you don't fancy the walk, you're welcome to borrow my bike,' May said, putting the teapot on the table and fetching milk and saccharine.

It was a gamble but, with a bit of luck, she'd have put her off going to into Parva. A scene between her and the Potties would be worth seeing, but the consequences could mean

233

hell for May's family.

Mrs Wallbanks was piling blackberry jam on her toast. The boys got a ticking off if they used more than a scrape and May resolved to make sure there were only a couple of teaspoons full in the pot tomorrow.

'Ain't there a bus to the village?'

'No buses run down the lane, I'm afraid. You could walk to the main road and get a bus to Magna. There are a lot more shops there; Parva only has a butcher, baker and the little post office-cum-village shop.' She got to her feet. 'Please excuse me, I have to check on the boys. I'll take Spencer with me. The chicken's in the oven, so just make yourself at home. Cliff wants to show you around the farm so he'll probably be in shortly.'

She cleaned up Spencer and put his eggy plates on the draining board. The little boy had been unusually quiet, staring at Mrs Wallbanks as if he couldn't make her out. But then, May mused, who could?

The boys had done a good job with the hens and she was happy Peter could cope with the new batch arriving in a few days.

The boys pitched in to help mucking out the stables, and in ten minutes, they had the job done. They walked together back to the house. Jesson's coming to eat with us,' she said. 'Peter, you're welcome to join us, if you'd like.'

'Thanks, Mrs Sheppard, but Mum's expecting me back.'

'Come in and get your wages and then you can get away.' She held the door for Cliff, who was trying to teach Spencer to use a blade of grass as a reed and make a noise blowing between his thumbs. Spencer didn't understand the principle and made his own sound as he blew into his hands.

234

The boys fell into the kitchen laughing. Mrs Wallbanks was standing at the sink, peeling carrots. 'I thought they'd be for our dinner,' she said.

'Indeed,' May said. 'And you've washed up, too. Thank you.'

'Can you come out and have a look around the farm when you've finished the carrots?' Cliff asked Mrs Wallbanks.

'Well …'

'It's fine,' May said quickly, coming back to the kitchen after giving Peter his pay. 'I'll take over the carrots. You go with Cliff. He's been dying to show you around the farm ever since he knew you were coming to stay.'

They persuaded her she'd need wellies and the thick coat that May sometimes used around the farm.

In the melee of Peter leaving and Mrs Wallbanks hopping on one leg pulling on boots, she took Cliff aside and asked him not to encourage Mrs Wallbanks to go into Parva. 'I can't explain right now,' she said, 'but please back me up by persuading her to go to Magna on the bus, if she wants to go shopping.'

He looked bemused, but didn't argue.

Cliff brought Mrs Wallbanks back indoors as May rummaged through drawers in the kitchen.

'Have you had my wooden spoons, Cliff? I've searched everywhere and I need to make the batter for the Yorkshire pudding.'

'I haven't touched them,' he said.

Mrs Wallbanks shook off her boots and hung May's coat on a hook. 'Yer wooden spoons're in the drawer with yer tablespoons. I sorted them out,' she said.

Ye gods and little fishes. 'Just the spoons?'

'Some other stuff, too. You'll find it easier to keep track, now.'

'I didn't have any trouble *keeping track* before, but I can see that it'll take hours to find things now.' The tablespoons clattered alarmingly as she yanked open the drawer.

'Mum—' Cliff pleaded.

She hadn't heard Jesson arrive. How much had he heard? Enough obviously, because he said, 'Shall I put the kettle on?'

Typical Jesson peacekeeping tactic.

'April, would you like tea?'

April? How did she manage that? Last night, they were Mrs Wallbanks and Mr Cobb.

'Thank you, Jesson. That would be lovely,' Mrs W. gushed.

'Cliff's just shown Mrs Wallbanks around the farm,' May told Jesson, as he reached round her to get out cups and saucers.

'Yes, I met them in the stackyard,' Jesson said, squeezing her arm and giving her a reassuring smile.

'A rat ran out right by our feet and it gave Mrs Wallbanks a shock,' Cliff said. 'Jesson calmed her down,' he added.

'Humph,' May grunted.

Chapter 42

'I'm so pleased to see you, Rose,' May said on Monday morning.

'How's it going?'

'Don't ask,' she whispered. 'Mrs W's a horror. Evelyn's getting on with the hens, but I must go back and help.'

'Why's she a horror?' Rose kept her voice low.

'Where do I start? She's still in bed and I'm afraid I can't clear the breakfast until she comes down and orders hers.'

Rose frowned. 'Orders?'

'Yes. And never a please or thank you. Correction. I got a "ta" yesterday.'

Rose laughed. 'You said she was offish when you first met her.'

'Offish I could handle, but the reorganisation of my drawers, I can't.'

'Don't say she's sorting out your underwear?' Rose dissolved into fits of laughter.

'You never change,' May said, laughing with her. 'And the answer to that is, she would if she got a chance.' She related the events of the weekend in low tones, watching Rose's face as she listened. 'Jesson can't see anything wrong with her, thinks I'm overreacting and Cliff thinks she's something between a saint and martyr. I think he's worried that by the time he gets back from school, I'll have done her a mischief.'

'How long's she staying?'

'Nothing's been said, but I'm not having her longer than a fortnight. She could go today as far as I'm concerned. For goodness' sake, persuade her to go to Magna for her shopping. She doesn't want us to have her ration card in case we lose it. I've tried to put her off Parva, saying how limited it is for shops, but I don't know if I've succeeded.'

'I'll do my best. Heaven forbid we upset the Potties.'

May shook her head. 'Sorry to leave you to it, but it's not fair to leave Evelyn on her first day. Spencer's still in bed, too. He's not keen on her ladyship, either.'

'You go, I'll cope,' Rose said, picking up a tea cloth.

Evelyn had finished mucking out the henhouses. As they walked back to the yard, May showed her some of the hens' favourite hidey holes for egg laying.

'They mainly lay in the nest boxes but, being able to wander around the yard, they find all sorts of secret places,' May said. 'If they can get in the barn, they sometimes lay in the horses' mangers, so we have to watch out when we feed Blossom and Ben.'

'Right. I'm sure I'll get to know me way round before long.'

May handed her an egg basket. 'We won't find many today but as soon as the poults start laying you'll find baskets full. In the meantime, you'll be able to get up to speed with the feeding and mucking out.'

They searched around the yard and Evelyn collected a dozen eggs before they returned to the henhouses and checked the nest boxes for more bounty.

She could see from Evelyn's face she experienced the same pleasure May did, even after years of tending the flock, when she lifted the nest box lid and discovered a clutch of eggs on the straw.

Both had a decent collection in their baskets when they

finished.

'Did you bring something for your elevenses?' May asked.

'Just a sandwich.'

'Right-oh. If you take the eggs to the harness room, I'll dash up to the house, grab a couple of drinks and come and join you.'

What would she find indoors? She opened the back door gingerly, but all was calm. Spencer greeted her. He was colouring in a picture of a cat and dog drawn by Rose. His scribble extended way beyond the outlines of the animals, but he loved his art.

Mrs Wallbanks and Rose were chatting; Rose with a sheaf of papers in her hand and their guest with a magazine on her lap. More magazines lay on the table. Rose had had the forethought to bring a stack to entertain Mrs W. She was a wonder.

'Hello, Mrs Wallbanks. Did you sleep well?' May asked, taking two beakers from a cupboard.

'Apart from that blessed bird crowing at the crack of dawn,' Mrs W. said.

'That's Lucky, our resident cockerel. Never fails to deliver our morning call.' May grinned.

'Country living,' Rose said. 'Anyway, do you like your room, April? I believe you're the first to use it since we redecorated it.'

April? Again?

Mrs W. said, 'I thought I could smell paint.'

Impossible. They'd painted the room over a year ago. Rose got in before she could say anything.

'A light colour makes all the difference to a room, don't

you think?'

May carried the beakers of tea to the door.

'It's better than that sleazy B&B the council wanted to put me in,' said Mrs W.

Tea slopped to the floor as May spun round and stared at Rose, whose eyebrows rose almost to her hairline.

May carried the beakers back to the kitchen. 'I didn't realise they offered you alternative accommodation, Mrs Wallbanks. Cliff said you had nowhere to go.'

Mrs W's cheeks were scarlet. 'Where they wanted to put me ain't accommodation, it's a dump. Overrun with bedbugs and the like.'

May didn't dare catch Rose's eye. 'I'd better take this tea out; Evelyn will think I've forgotten her,' she said.

Rose followed and opened the back door for her. 'I can't believe it,' she said.

'I can,' May said, 'but I didn't think she'd stoop so low as to manipulate Cliff.'

Chapter 43

He felt bad. He'd done the wrong thing asking Mrs Wall-banks to stay and everyone was upset. Mum had stopped even trying to be friendly to her. Mrs Gale chatted to her, but not in the way she did with Mum. Jesson called her April and listened politely, but it was obvious he'd rather talk to Mum, or be out on the tractor.

Mrs W. was twiddling her thumbs. When he'd got back from school yesterday and asked her what she'd done, for the second time she said she'd been reading magazines in the kitchen. He'd asked her if she wanted to go to Magna – said he'd find out the bus times for her – but she said she'd rather go somewhere nearer.

He didn't know what to say. Mum had asked him not to encourage her to go into Parva, so he just muttered that Magna was nice, even though he'd always found it snobby.

When he'd got off the bus today, old Misery Guts was biking down the main road towards him. Cliff shouted good-bye to the twins and hurried into the lane. Old Potty mostly ignored him nowadays but, after the scene in the post office with Victoria, he didn't want to listen to her brother's reasons why he should have gone back to Southampton and not stayed in Parva sabotaging shops.

He was jogging down the lane when he heard a shout behind him. He jogged on until another shout came. His name. Heck, he'd have to face Old Potty.

The ancient boneshaker's brakes squeaked as Ephraim pulled up alongside him. 'Is 'ee deaf? I shouted way back.'

'Sorry, I was thinking,' Cliff said, instantly knowing it

was a stupid thing to say.

'Thinking? Can't 'ee do that and use 'ee's ears?'

'What did you want me for?' Cliff looked at the sulky mouth and the straggly moustache that used to be ginger but was now grey, and waited for the flak that was sure to be coming his way.

Old Potty gave him a message for his mother.

Cliff wondered why on earth Mum would want to know that, but said he'd pass on the message, not quite believing he'd got away so lightly.

He'd persuaded Mrs Wallbanks to come with him to feed the horses in the paddock; the weather had warmed up, and the animals were going to stay out at night.

'They don't get much,' he told her, as he dropped two feed buckets over the fence; a handful of sliced carrot and chaff in each, 'because the spring grass is coming through and they can get laminitis, a painful problem with their feet, if they eat too much rich stuff.'

'Proper little vet, you are, Cliff. You'll be a good one, too,' Mrs W. said, smiling at him.

He flushed; he very much wanted to be a good vet.

As they walked back to the house, he said, 'I hope you like being here, aren't too bored?'

She was quiet for a moment before saying, 'It's different, Cliff. The only time I've been in the country before was in service and I was too busy to take walks or anything. Got there on the bus, slaved, left on the bus. That was about it.'

He thought she'd lived in Soton all her life. It gave him an idea.

Mum had talked Jesson into having his tea with them. He

knew it was to make it easier with Mrs W., but he had a plan.

Once Mum sat down and everybody was eating, he said, 'Mum, did you know Mrs Wallbanks has lived in the country before, when she was in service?'

Mrs Wallbanks looked a bit surprised, but Mum must have had something go down her throat the wrong way because she coughed and grabbed her glass of water.

'Sorry,' she said. 'I think those carrots would be better off going to the horses.'

Cliff hadn't found anything wrong with the carrots.

'Whereabouts were you in service, April?' Jesson asked.

'Just outside Romsey,' she said.

Jesson looked questioningly at Mum.

'It's between Salisbury and Southampton. Lord Mountbatten lives there,' she said.

'I weren't at Broadlands, where the Mountbattens live, but it was a big house in the country and it was owned by a lord,' Mrs W. said, pink-faced.

'What job did you have?' Mum asked.

'I were a tweeny.'

'What's a twinny?' asked Jesson.

'Tweeny,' Mum said.

'It's a maid what does upstairs and downstairs, helping the housemaids and the cook. Means you never stop work,' Mrs Wallbanks said bitterly.

'Did you ever see anyone famous?' Cliff asked.

'The Mountbattens came to dinner, and we peeked round the servant's green baize door to see them going into the dining room. She had on a beautiful shantung dress, pale green it were, owe der kneel, Cook said that colour was called.'

'Pretty,' Mum said.

'And once the Prince of Wales, Edward the Eighth he

243

was to become for a while, came shooting. I only saw the back of him as he got in the motor.'

'Cor,' said Cliff. 'Fancy seeing a prince. Have you seen anyone famous, Mum?'

'I once saw Winston Churchill in Salisbury. He was in a car with a flag on the bonnet on his way to talk to an American general. All I saw was a black hat and a fat cigar.' She laughed, and Cliff was glad to see Mrs W. join in.

'How long were you at Romsey, Mrs Wallbanks?' Mum asked.

'Three years. I went home one Mothering Sunday – we was all allowed that day off – and I met Owen. He was on shore leave. He proposed the same day. We wasn't allowed to be married in service, so I gave in me notice. We was married just before he went back on his ship in 1914. He went away to war and his ship went down eight months later. I never saw him again.' She looked sad; Cliff wished he'd never started trying to get them to talk.

'I'm sorry,' Mum said, 'that must've been terrible.'

'Sad to hear that, ma'am,' Jesson said.

They meant what they said – Mum's husband had died and Jesson's plane had been shot up – but Mrs Wallbanks just nodded her head. Then she said, 'Did you say bread and butter pudding, Mrs Sheppard? My mother used to make that. Hers was unbeatable.'

'I expect she had more dried fruit than I can get hold of,' Mum said.

'Not in 14–18,' Mrs W. said.

Cliff hoped he was the only one to hear his mother's sigh as she stood up. He got to his feet to clear the table and caught Jesson's eye. He winked.

Cliff grimaced. Nothing he tried worked out.

Chapter 44

'When Cliff said she'd been in service, I nearly died; I was waiting for the story she wrote in that letter – telling me about Isobel Bullock harming a child while Mrs W. was in service – to come out.'

May and Rose were in the study, leaving Mrs Wallbanks and Spencer to enjoy breakfast together.

'But it didn't?'

'No. What she said was heart-rending; she lost her husband at sea only eight months after they married. He sailed after the wedding and she never saw him again.'

'That explains a lot,' Rose said.

'In what way?'

'The way she's resentful of you; she must think you have it all compared ter her: property, a son she'd love ter have had as her own, a second child that's almost your own and a wedding on the horizon.'

And I might lose what she's most jealous of – the farm. The thought brought a lump to her throat.

'I ought to be more sympathetic,' she said after a moment, 'but she's so irritating. Yesterday, I was all set to sympathise over her loss, but she demanded pudding and announced that her mother's version was better than mine before she'd even tasted it.'

Rose laughed. 'I'm afraid there's something else,' she said. 'Before you came in from the yard, she said she's going shopping this morning.'

'Hell. I can't take her. The poults are due anytime. I've got to be here.'

'The bus to Magna goes at eleven. I'll suggest she catches that,' Rose said. 'Touch wood, she takes the hint.'

They discussed farm matters before returning to the kitchen. Mrs Wallbanks was washing up, and Spencer engrossed in drawing.

'Sorry we've been so long. Thank you for clearing up,' May said to Mrs Wallbanks' back; she hadn't turned round when they entered.

'The bus ter Magna goes at eleven; I'll finish the washing up and you can get ready. You've lots of time,' Rose said, picking up a dish to dry.

'I'm not sure I want to bother with buses, the walk's bad enough.' Mrs W. picked up a towel and wiped her soapy hands. 'I might just—'

Before she could continue, May cut in, 'I know, Bill Tyler's due any minute to deliver the poults. He lives in Magna and could give you a lift there. That way, you'll only have to get the bus back. You could walk, but it's over Magna Hill, which is a bit of a killer.'

'Super idea,' Rose said. 'He's very handsome. Lucky you.'

Mrs Wallbanks' face lit up.

May bit her tongue until Mrs W. had gone upstairs to get ready.

'You're naughty,' she whispered to Rose.

'Did the trick, though, didn't it?' said Rose with a grin.

May, Evelyn and Bill unloaded the poults and carried the crates to the poultry yard, opening them inside the henhouses with the doors closed.

When Bill's lorry had been stacked with the empty crates and Evelyn was back in the poultry yard, May asked Bill for a word in confidence.

'What's the matter? Not getting cold feet about the wedding, are you?'

That was a bit near the knuckle from someone who'd once set his cap at her, but she needed a favour and laughed off the remark.

'Remember that chap you and Seth used to know, Ingles, wasn't it? The one who joined the army before the war and became an officer.'

'Basil Ingram? He's a colonel now. Got a desk job in the War Office.'

'Are you still in touch with him?'

'On and off. Why?'

May had just finished giving a cursory explanation when Mrs Wallbanks tottered into the yard, examining her shoes as she attempted to avoid the evidence of so many chickens unhappy at being cooped up in slatted crates.

Mrs W. wasn't back by the time May and Jesson came in to eat at one o'clock.

Rose put a plate over the sandwich she'd made for her. 'She should be back soon if she caught the twelve-thirty bus.'

'She could have walked into Parva for a look around,' Jesson said.

May prayed she hadn't. 'She'd have used up her rations in Magna, so there'd be no point,' she said. But what if that wasn't the case?

'Perhaps she's in The Crown, having a quick nip,' Jesson joked.

Rose laughed. 'A hasty port and lemon?' she suggested.

'You two, really,' May said, not being able to stop herself smiling.

Suppose she had ventured into Parva and come face to face with Isabella?

She and Rose had put the story of a young woman, once dismissed from her job and investigated by the police for an incident with a child, together with what they knew of Isabella's arrival after the Great War as Ephraim's bride.

All Mrs W. had known of the woman was that she'd married a soldier and moved to "Crompton".

The agreement she had with Ephraim was that she'd never mention Isabella's history if he stopped verbal attacks on her and her family.

If Ephraim restarted his slurs just as she was about to get married, their future happiness would be ruined.

She'd tried to divert the risk of Mrs W. quizzing Bill, by suggesting he tell Mrs Wallbanks about her role as midwife; a frantic attempt to distract conversation from the residents of Parva.

Their guest hadn't returned by the time the meal was over. 'I'm getting worried,' May said. 'Should I look for her?'

'Why don't you call Magna Farm?' Jesson said. 'Bill could tell you where he left her.'

She went to phone, imagining her call ringing in Sally's spotless kitchen.

'I dropped her outside the grocers,' Bill said, when Sally called him to the phone. 'She'd got the idea Magna would be a smaller version of Southampton, but she went off cheerfully enough when I told her people come for miles to shop here.'

He sounded like the worst of the Magna inhabitants, all believing their snooty village the best in the county. If he'd convinced April Wallbanks it was better than Parva, though, he'd earned the right to brag.

'Did she say which bus she'd be catching back? She hasn't arrived yet and, even in the enormous metropolis of Magna, she can't have found that much to do.'

'Spoken like a true Parvaite,' Bill said, laughing. 'But no, she didn't say. I wouldn't worry. She probably got tempted into the tea shop and got chatting. She's an ardent chatterer.'

'Hmm. I'm sure she'll turn up,' May said through clenched teeth. 'Thanks for giving her a lift and thanks for delivering the poults; they're all in the houses and settling in.'

'Pleasure, May. Before you go, I've had a word with Basil Ingram. He says if you write to him at the War Office, he'll help.'

He gave May the address.

Returning to the kitchen, she said, 'Bill says she might have gone to the tea shop. He thinks she's a chatterer.'

'Better that than a questioner,' Rose said, as Jesson called out, he'd see them later.

'The flaming tea shop – when you've got a sandwich here for her? I hope she brings some rations back with her; there's no cheese left, and she's eaten almost a jar of the homemade jam.'

'She is rather thoughtless,' Rose said. 'At least, if she's in the tea shop in Magna, she can't be nosing around in Parva.'

'I suppose so,' May said.

She was just off to help Evelyn with the expanded flock when Mrs Wallbanks sailed into the kitchen carrying a bulging shopping bag.

'I could do with a cuppa after that walk,' she said, dumping her bag on the kitchen table and flopping into the armchair.

'Did you come over the hill from Magna, after all?' May asked.

'Not flippin' likely. I waited for the bus and trekked down the lane.'

'Did you have a nice day?' Rose asked. 'I saved you a sandwich and the kettle's on.'

'I've eaten. A lovely tea shop in Magna that Bill pointed out. He's a lovely fella, isn't he? A real treat it were to sit in a caffee that weren't WVS.'

'I've got to go back to work,' May said. 'I'll see you later.' She closed the door behind her. Only just over a week before her ladyship went home; it couldn't come quickly enough.

Evelyn rubbed her back as she stood up from heaving a meal sack on to the wheelbarrow.

'All right?' May asked. Was Evelyn up to the rigours of carrying heavy feed sacks and pushing barrow loads of smelly chicken manure five days a week?

'Muscles aching a bit. Just need to get them accustomed to lifting.' Evelyn smiled.

'You'll soon adapt to it. I ached all over the first few weeks when I started. My late husband used to massage my shoulders. Get your Janice to do it for you,' May said.

'She's hardly ever in. You'd think I was going to poison her, the fuss she makes when I say I'd like us all to have a meal together for once.'

May waited while Evelyn filled a scoop from the sack and carried it to the henhouse, where May opened the door and prevented the hens from escaping. It was reassuring to see Evelyn move cautiously, so as not to startle the new birds.

'Janice getting the taste of freedom, is she?'

'I worry because the other factory girls are older than her and I don't want her tempted into bad ways.'

'She's always struck me as a sensible girl,' May said. 'I'm sure she'll settle before long.'

'I hope so.'

They moved on to the next house, May pushing the barrow.

The pleasure May felt returning home at the end of the working day had abated now April Wallbanks was in residence. She must stop being irritated by the woman, but she'd been brought up well; taught to say please and thank you and consider other people's feelings. Mrs Wallbanks hadn't had that upbringing, but it was incredible she remained oblivious to good manners.

She sighed and went indoors to wash her hands in the back-kitchen. Glancing through to the main kitchen, she saw a pot of jam and some greaseproof wrapped packages lying on the table alongside Mrs Wallbanks' bag. She'd brought some rations. Perhaps she'd misjudged her after all.

Rose came in from the study, her coat on. 'Here it is, April. Sorry, I took it through with the business post.' She handed over a letter.

May frowned. She was having her post sent here?

Mrs Wallbanks took it warily. She tore the envelope open and Rose and May began a desultory conversation, pretending not to be interested.

'Oh Lor,' Mrs Wallbanks jumped from the chair and

began ramming the groceries back into her bag. 'Me flat's ready. I'll have to leave tomorrer. I'll need these, I won't have any food in the place.' She grabbed the jar of jam and made for the stairs. 'I've gotta go and pack.'

May and Rose stared at each other, speechless.

May didn't know whether to cheer or rant about rations used and not replaced. In the end, she settled for joy. "Thank heavens," she mouthed to Rose.

Chapter 45

Cliff watched Mrs Wallbanks, suitcase in hand, walk away towards the station. Their lives were now different; would he ever see her again? He'd meant well when he'd asked her to stay, but it hadn't worked out. She hadn't liked staying at the farm, and Mum had only put up with her for his sake.

They'd parted as friends; she'd given him a red leatherette-covered notebook for his veterinary jottings. She'd bought a paintbox for Spence, but he wished she'd given Mum something. Just a bunch of flowers would have been nice. Mum wouldn't mind – she'd be grateful he and Spence had got presents, but it wasn't kind to leave her out.

'You coming, Cliff?' Pete called.

The bus had driven off, and the twins were waiting a few yards ahead.

'Yeah,' he said, jogging to catch up.

'Sorry to see her go?' Bob asked.

'Yeah, but she didn't fit in at home.'

Pete nodded. 'Mum said she was a bit of a tart.'

Cliff had a mental picture of his first mum with her painted red lips and dresses that showed half her chest. Mrs W. wasn't like that. Surely Mrs Gale wouldn't—

'Tartar, not tart, you clot.' Bob cuffed his brother light heartedly around the ear.

Cliff felt relief flow through him like the swig of brandy he'd pinched at Christmas. He punched Pete on the arm. 'Twerp,' he said, grinning.

There was pandemonium in the classroom, the boys crowded

around a notice pinned on the wall.

'What is it?' Bob called to Pete, who'd shoved to the front.

'Cricket team list.'

'Am I on it?' Bob asked.

'No. But I am.' Pete pushed his way out wearing a huge grin. 'First eleven.' He looked at Cliff. 'Sorry, mate, not you either.'

'That's okay. I'm not bothered.' He was glad. Cricket finished late and sometimes they had Saturday games. He'd rather be at the surgery than on the cricket field.

At dinnertime, Pete went off to practice bowling with some of his team, and Cliff and Bob mooched around the school field.

'I'm glad Pete's in the team. About time he had some good luck in this place,' Bob said.

'Yeah, he's had a rough time. Your old man better with him now?' Cliff asked.

'On an' off. He's pleased Pete's earning some money, but he's not keen on him workin' on a farm. Reckons he'd do better at a garage or with an engineer. So's he can go straight into the Forces when he leaves school.'

'He'd hate it,' Cliff said.

'Try tellin' my dad,' Bob said.

That was the problem. No one could tell Len Gale anything. Cliff would've hated the Forces, too.

'Let's go an' watch Don Bradman practicing, shall we?' Bob said.

Cliff grinned, and they walked over to the cricket nets.

Chapter 46

Rose was coming in late because she was picking up the shopping. May dressed Spencer in his outdoor clothes. 'We're going to see the new hens. You'll help Mrs Harris and me feed them, won't you?'

'Henny Penny, Chicky Licky,' Spencer chortled, dancing around as May tried to pull on his boots.

'We'll read the book again when we get back. Come on, Mrs Harris can't do all the work on her own.'

Once Spencer was ready, they set off down the track, waving to Jesson, who was in the Dutch barn giving orders to the POWs.

Spencer pointed. 'See Dada,' he said.

'Not now, Daddy's busy. We've got to see Mrs Harris and Henny Penny, remember?'

'Chicky Licky!' Spencer slipped from her grasp and ran ahead to where May could see Evelyn upending the wheelbarrow on the muck heap.

'Hello, Spencer,' Evelyn called. 'Morning, May.'

'Sorry I'm a bit late. Rose is picking up some shopping and won't get here until later. Our guest has left and we've got to replenish the larder.'

'Ate you out of house and home, did she?' Evelyn said with a laugh.

'Something like that,' May said. 'She seemed very fond of our homemade jam.'

Evelyn righted the barrow and set off back to the poultry yard. Spencer held on to the barrow handle. Every few steps, he glanced at his feet and the lace-up jumble sale boots he'd just grown into. He looked bottom-heavy, and May smiled as she walked alongside.

'Can't get blackberries in the city,' Evelyn said. 'She'll be back on rationed stuff: raspberry jam with wooden pips.'

'Ugh,' May said, holding the gate for them.

They'd fed the birds and cleaned out all but one house when May's attention was drawn to Rose stumbling through the gateway, coat and hair awry. Asking Evelyn to keep an eye on Spencer, she ran to meet her friend.

'Rose, what's happened?'

'It was awful.' She was unsteady on her feet, her face ashen. May put an arm around her shoulders and called to Evelyn to help; the ground in the poultry yard was no place to take a tumble in decent clothes.

The two women, Spencer behind, supported Rose across the farmyard and into the barn, where they sat her in a chair in the harness room. Evelyn fetched the flask from her saddlebag and poured a cup of tea. She handed it to Rose. 'No sugar, I'm afraid, but it's warm.'

Rose's hands shook as she took the cup, and May draped her own coat around her shoulders. It was a miracle Rose hadn't had an accident, riding her bike in this state.

Laying a hand on Rose's shoulder, May said, 'Can you tell me what's happened. Is it the boys? Or Len?'

Rose shook her head. Before May could stop him, Spencer wrapped himself around Rose's knees.

'Arn Roe sad,' he said, laying his head in her lap.

'It's all right, Spencer. I had a shock, that's all. Could you see whether you could find me a feather ter make me feel better?'

The little boy stomped his big boots off to the yard.

More composed, Rose turned to May and Evelyn. 'I was in the shop getting the food when Isabella burst in. She was in a real temper and tore Victoria off a strip because some magazine hadn't been delivered.'

Evelyn interjected, 'She's mad about that flippin' magazine. It's more important than anything in her life.'

'Not anymore,' Rose said, wiping a tear.

A sense of dread ran through May; something bad was coming.

'Isabella and Victoria were still involved in their set-to when I was leaving,' Rose continued. 'Victoria told her they would deliver the magazine tomorrow, but Isabella was determined ter have the last word and snapped tomorrow was no good. She marched over to the door and shouted over her shoulder, she was cancelling the order. Victoria had a face like thunder – Isabella had shown her up in front of her customers. Before she could say anything, Isabella shoved in front of me and swept out of the door …' Rose's voice faltered. She cleared her throat. 'I was behind her when she walked straight in ter the road,' her voice broke, 'in front of a lorry.' She sobbed, head in hands.

May and Evelyn stared at each other, stupefied.

'Is she … is she …' May couldn't say the word.

Rose's voice came between sobs. 'Killed outright,' she whispered.

'Dear Lord.' May dragged out another chair and slumped down.

Evelyn stared into space.

They were back in the farmhouse. Rose refused to be driven home, insisting she wanted to work. She was in no fit state, but she probably preferred company to being at home alone.

257

They sat with the teapot and a pile of bank statements in front of them. May had said she needed to calculate some figures, but neither had lifted a sheet of paper.

At the other end of the table, Spencer sat with his crayons, making more of his scribbled pictures on the backs of old letters.

Mid-morning Jesson came indoors to collect the key for the fuel store. May explained what had happened and offered him a coffee.

'Wow. Poor old Isabella. Victim of her own crankiness.'

May nodded pointedly at Rose, who was mindlessly twisting a pen between her fingers. Using the noise of the boiling kettle to mask her voice, she whispered, 'She's in shock.'

When she brought fresh drinks, May again insisted Rose took real sugar in hers, accepting no argument about using up their rations.

'On that note, I misjudged Mrs Wallbanks,' she said. 'She's left us something for the larder.'

Rose looked up, curiosity overcoming distress. May went to the larder and brought out a tin to show them.

'You are joking,' Rose said, wrinkling her nose. 'Snook?'

'If you serve that, I'll eat at the cottage,' Jesson said.

May put the tin aside and said, 'I think we'll let Bess have it.'

The dog raised her head at the sound of her name. Bess would like it, but May had never met any human who enjoyed the foul smelling, foul tasting fish, no matter how many recipes the Ministry of Food came up with.

She hadn't wanted to ask about the details of the

accident, but Jesson had no such compunction.

'What did the truck driver do?' he asked.

'He couldn't be faulted,' Rose said. 'He reacted instantly – he was already slowing down ter deliver ter the shop.'

'Not magazines?' Jesson said.

May gave him a look.

'Vegetables,' Rose said. 'He braked so hard the tyres left rubber on the road, but it wasn't any good. He hit her. Poor man. He was distraught.'

'Was it the impact that killed her?' May said. Asking whether Isabella had been run over was too awful. They'd experienced tragedies in the war, but in peacetime, such events took on a different perspective.

'No. The lorry knocked her down, and she hit her head on the road. There … there was a lot of blood …' Rose put her hand over her mouth.

'Did someone call the cops?' Jesson asked.

'We don't have to talk about it,' May said, frowning at Jesson.

'It's all right.' Rose blew her nose. 'Len and the boys will quiz me tonight. If I've already talked about it, it won't be so bad a second time.'

You can always hope, May thought, knowing Len's hunger for detail.

Rose insisted on doing some proper work after she'd picked at a sandwich. She'd told them that Victoria had veered between guilt and defence, saying it wasn't her fault Isabella had marched out in a huff. Seconds later adding she'd never be able to make it up to Ephraim for the loss of his beloved wife.

She said an ambulance had arrived, as well as the village

bobby, and someone went to fetch Ephraim.

Feeling overwhelmed and not able to face Ephraim's distress, Rose gave her name to the policeman and left.

She'd composed herself when May left her working in the study while she and Spencer joined Evelyn for the afternoon's work.

'The village is in shock,' Evelyn told her. 'The shop is shut, of course. Victoria is with Ephraim and everyone's makin' out like Isabella was a saint.'

'They don't like to speak ill of the dead. She did have a terrible end,' May said.

Evelyn nodded. 'No one would have wished that on her. They say Ephraim is inconsolable. Victoria's the only family he's got now.'

What about Isobel Bullock's family; did they keep in touch?

Spencer joyfully searched for the hens' secret laying places. May fondly recalled showing Cliff where to look when he'd first arrived. He'd been as excited as Spencer when he'd found a cluster of warm eggs.

After work, they found Cliff in the kitchen with Rose. May gave her a quizzical look. She shook her head; she'd left May the job of breaking the news.

'Time you left, Rose. The twins will be home by now. Sure you don't want a lift?'

'I'll be all right, thanks. And I'll catch up with the work tomorrow.'

As Rose passed her, May said quietly, 'The shop's shut. Ephraim's taken it very hard.'

'Right. Thanks. Bye.'

Cliff was admiring Spencer's pictures. 'Why did Mrs

Gale need a lift?' he asked. 'Something wrong with her bike?'

'No. She had a shock this morning.' She turned to Spencer. 'Why don't you have a game with your toy cars?'

He ran over to the settle, gathered his cars from the seat and spread them across the rug.

May drew a deep breath. 'Mrs Gale was in the shop this morning. Mrs Potts came in and started a row with Victoria. To cut a long story short, Mrs Potts stormed out. Sadly, she got hit by a lorry.' She laid a hand on Cliff's arm. 'She's dead, I'm afraid. Mrs Gale saw the whole thing, and it was a terrible shock for her.'

Cliff seemed momentarily stunned, but then frowned and said, 'Didn't Mrs Potts go on holiday then?'

'What? What holiday?'

'Old Potty told me. They were going to Christchurch,' Cliff said, not meeting her eyes.

'Why did he tell you that?'

'He … he asked me to tell you.' He rushed on. 'I didn't think it was important. I thought he was just showing off. When I got home, Mrs W. was here, and I forgot. I'm sorry.'

May gave a shuddering sigh. Why did every event have complications for her? 'Cliff, you must pass on messages.'

'It wouldn't have made any difference to the accident, would it?' Cliff said, lip trembling.

How could she tell him she'd persuaded Ephraim to take Isabella on holiday and maybe she wanted the blessed magazine to read on the journey? If they hadn't been going away, the row may never have started.

'I don't know, but that's not the point, is it?' she said.

'No. I'm sorry, Mum.'

'All right. Look after Spencer, will you? I'm going out

to the yard.'

Jesson grasped how upset she was at first glance and dismissed the POWs without ceremony. He led her into the barn and, once again, she sat at the harness room table. She'd tried to protect him from finding out just how aggressive Ephraim's persecution had been and she'd succeeded for nearly two years, but now she'd reached breaking point. A woman had died and her actions could have set off the chain of events that triggered it.

She spilled out the whole story of her and Ephraim's agreement.

'The fact is, I didn't know what Isobel Bullock had done.' She described the contents of the letter. 'But just saying the name was enough to get Ephraim shaking in his boots. It was easy to get him to hold his malicious tongue in return for my silence, even though I didn't know what I was silent about.'

She explained how she'd gone to the allotments to warn Ephraim that Mrs Wallbanks was coming to stay. She told him she'd suggested he take Isabella away, and had just discovered he'd planned to do it.

'If she hadn't been going away, she wouldn't have stormed out and been killed.'

'Whoa, May. You can't believe you have any responsibility for Isabella's death. That family is poison. If they're not stabbing other people in the back, they're tormenting each other. None of this is your fault. And not Cliff's either.'

'But—'

'No buts. If you'd known they were going on vacation, what would you have done, hightailed up there to stop them when you heard April was leaving?'

'I … I don't know.' She put her head in her hands.

Jesson pulled her to him. 'You need to offload, May. Let me help – we'll soon be husband and wife. I want to protect you, too, but I can't if you hide things. Old Ephraim's abuse is nothing compared to what I had slung at me in the States. I know it's new to you, and you hate it, but we'll face it together from now on. Okay?'

She looked up at him and nodded. 'Okay.' She crossed her fingers, desperately hoping Mr Leadbetter would have a way of resolving the other problem she hadn't revealed.

Chapter 47

Rose's face was tear-stained when she arrived for work. She went straight to the study and May didn't question her.

All morning, the thought of Len grilling her over the accident played on her mind. Would he have said she shouldn't have been doing May's shopping, or told her she should have intervened in the row? More likely, he'd told her not to be wet about what she witnessed.

Mid-morning, she popped her head around the study door. Rose sat at the desk. Beside her, Spencer tried to fit together the big wooden pieces of his zoo animal jigsaw.

'Would you like me to take him with me, give you some quiet?' she asked.

Rose shook her head without turning round. 'I'm all right,' she muttered.

May walked over and put a hand on Rose's arm. 'But you're not, are you?'

The dam burst and tears flowed.

May perched on the spare chair. 'Is it the accident?'

'No. Although I keep seeing her lying there in a pool of her own blood. It's … it's bloody Len.'

May couldn't remember ever before hearing Rose swear.

'Sorry. Hell, Spencer's here.' Rose lowered her voice, but the boy was absorbed in trying to force an elephant into a space designed for a monkey.

May said, 'He's all right. What has Len done? Wasn't he understanding about Isabella?'

'Understanding? Yes, if you want ter hear how many bodies he saw in the war and how badly mutilated they were.

In detail.' She mopped her face.

What could she say? It was a monstrous way to comfort his wife.

'That's not the worst of it, it's what he's done ter Peter.' She blew her nose. 'The lad came home floating two feet off the ground. They have picked him for the first eleven cricket team. He was happier than I've seen him for … for … since Len was demobbed.'

Considering the state the boy had been in, anything that raised his spirits had to help him. 'That's marvellous. Just what he needs; a boost to his confidence,' she said.

'You'd think so. You'd think his father would be pleased – for once – wouldn't you? But no. His father told him he couldn't play for the team; said he needs the time for extra maths and he's written ter the headmaster telling him as much.'

Bloody Len. How could a man be so heartless about his own son's well-being?

'I'm so sorry, Rose. I can't understand Len's attitude. If there is anything I can do, you've only got to ask.'

Rose mumbled something.

'Sorry, I didn't catch that,' May said.

Rose faced her, eyes bright with tears. 'I said, I'm not sure how much longer I can bear it.'

'Hello. Anyone home?'

Both women jumped, but Spencer was on his feet. ''ello,' he called, running to the back door.

May followed, to find Redvers Norton disentangling Spencer from his knees.

'Hello to you, too, Spencer,' he said, smiling. 'I hear a lot about you from Cliff.'

'Kif.' Spencer gave his banana grin and Redvers tousled

his hair.

'Sorry, May. Good morning,' Redvers said.

In her mind's eye, she saw Seth and the child he never had.

She said, 'We haven't got a sick animal, have we?'

'No. I just wanted to talk to you. However, if it's not convenient …'

'No, no. It's fine. It's good to see you,' May said, feeling herself blush.

'I'll put the kettle on, shall I?' Rose asked, appearing beside her. 'And then it's time for Spencer's walk.'

Spencer didn't have a particular time for a walk, but May appreciated Rose's discretion.

Alone, May and Redvers talked about Cliff and the weather until they ran out of small talk.

'I'd better explain why I'm here,' he said, at last. 'It's about what you told me about my resemblance to Seth.'

'Right,' she said, trying to ignore the fluttering in her stomach.

'I had a quiet chat with my father. We get on well and he's always been honest with me but, when I told him a client had mentioned I had a strong likeness to someone she'd once known, he was very evasive and clammed up. That's when I knew you were on to something.'

'I never intended to come between a father and son,' she said, beginning to regret mentioning his resemblance to Seth.

'I know, but there had to be truth in what you'd said, so the next step was to approach my mother.'

Poor woman. 'That can't have been easy,' she said, pouring them more tea without asking Redvers.

'I caught her when she was baking. We always used to

chat while she cooked when I was a boy. As soon as I began, she knew what I was going to say; Dad had warned her, I think. She poured out the whole story.

'She met Hector Sheppard, Seth's father, in 1914. He was having a last fling before joining up as a volunteer—'

'Seth told me his dad had volunteered. His mother, Florence, was furious. I don't think she ever forgave him.'

'Perhaps that's why he went out on the tiles ...' He cleared his throat. 'It was a one-night stand. Mum said she never heard from him again, although she'd given him her address.

'When she found out she was pregnant, her family disowned her – which is why I never met my grandparents. She was a secretary and George, my dad, worked with her. He'd always admired her and when he discovered her predicament, he asked her to marry him. He told her they could call him up at any moment and he might never come back, but he'd have given her a name and status and, if he survived, he would treat her child as his own.'

'What a decent man. He must have truly cared for her.'

'He did – does – and now the feeling is mutual, I'm sure.'

'Was your mother all right after she told you? She must have been upset.'

'Actually, she was quite sanguine. She said she knew she'd have to tell me one day. I think she was relieved to get it out in the open after so long.'

May had to ask the next question. 'And what about you? This must have come as a terrible shock. I'm so sorry I forced your family to drag those old skeletons out of the cupboard.'

Redvers stretched back in the chair. 'It was a shock at first, but I'd known something was odd ever since you showed me that photograph of Seth. There had to be a family

267

connection. I don't think any differently about my father – in fact, I admire him for taking Mum in.

'The person who doesn't come out well is Hector Sheppard, but I've thought about it a lot and I reckon he was trying to take his mind off the terror he was about to face – especially if his wife was angry with him for joining up. It's no excuse, of course, and I want to believe he acted out of character.'

May nodded. 'From what I know, I would agree. Hector was killed in Ypres in 1915 and Florence remarried. Tom Arrowsmith was good to Seth and his mother.'

One of Seth's blood relatives was alive; she tried to take it in. Even if they'd never known each other, there was a link. It had caused heartache, but she was glad she'd found out the truth.

She slid open a dresser drawer. Taking out a photograph, she handed it to Redvers.

'It's Hector.'

He examined it closely, and she told him he was welcome to keep it. He'd have to play it by ear when it came to showing his mother, though. A thought occurred to her.

'Are we related?'

'My late half-brother's widow? Hmm, sounds rather tenuous. But, even if it's unofficial, we have a connection through Seth. My half-brother.' He gave a rueful grin. 'I wish I'd known him …'

The back door burst open and, in usual style, Spencer raced in, Bess at his heels. Rose closed the door behind the excited child.

'Look.' Spencer held out a little egg; buff coloured with reddish spots.

'That's a robin's egg, Spencer,' Redvers said.

'Wobbin.'

'That's right. A baby bird lived in there and now he's come out.'

Spencer frowned and shook his head. 'No,' he said, turning away.

'I stand corrected.' Redvers laughed.

'A professional in the family, able to educate the boys. That's a real boon,' May teased.

Redvers gave a wry grin. 'I'll try to do better with Cliff.'

May's appointment with Mr Leadbetter was his last of the day. She refused tea, wanting to get back for the boys' supper.

She described the visit to Dorothy and her discovery of the recently returned Frank. 'I didn't believe her about him being only just demobbed,' she said. 'Dorothy was far too evasive and clearly irked that I was scrutinising his photograph.'

'Were you able to ascertain his regiment?' Mr Leadbetter asked.

'No. But Seth had a friend who has since become a colonel and works at the War Office. I contacted him and he sent this.' She handed him a letter.

Mr Leadbetter scanned the typewritten sheet and looked up over his glasses. 'That's a turn up for the book. Private Ottaway served time in military prison for looting. Well done, Mrs Sheppard.'

'Thank you. He would have been released in February this year.'

'Time enough to convince his mother to question her brother's will and put pressure on her to query your inheritance.'

'Exactly my thoughts. And if he threatened to move away again if she didn't comply …'

'Quite a manipulator.' Mr Leadbetter removed his glasses and laid them on the desk. 'I've done a brief investigation myself through a fellow solicitor practicing in Basingstoke.

'My colleague had never heard of the practice who wrote to you, but it intrigued him and he visited the address. He reports it's a dingy office in a seedy side street. There is no brass plate, and he is of the impression it is a correspondence address only. And none of the people mentioned on the letterhead are registered with the Law Society.'

'Criminals?' She'd fallen victim to criminals?

'It would seem so. During the war, as you know, a criminal element made a profession out of the black market. If Frank Ottaway was involved in that, or became involved in it in jail—'

'Wait a minute. In the war, Dorothy always seemed to have access to petrol and nice food – hams and so on; she brought one to Tom's funeral. I always wondered …'

'Then perhaps he, or even she, had local criminal connections. If Frank met up with this Basingstoke shower through prison – he was in Aldershot, not far from Basingstoke – he could have moved up a league into coercion and fraud.'

It made sense, but May had reservations. 'I don't think Dorothy can have been the instigator. She may have used Frank's contacts to get under-the-counter food and petrol coupons, but I can't believe she'd knowingly try to defraud me and her own brother. Frank must have bamboozled her.'

'Hmm. You'd be surprised what a mother will do to retain the love of a child.'

No, I wouldn't, she thought. She'd run through fire for Cliff or Spencer.

They left it there. Mr Leadbetter would write a letter to the specious firm refuting their claim and making it clear they expected to hear no more from them. He would also inform them they were being reported to the Law Society for impersonating a law practice.

He wouldn't tell them he was also reporting them to Scotland Yard for attempted deception.

May returned to the lorry feeling sullied by the experience; the people responsible deserved to be prosecuted and if that meant jail, so be it.

Her thoughts whirled. What if it had been Cliff? Perhaps Dorothy didn't know what Frank was up to. If she did, she deserved what was coming as much as he did, but what if she didn't?

She parked outside the house with the sunray fanlight and banged on the door. The bay window curtains twitched, but no one came. She banged louder. The curtains twitched next door.

'Dorothy,' she shouted.

The door opened instantly.

'I told you before, I've nothing to say. Leave me alone,' Dorothy hissed. 'I don't want my neighbours knowing my business.'

'Your son's dirty business, you mean.'

'How dare—' Dorothy gasped. But then moved back, hissing, 'For goodness' sake, come inside.'

As she stepped indoors, May realised she was hoping Frank wasn't at home. Who knew what he might do? She should have told Jesson about all this, and he could have been with her.

'What now?' Dorothy snapped, standing in the hallway.

'My solicitor thinks you may be behind these people making false accusations and he's taking action. I don't think you would do that, but I'm certain Frank knows all about it. Is he here?' She held her breath, longing for him to be out.

'No. And I don't know what you're talking about. Frank's a good lad. He looked after me throughout the war, made sure I had everything I needed.'

'Through his black market pals, now doubt.'

'I don't know what you mean.'

'Yes, you do, Dorothy. They jailed him for looting. For five years. Now, he's trying to swindle his late uncle. He's a bad lot, you must see that.'

Dorothy seemed to sag. She gave a great sigh and dropped on to a small upright chair. 'I told you my husband died in the Great War. That was eighteen months before Frank was born. Ottaway left me two things: his name and his life insurance. Frank's father left me one thing: an unborn baby. He left his name to his wife.'

Frank was illegitimate. That was why she'd kept him hidden. May tried to sound sympathetic. 'I can see Frank's presence would have embarrassed you, but that has no bearing on what you are accusing me of.'

Dorothy seemed to have aged ten years since May had arrived. 'The first war took everything from me. The second could have taken my boy, but it spared him. He left me once, but now he's back and I'll do anything to keep him.'

'Even if it means colluding to deprive an innocent person of what's rightfully theirs?'

Dorothy stood up and looked into May's face.

'Anything.'

Driving home, she felt lighter of heart. She hoped Dorothy would be all right, whatever the outcome. She'd done all she could and Mr Leadbetter wouldn't approve if he knew she'd tipped Dorothy the wink about the police, but at least her conscience was clear.

Chapter 48

'It'll make the old place something special,' Jesson said as she returned from showing the builder out of the cottage.

'It was embarrassing having him come to measure up on a Sunday – the churchgoers would be horrified. Still, a job cancelled at the last minute was lucky for us, although I worry about you living in a building site,' she said, looking around and trying to imagine the house with the old scullery replaced by a modern bathroom. The old lean-to outside lavatory was to be demolished and a "laundry room" built on; all the thing, according to Sally.

'As long as I've still got a john and somewhere to wash, I'll be okay,' Jesson said. 'Having the range taken out was your best idea.'

He hated the thing. He just wanted to flick a switch and have warmth and hot water.

The kitchen work would be done after the wedding, when the cottage would be empty. With an immersion tank for summer and a boiler instead of the range for the winter, the cottage would be cosy all year round.

The alterations would be expensive, but the income from renting out the place would be worth it.

'Let's check out what else you want to move to the farm,' Jesson said.

As well as meeting the builder, the purpose of the visit was to decide whether she wanted to keep any of the cottage furniture, or to leave it for the tenants.

'We'll look upstairs,' she said. How small the cottage seemed after the rambling farmhouse.

She stepped into her old bedroom. She'd thought memories would flood back, but this was a man's room now: shirts draped over a chair, a bottle of cologne on the tallboy. A Raymond Chandler novel lay on the bedside table alongside a framed photograph of May, Cliff and Jesson atop a haycart.

'You've still got this?' she said, picking up the picture and sitting on the bed.

'Of course. My first picture of you.' He sat down beside her.

'So much has changed since that summer,' she said. 'New people working here, some people gone …'

'Still thinking about Isabella? You weren't to blame, even Ephraim told you that. You did everything you could after the accident – even thinking about inviting him to the wedding breakfast.'

'He's lonely. I didn't do it, though. If I had, I'd have to invite Victoria.'

'There wouldn't have been a wedding if you had!'

'I'm safe then, am I?' She put the picture down and faced him, smiling. What a dish he was.

He put his arm around her. 'Amazing the way things pan out. Old Isabella paying for her sins by the thing that caused them.'

May rested her head on his shoulder. She'd never forget the conversation she'd had with Ephraim the day after Isabella had died.

She'd found him at the allotment.

He was forking over the ground. A few hearty savoy cabbages remained in a bed from which most had been harvested. Next to them, bushy green potato plants, earthed up in immaculate mounds, had all the promise of a bumper crop.

She expressed her condolences. It wasn't a surprise to see anger on Ephraim's face. Here it comes, the tirade blaming me for suggesting he take Isabella away.

But there wasn't a tirade, or not directed at her. 'That bliddy magazine,' he spat, 'it ruined her life, and it were the death of her.'

What on earth?

Oblivious to her confusion, Ephraim went on, ''ee knows all about the shame of her getting sacked by the toffs, a course. But she'd told the police she was fetching food for the kiddie when the girl's nightgown caught alight.'

What? May recoiled, appalled. A child had been burned? No wonder Isabella got sacked. She couldn't reveal her horror; Ephraim believed she already knew about it.

'Her admitted her should've put up the guard, but the toffs still got rid of her. When she got back to Soton, they all knew what'd happened.'

Which was worse, leaving the child alone or leaving her without a fireguard?

'Her couldn't bear the gossip, always was proud. When I met her, she'd have cut off her arm if it meant getting out of there. I asked her to marry me and she said yes, as long as we wed fast and got right away.'

'What happened to the child?' She couldn't stop herself from asking, if only to stop the terrible pictures in her head.

'The kiddie got burns on her legs that'd mark her for life. Isabella told all of 'em she'd come back in the room and saved the child. It was the saving her that did the trick with the coppers, else she would've got a prison stretch.' He wiped his arm across his face. 'If she hadn't done it, I'd never have met her, but when she told me the truth, I almost hated her.' He threw down his fork.

What could be worse than a child scarred for life? He went on, 'It were that bliddy rag.' Ephraim stamped his foot. 'She weren't out of the room, she were reading that bliddy tripe instead of watchin' the kiddie.'

May wished she could sit; her knees were quaking. She'd never liked Isabella, but this? Was that why she'd hated children, because she'd lost her job? Could she never see it was through her own neglect? She should have gone to prison.

'I don't know what to say, Ephraim. I could never have imagined anything so … so … serious.' Horrific, she wanted to say. 'And such a dreadful end …'

'It ain't your fault, May Sheppard. 'ee tried 'ee's best for her, protecting her from that visitor from Soton. No, it were the bliddy rag what killed my Isabella.'

May shuddered. An old saying sprang into her head: what goes around, comes around.

Leaving as soon as she could, she glimpsed the plot Ephraim had been "watering" when she'd been there before. All the plants looked dead.

'So, Mrs Sheppard, what else do we have to move to the farm?' Jesson dropped a kiss on her forehead. 'This bed?'

She switched her thoughts back to the move. 'No, I took my bed when I moved out. This one came from the farm.'

Jesson took his arm away. 'You mean you've never slept in this one? And every night I thought I was lying right where you had.' He put on a sad face.

'Sorry to disappoint you.'

'It's easily resolved.' He pulled her down on to the pillows and began kissing her neck.

She let out a shriek of surprise, before wrapping her arms around him and laughing into his shoulder.

Chapter 49

Wedding nerves. Cliff had never heard the phrase until he and Mr Norton were chatting over their sandwiches.

'No one can do anything right at home,' Cliff complained. 'Things that Mum never moaned about, like forgetting to get out more lavvy paper, gets you in the doghouse, nowadays.'

'It'll be wedding nerves,' Mr Norton said. 'She'll get back to normal once it's over.'

'I can't wait for it to be over. All anyone talks about is wedding this, wedding that. Parcels keep turning up that only Mum and Jesson can open. Bits of paper with sitting plans on them are all over the table and if you touch them, you're for the high jump.'

Mr Norton laughed. 'You have my sympathy. I'm just glad that my bride is miles away and her mother's arranging all this stuff. All I have to do is turn up. And make a speech.'

Cliff groaned. 'Me too. I don't know what I'm gonna say. The best man's supposed to tell funny stories about the bridegroom, and I don't know any about Jesson.'

'Of course you do. You told me about him being mad to drive the tractor and not letting anyone else do it. Use that sort of thing and ham it up a bit.' He sighed. 'At least you don't have to tell everyone how wonderful your bride is – she is – but saying it in public without feeling a chump won't be easy.'

They ate in silence for a while, Cliff trying to think of funny things Jesson had done.

The doorbell rang just as Cliff poured tea. Mr Norton

called him; a terrier had been injured and was in a bad way.

The owner, a rough-looking man with his trouser legs tied over his boots with twine, waited in the corridor, tapping his foot.

The wire-haired terrier lay on the examination table. His eyes were closed and his breathing was weak. Mr Norton gently removed the bloody neckerchief tied round the animal's chest. Immediately, blood bubbled from the jagged wound.

'Mr Fielding is a ratcatcher,' Mr Norton said. 'He and Jack here dispatch vermin. Jack chased a rat inside a barn and got impaled on a piece of machinery.' He examined the injury.

'He's not going to be all right, is he?' Cliff asked as he stroked the little animal's head.

'I'm afraid not. Can you fetch Mr Fielding, please?'

Cliff brought Mr Fielding into the consulting room.

'It's bad news, isn't it?' he said.

Mr Norton nodded. 'The spike punctured his lung, I'm afraid. The kindest thing is to put him to sleep immediately.'

Mr Fielding nodded. Cliff looked away as a tear rolled down the man's face. When he glanced back, the man was bent over his dog, talking quietly. He kept his hand on the little creature while Mr Norton gave the injection, only removing it when the vet told him Jack had gone.

Cliff kept his eyes lowered. He didn't want either of the others to see the tears in his own eyes.

'I don't know what I'll do,' Mr Fielding said. 'Jack was my partner. I'll have to look for another dog now, it won't be the same.'

'I'll let you know if I hear of anything,' Mr Norton said, accepting what Cliff knew to be a meagre fee for the job.

'Mr Fielding,' Cliff said, as the man turned to leave, 'a boy at school was talking about his terrier bitch having a litter of pups a few weeks ago. I don't know if they've still got any, but he lives at Martin's Farm on the Dorchester road.'

'I know it. Thank you, lad. I'll stop by and ask. Can't do no harm.'

Cliff went to the front door with Mr Fielding and was astounded when the man handed him a thruppenny bit.

'Thank you,' he called, as the client descended the steps.

Mr Fielding raised a hand.

Cliff showed the coin to Mr Norton.

'A tip? Well done.'

'But I didn't do anything.'

'You were professional, and you suggested the place for a pup. It doesn't happen often, but when someone shows gratitude like that, it makes up for all the Mrs Colindales. Enjoy your thruppence.'

Cliff put the coin in his pocket. You couldn't tell what people were like: ones with furs and money could be mean and rude, and ones who had just lost an animal dear to them and probably had little money, gave you a tip.

Putting an animal down was horrid and upsetting, but the owners were a worse problem. Mr Norton was right when he said you have to treat them all the same; it's the animals that count.

Chapter 50

She sat in the back seat of the car, still fuming that Len had let them down. Beside her, Rose could barely speak she was so embarrassed and upset.

The bouquet of pink roses lay on the seat between them. Their heavy fragrance mingled with the clove-like scent of the pinks in the corsage pinned to Rose's jacket.

'I'm so sorry, May,' Rose said again, wiping a tear from her eye.

'At least he let us use the car, and Andy is an experienced driver. Don't worry, we've got plenty of time,' May said, thinking she'd like to strangle Len for refusing to drive the car half an hour before he was due to pick her up. What would they have done if Rose's next-door neighbour hadn't stepped in?

And how could Rose not worry? Her selfish husband was causing problems all round. May didn't know why he'd refused to drive the car; another family row, she supposed. But with Rose and the boys moving into the farmhouse while she and Jesson were on honeymoon, they'd all get some breathing space.

'He couldn't stop you having the car, even in his temper, since Jesson had already paid for it,' Rose said with a sigh.

They drove on in silence. May tried to relax. Nerves had been fluttering in her stomach since she'd got up. The sight of a long buff envelope in the morning's post hadn't improved her confidence.

She'd ripped it open with trembling fingers, only to discover the paperwork for transferring just under half of the farm's ownership to Jesson. Mr Leadbetter reassured her the police were investigating the criminal firm, and he'd heard Dorothy's house was on the market. He sent his congratulations to her and Jesson.

Dorothy was her last connection to Tom, and she'd done what she did for him, not his sister. Dorothy had made her own choices and May wished her well taming her maverick son.

The landscape they passed shimmered in dazzling sunlight. It was a beautiful day. Her wedding day.

What would Jesson think of her outfit? Her cream dress was impractical, but it had felt wonderful when she'd tried it on in *Miss Martin's Modes*. The "New Look", the assistant had told her. The flowing skirt felt glorious after years of straight, fabric-saving styles patched and mended time and time again.

A matching tightly waisted jacket with a full peplum was like nothing she'd ever worn before. Sally had lent her a tiger's eye brooch that reflected the tan of her slim leather belt and her heeled court shoes.

Cream lace gloves and matching mushroom-shaped hat completed the ensemble.

She caught her breath at the sight of the row of menfolk waiting outside the registry office. Cliff was smart, looking so much older in the suit she and Rose had bagged at a jumble sale in Magna. A seamstress in the village had altered it to fit his slim figure.

Peter and Bob were wearing jackets, bought at the same jumble sale, and school trousers. They looked dapper but uncomfortable; not surprising after their father's behaviour.

And then there was Jesson. His parents had sent him a

suit, which had arrived among several large boxes they'd shipped over during the previous few weeks. May had still to get to grips with the principle of a percolator, but Jesson was ecstatic to have received it as their wedding present.

His suit was a shade lighter than his skin, single-breasted and slim fitting. With a snow-white shirt and boldly patterned gold tie, he looked wonderfully suave. Beside him, in his navy chalk-striped, double-breasted former wedding suit, Bill looked outdated.

Jesson caught sight of her. His jaw dropped, and he shook his head, staring at her as if he'd never seen her before. She must look a little different from the woman who sat on a tractor in a tatty man's trench coat and muddy wellies.

Under his gaze, she felt nervous. Stupid, it's not as if we don't know each other … she stopped her thoughts, feeling herself blush.

'May. You look a million dollars,' he said, eyes shining.

'So do you,' she said, no doubt wearing a silly grin.

She was desperate to tell him she was giving him a partnership in the farm as a wedding present, but she'd wait until they were alone this evening.

'They're ready for us,' Cliff called. Spencer tugged at his hand.

She waved to the wide-eyed child in shorts, pullover and a tiny bow tie he adored. How lucky she was to have two such wonderful boys.

In the ceremony room, rows of chairs faced the table where the registrar sat. They stood in front of him, Rose and Cliff slightly behind.

She was glad it was so different from her first wedding; two separate events, two separate lives.

She handed her bouquet to Rose before taking her vows. Cliff passed the ring to Jesson, who slid it on her finger. He'd returned to Mr Dawson and accepted his recommendation for a style to fit with the engagement ring. He'd remembered her size and the domed gold band fitted perfectly. She loved it.

The registrar pronounced them man and wife and led them to a side table to sign the register. Sally and Doreen stepped up to witness their signatures. Doreen wore her best navy dress and a rather lumpy hand-knitted jacket in a startling acid yellow.

Sally was a vision in powder blue, full skirt and enormous hat. Her outfit certainly hadn't come from *Miss Martin's Modes*. Had she upstaged May? Possibly, but May wasn't concerned. It was a puzzle, though, where the money came from; Magna Farm couldn't be much more prosperous than Elem.

Jesson caught her arm, and they walked down the aisle between the chairs. She could barely believe she was Mrs Jesson Cobb.

The photographer stood just beyond the arched doorway and snapped them coming out.

Cliff and Spencer joined them.

'Congratulations, Mum,' Cliff said. 'You look beautiful,' he added, blushing.

'Gratshions, Arn Mee,' Spencer said. 'Gratshions, Dada.' He wrapped his arms around Jesson's leg. His father swept him up, and the photographer snapped a laughing family photograph.

Once the photography had finished, the guests stood around chatting in groups. May scanned around for Rose and discovered her with the twins at the side of the church, all looking glum faced.

'I think Cliff's looking for you, boys,' she said. They went to find him. 'What's happened, Rose? You all seem shaken up.'

Rose shrugged. 'I didn't want ter upset you on your wedding day, or not more than my wretched husband has already done.'

'That's forgotten. We got here, didn't we?'

'I suppose so.' Rose took a deep breath. 'It was last night. You know I walked up the lane with Walter and Alwin as usual?'

May had a sinking feeling. She'd always wondered what Len would think of his wife associating with the POWs.

'Len left work early because he'd got the car. He says he was coming ter meet me from the farm and that's when he saw me standing at the crossroads with them. Their truck hadn't arrived, and Walter was telling me something when Len came along. He was so rude, May. He threw the car door open and dragged me in. It shocked Walter – he's such a gentlemanly soul. He asked me if I was all right and tried ter tell Len we were just talking, but Len swore at him so foully … I'm not sure how I can face him or Alwin again.'

May prayed she'd find a way; Rose was running the farm for the better part of the following week.

'Once you've all had a break from each other, I expect things will settle down,' she said.

'I'm not sure. Len said some terrible things in front of the boys. They don't know what ter think. They know Walter and they like him, but the things Len accused him of – all the crimes of the Third Reich and adultery with their mother.' She stifled a sob. 'May, I don't think I can go back. The boys are scared and I have ter protect them—'

'There you are, Mrs Cobb. It's time to head for the reception.' Jesson appeared beside her. 'Is everything okay?' His smile faded as he took in Rose's distress.

'Yes, fine. I'm just coming,' May said.

Jesson hovered for a second and then walked away.

'Would Len ever leave – move back with his parents?' May said.

'Not a hope,' Rose said. 'The mood he was in, I'd be amazed not ter find the locks changed.'

'Try not to worry. Enjoy being with the boys, away from Len, for a few days and when we get back, we'll sort this out. I can tell him it's ridiculous to think there was anything between you and Walter.'

A little cheer went up as May joined the guests ready to escort her and Jesson to the waiting car.

Andy had lowered the hood of the Wolsey, the white ribbons gleamed in the sunshine and, as Jesson put a hand under her elbow to help her into the car, someone called out, 'Mr and Mrs Cobb.' They turned and met a deluge of confetti.

Chapter 51

Cliff wondered what Mr Tyler thought of the three of them. Sitting in the passenger seat, Pete and Bob in the back, he silently rehearsed his speech again and again, terrified that if he chatted, he'd forget everything. The twins didn't speak; it was something to do with their dad. Again. This time it was different because they hadn't wanted to travel with their mother in the car Sally had borrowed.

He was just running through the punchline of a joke Mr Norton had told him when Bob blurted out, 'D'you think that German, Walter, is a decent bloke?'

Cliff twisted round in his seat and was alarmed by the haggard look on Bob's face. Pete, too, craned forward to hear Cliff's answer. Mr Tyler glanced across.

'Yeah, I like him. Why?'

'But is he a blighter?' Bob demanded.

Cliff stared at him. 'No. I don't think so. He works hard, and he's friendly. He's nice to Spence. Jesson doesn't like him and Alwin much, but that's because he fought the Germans in the war.'

'Humph.' Bob slumped back in his seat.

'Has this man done something to hurt you, boys?' Mr Tyler asked.

'Na,' Pete said, 'nothin' like that. When I worked with him on the farm, he was bang on.'

'That's not what Dad—' Bob stopped himself short.

'I don't know what your father has against this man,' Mr Tyler said, 'but I believe he was in the Navy. It's difficult for men who've seen their fellows killed by the enemy to forgive them but, don't forget, there will be people in Germany who think the same about your father and about Jesson. They had family members killed by our actions. We all have to put it behind us and realise not all the enemy are evil, any more than all of us are.'

'Yeah.' Bob hung his head, and Pete stared out of the window.

Mr Tyler parked at The Crown. Mum and Jesson were talk-ing to people just inside the garden. He'd never been in the pub and had hoped they'd be going to the bar, but Jesson said he was to show the guests straight into the garden.

Half the village had turned up, and Cliff soon tired of pointing out the way to the drinks and the sitting plan.

The tables formed a U-shape, seats either side, except along the narrow part where Mum, Jesson, his and Spence's names were on pieces of card. Mrs Gale's name was on the end, next to Spence, with Pete and Bob facing each other just round the corner.

Andy's name was pencilled in at the bottom of the plan and Mr Gale's name had a line through it. Served him right.

Knives and forks and glasses gleamed on white cloth-covered tables and bowls of bright-coloured flowers, daz-zling in the sun, dotted the tables.

It looked so posh; Mum and Jesson looked so posh, even he and the twins were dressed up like dog's dinners. And all these people were going to listen to his speech.

He heard his name being called. It was Jesson giving him the signal to call everyone to the table. Heck.

He coughed, but the words seemed stuck in his throat. He tried again, and only a croak came out. Mr Tyler was close to him; Cliff could have hugged him when he picked up a spoon and rapped it on a table.

'Ladies and gentlemen, please take your places for the wedding breakfast,' Cliff called out. His voice quivered but, incredibly, everyone began moving towards the tables.

The guests stood by their chairs until Mum and Jesson were in place and then Cliff announced the grace.

Everyone bowed their heads as he said the prayer.

As soon as he said amen, everyone watched as the family at the top table sat, then they all sat down too.

"Well, done," Jesson mouthed.

This was super; he loved the power of everyone doing what he told them, but there was still his speech to come. He looked at plates of ham salad and new potatoes being handed round and knew he couldn't eat a thing.

Sally had found some early strawberries. Everyone oohed and aahed as the waiters brought the fruit with the clotted cream she'd had sent up from Devon. Earlier, he'd overheard someone whispering that her family had loads of money. It was probably true because she always had things no one else had, but he didn't care; she used to be a land girl and she'd always been kind to him. Anything else was none of his business.

Heck. Everyone had finished their pudding, and their glasses were being topped up – Jesson whispered it was for the toasts. It was almost time. As there wasn't a bride's father to give a toast, Cliff was first.

He'd eaten almost nothing and his knees shook as he got to his feet. He laid his written notes on the table – in his hands, the paper trembled like a flame in a draught.

'Ladies and gentlemen, on behalf of the bride and groom, I'd like to thank you all for coming this afternoon.

'When Jesson asked me to be his best man, I didn't know what it meant and why everyone kept telling me not to lose the ring …'

Laugher rippled through the group, and he felt a surge of relief. He told them how Jesson had turned up out of the blue one evening. 'I was a bit scared of him; he was so smart in his uniform and I'd never talked to an American pilot before. I liked him right away. I think Mum did too.'

His mother gasped and blushed, and everyone laughed. He told them how Jesson had become invaluable on the farm. 'The only thing is, he hogs the tractor *all* the time. We have to drag him off it for food.' Mr Norton smiled and nodded at this.

It was going all right. Halfway through and no disasters yet.

'As a family,' he loved saying that, 'we hadn't had much to do with Americans and some things were confusing. For example, we start early on the farm and eat breakfast after we've worked a few hours. Mum once asked Jesson how he liked his bacon cooked and he said, "broiled". Mum thought he said "boiled" and served up a couple of slimy rashers.' More laughter. 'In America, broiled means grilled!' People roared. He felt marvellous.

After a couple more jokes, in a more serious tone, he said, 'Jesson is going to talk about Mum, but I want to say thank you for looking after me and Spence so well.' He looked at his mother, who smiled at him, eyes shining. Still looking at her, he went on, 'I'm glad you've married Jesson because I know he'll make you happy and you deserve it.' His mother dabbed her eye.

He turned to Jesson, 'It's going to be great having you as my dad, even if you do hate ginger beer.'

Everyone laughed and clapped madly. He felt ten feet tall. He was about to sit down when he remembered what was left to do.

'Ladies and gentlemen, please stand for the toast.' Everyone pushed back their chairs and stood.

Cliff lifted his half-glass of fizzy wine. 'The bride and groom.'

After Jesson had made his speech, saying nice things about Mum, and thanking him, Mrs Gale and anyone else who had helped, they cut the cake. It was small, but the WI ladies had raked up enough sugar for icing and some fruit for the inside.

The little band that played at village dances started up. Mum and Jesson danced and everybody clapped, then other people joined in.

Cliff had no intention of making a fool of himself trying to dance and went to find the twins.

Pete and Bob were much happier; they'd not only drunk the fizzy wine for the toast, they'd found a supply of booze.

'I'm starving,' Cliff said, 'I was so nervous I couldn't eat the dinner.'

'There's food there too, come on,' Pete said and led them to a lean-to at the back of the pub.

The waiters had been using it as a makeshift servery and platters still contained bits of ham, salad and new potatoes. Cliff picked up a plate and piled it up.

Pete held a beer bottle up to the light, then handed it to Cliff. He passed another to his brother and grabbed one for himself. 'Cheers, mate. You did smashin'. Did your ma really give him boiled rashers of bacon?'

Cliff took a swig. The bitter beer hit the back of his

throat and he spluttered.

'Shhh,' Bob hissed. People were talking just outside.

All three froze as they recognised their mothers' voices. They'd be dead ducks if they found them here. As one, they put their drinks down. Cliff thought he couldn't be in trouble for eating, so he crammed food into his mouth.

His mother's voice: 'I just wanted to suggest something, Rose, if you decide not to go back to Len –'

Bob clutched out at the table; his face as white as the cloth. Pete grabbed his arm and steadied him. Cliff put down his plate, no longer hungry.

'– I've talked it over with Jesson and we wanted to offer you and the boys the cottage. The work won't be finished for a few weeks, so you'd have to camp out for a while with no stove or proper bathroom—'

'Do you mean it?' Mrs Gale sounded shocked, although less than her twins, who gawped wide-eyed. Cliff thought he saw the hint of a smile on Pete's lips.

'We can't afford a lot of rent, and I doubt Len will chip in much for the boys, but it would be wonderful. Thank you, thank you.' There was a small gasp as if the women had hugged.

'We'll come to some arrangement when I get back,' Mum said.

'Telling the boys will be difficult – at least for Bob – but I must make it clear ter them and ter you, there's nothing between me and Walter.'

Cliff gulped. *Walter?*

'What he was telling me when Len came along in the car was that he's being repatriated in the next batch. He's excited about seeing his family, and his fiancée, again. Len wouldn't let me explain.' The two women moved off.

In the lean-to no one spoke, Cliff didn't know what to say; Pete and Bob had opposite reactions. He was in the middle.

Bob made the first move. He turned on Pete. 'You're glad, aren't you?' he said, poking Pete in the chest. 'He's our dad and I'm stayin' with him.' He grabbed a half-empty beer bottle, upended it and, with liquid running down his chin, stalked out.

'You *are* glad, aren't you?' Cliff asked, picking up his beer.

'I bloody am,' Pete said, downing the dregs of a wine bottle. 'I hate that old devil and I never want to live with him again.'

Mum and Jesson had changed into different clothes. Mum had on a pinky-blue jumper and cardigan he couldn't re-member seeing before and her new light grey skirt, "dove" she called it. It swished as she walked. Perched on the side of her head was the funny little grey hat she'd got at the jumble sale. A bit of purple netty stuff was now stuck on it.

'Do I look all right?' Mum twirled in front of him.

He felt a lump in his throat. 'You look lovely, Mrs Cobb.'

'Oh, Cliff. Thank you,' she said. 'Do you think May Cobb makes me sound like a type of nut?'

They both burst into shrieks of laughter that had every-one turning to look.

'Thank you for what you said in your speech,' Mum said, when they'd got their breath back. 'I am so proud of you. You couldn't have done it better if you'd been best man ten times before.'

He felt heat in his face. 'Thanks, Mum.'

'About names. I know you're happy for Jesson to be your stepdad, not your adopted father. But you can still change your name to Cobb. It's up to you.'

'I don't think I will change it; I'm used to Erwin and I'm not sure about Cliff Cobb. They'd probably call me "Clip Clop" at school.'

She laughed again. 'I can see that being a problem.'

The twins were signalling him from the lean-to. They were obviously speaking again.

'We talked to Mum,' Bob said, 'asked if she was gonna go back to Dad. She told us about the cottage and we've agreed if she and Dad can't work things out, I'll stay with him at weekends and Pete'll live with Mum in the cottage all the time. As long as Dad agrees.' He sounded doubtful.

'Course he will,' Pete said, punching him lightly on the arm. 'Someone's gotta cook for him!'

Bob shook his head and raised his eyebrows.

'All sorted out, then,' Cliff said, relieved they were going to be okay.

'I'll be handy for work,' Pete said with the great grin Cliff recognised from before Len Gale had come back from sea.

Mum and Jesson were going away in a car Sally had borrowed. Mrs Gale told him they were leaving it at Dorchester station for the owner to pick up. Mum didn't know where they were going and Jesson wouldn't tell anyone. Cliff suspected Mrs Gale knew but was keeping shtum.

People threw more confetti as the bride and groom went to the car. Spence wriggled in Cliff's arms, calling out for Mum, but Cliff distracted him, pointing out the old shoes and tin cans tied to the back bumper. He told him to wait and see what happened when the car drove off.

Before she got in the passenger side, Mum threw her bouquet over her shoulder. Janice Harris lunged forward and caught it, waving the pink roses in the air as if she'd found buried treasure. Mrs Harris looked like she'd sucked on an orange and found it was a lemon.

Finally, they drove off. Spence shrieked with delight as the shoes leapt and bounced behind the car. The clanging of the tins gradually faded and Cliff felt an emptiness inside him he hadn't felt since the day he'd stepped off the evacuees' charabanc.

Within seconds, the Tylers, Mr Norton, Mrs Gale and the twins surrounded him and Spence, all chattering at once, offering tea, cake and even beer (Mr Norton) and the emptiness just evaporated.

Chapter 52

May lay in bed facing the window, watching snowflakes flutter past.

Spencer's yells and giggles came from the garden where he and Cliff were having a snowball fight. The little boy was three now. How was that possible? How was it possible that an entire year had passed since that dreadful winter when it snowed for three months? Pray to God this one wouldn't be as bad.

She turned her head on the pillow and gazed at the double silver photo frame standing on her bedside table beside the telephone. The nearest picture was of the four of them on her wedding day. They all looked so smart; Cliff and Spencer dressed up to the nines, herself and Jesson the fashionable bride and groom. It had been a wonderful day.

The second photo depicted another lovely day. She and Jesson stood at the gates of Buckingham Palace. Before the royal wedding, before even the royal engagement.

A honeymoon in London had been an inspired idea; she'd only ever passed through. Jesson had never been. He had still been in a state of shock after she'd presented him with the documents transferring a share of the farm.

The passer-by they asked to take their photograph had guessed they were a honeymoon couple. He'd wished them every happiness. And they had had every happiness, especially now.

A wail from beside the bed personified the latest happiness but, before May could turn to her daughter, the bedroom door opened.

'Don't try ter lift her, you know what the doctor said.' Rose reached into the crib Jesson had built by hand, and gently lifted out the baby. She smiled tenderly. May knew the one thing she regretted about leaving Len was the loss of the possibility of another child; Rose had always longed for a baby girl.

May struggled to sit up without pulling her stitches. The penalty of being a first-time older mother, the midwife had told her. It could have been worse; they didn't take her into hospital, just put her on five days' bed rest after a long and painful delivery.

Rose changed the baby's nappy before handing her to May, who settled her on her breast.

A tap sounded on the door and Jesson peered round. 'Did I hear my baby girl?'

May smiled. He doted on his daughter and made any excuse to spend time with her. Cliff told him the tractor would get jealous.

They sat chatting while the baby fed. 'She's doing so well,' Rose said. 'The midwife will be pleased next time she sees her. Pity about the weather; looks like it'll be a while before you can show her off around the village.'

A good job, May thought. With a bit of luck, by then no one would spot that the supposedly early baby was well-grown enough to have been born full-term, which she had been. Rose must have guessed, but she said nothing.

The afternoon they'd checked the cottage for the furniture she'd wanted to keep had a lot to answer for. She smiled at the memory.

'Has Pete finished the hens?' Jesson asked.

'Yes,' Rose answered. 'He's gone back to the cottage. Homework, he says, but I think he enjoys having the place to himself when I'm at work and Bob's with Len.'

Footsteps thundered across the landing and the bedroom door burst open, revealing Spencer, red-nosed from the cold.

'Mama!' He made a dash for the bed. Jesson caught him and sat him on his knee.

'Be careful near your sister, Sprout,' he said. 'Would you like to hold her?'

He took his daughter from May's arms. 'Hello, Clara Elizabeth,' he said.

Everyone will think we've named her after the princess, May thought, not her maternal grandmother. And Jesson's mother, Clarabel.

Cliff came in as Spence took the baby in his arms, staring down at her in wonder. They could have had identical parentage; Clara's skin the same shade of honey-brown as Spencer's.

'Wait,' Cliff said, dashing out of the room.

May and Jesson looked at each other. 'The camera,' they said in unison.

Ever since they'd returned from honeymoon with the camera Jesson had given her as a wedding present, Cliff had been obsessed by it. The family, the dog, the horses and even the chickens weren't safe from forced poses.

He ran back in and, oblivious to her cries she was in her nightgown, set them up for a photograph: Jesson sitting on the bed beside her, Spencer between them nursing Clara.

Rose intervened, insisting Cliff sat on the other side of May while she took a snap of the whole family.

May beamed. "The whole family". *Her* whole family. Everything she'd ever wanted.

Acknowledgements

No writer can produce a book without help, and I have been fortunate in receiving invaluable advice and support from a range of good friends and professionals and some who are both.

My thanks to Robert Hill MRCVS for his advice on matters veterinary. All remaining inaccuracies and factual departures are my own.

Laura Burkin, Katheryn Sareen, Michael Brown, Edward Field, Su Sareen, Helen Baggott, Nick Brown and Debbie Calderbank have provided excellent feedback, generous assistance and professional advice to enable this project to come to fruition. Sincere thanks to you all.

Last but not least, thank you, the reader. I hope you have enjoyed May's story. If you could post a few words of review on Amazon or Good Reads, it would help me a great deal and I would be immensely grateful.

Reader Acclaim for May's Boys
A boy wants a mother, a woman wants a son ...

Beryl P. Brown's novel focuses particularly on the role of
the women, whose world is in turmoil
*****

… a heart-warming story about an evacuee from Southampton to a very traditional Dorset village
*****

The senses are beautifully evoked, the dialogue crackles on
the page and the tension builds up wonderfully, along with
countless surprises.
*****

… it takes on themes like prejudice, loneliness and of
course, the power of love.
*****

… surprisingly moving and quietly un-put-down-able!
*****

We are there in that muddy farmyard back in the Forties,
with all its problems, smells, etc., and we get particularly
fond of the hens!
*****

May's Boys
A boy wants a mother, a woman wants a son ...

Losing her husband just before WWII shattered May Sheppard's dreams of having a family. Her life is transformed by the arrival of Cliff, an evacuee from the city who has never known a loving home.

Already struggling with the hardships and deprivations of wartime Britain, May must now fight prejudice and defend Cliff against vindictive locals. She finds her strength stretched to breaking point when she is caught unawares by a manipulating visitor.

May and Cliff dread the day evacuees must be returned to their parents. If Cliff is sent back, the boy who longs for her to become his new mum will disappear from May's life for ever.

Printed in Great Britain
by Amazon